COUNTERPOINT

A Jack Connolly Novel

coun-ter-point, *n.* contrasting, but parallel events; events combined in order to establish a relationship while retaining their unique individuality;

Follow the author on Twitter:
@McharlesMcBee

Published by:
MCM Productions, Inc.
Advance Mills, VA 22968

Fourth Edition March 2016

Chapter 1

The Middle East
Southern Coast of Yemen – The Gulf of Aden
Wednesday, 0049 Zulu, 0349 Hrs. Local Yemen Time

First of all, it's a pitch black, moonless night. The beach appears to be deserted in both directions. Although the darkness does obscure ones visibility. The sand is comfortably smooth and fine with a richness only found on the south shore beaches of Long Island, New York. Not like the sand found on the Mediterranean beaches. Of course, Yemen is not exactly a vacation destination for Europeans on holiday. Known as a breeding ground for homegrown and imported terrorists of all stripes, Yemen shies away from those glossy ads in Travel & Leisure magazine.

The only sounds within earshot are waves that lap on shore. The sounds are soothing, calming. Not intrusive or striking. And it's these gentle sounds that calm the nerves of VASILI, a tall, yet trim and muscular pure breed Russian who moves slowly from the saw grass onto the beach.

He's followed by two other men – CHEKHOV and ZOYAN.

No one speaks. They just look. In all directions. But as if expecting not to be expected by the local authorities. The men are dressed in black, head to toe. Although not in black face. The moonless night has taken care of that extra measure of protection. Chekhov and Zoyan carry soft bags, medium in size. If there's weight to these bags, neither man shows it. Chekhov carries a smaller bag slung over the same shoulder, and has his free hand concealed in the cargo pocket of his trousers. Likely gripping a weapon of some serious business. His look is more threatening than the other two. Perhaps Chekhov is more interested in attracting trouble than a casual stroll on the beach.

Chekhov mumbles. It's hard, guttural Russian.

"Too fuckin' quiet. You could hear a hooker fart."

Vasili takes a moment. "…yeah."

Vasili stops at about mid-beach and gazes intently out onto the Gulf of Aden, scanning a wide expanse of the waters' surface. And from a pocket he removes a long chain. The kind you'd find with dog tags attached. Perhaps twelve inches in length. It holds a key. Its finish chrome. Average size, maybe for a door, it appears.

But this is no ordinary key. On closer examination there are small indentations. Tiny depressions that a trained individual familiar with such a key would recognize as a key that not so much is a mechanical device, but one that is read by a laser.

Vasili spins it absently around his index finger. Then reverses the process. Then again. It's clearly a habit, but not a nervous one. A habit for Vasili that's more of a little reminder of where the mission might be heading.

Though, at the moment, scanning the surface, he's more interested in what cannot be seen than what can be seen. Vasili has carefully planned this mission, coming out of retirement after working many years undercover in Chechnya, at times directly for Mister Putin, a.k.a., *el jefe*.

Vasili was once part of the Russian equivalent of the U.S Navy seals, but later moved onto submarines. A life he thoroughly enjoyed, and excelled at, reaching the position of weapons commander. A trusted confidant of those in power in Moscow, he exudes an inner strength not commonly associated with former Russian military senior officers. Usually, these individuals end up in some form of corrupt activity, using their knowledge and extensive contacts to further their own personal riches.

Not Vasili. He's a true patriot. And will do whatever it takes to protect and defend mother Russia. A Russian with a conscience willing to do the right thing. If it means the ultimate sacrifice. This is perhaps the rationale behind Mister Putin's selection of Vasili for this critical mission.

However, at the moment what bothers Vasili is why he had to take along that thug Chekhov and his demented sidekick, Zoyan. He protested, but lost the argument, opting to make the best of it. Typical of Vasili. But make no mistake. These two were Russian Chechnyan thugs. Particularly Chekhov. The guy's a loose cannon. Despite their intense knowledge of submarine warfare – they were both part of the Russian Naval fleet towards the end of the cold war, and were both summarily dismissed from duty for a variety of less than pleasant incidents. Vasili's "employer" insisted they be part of the mission. His "employer" was shrewd. Not one to arbitrarily issue orders without some real purpose. Figuring out the end game was something Vasili was usually good at. In this case, it remained a mystery. But he assumed that somewhere along the line he'll be sent updated instructions. Instructions that should include new "orders" for Chekhov and Zoyan.

So, that was it. Vasili pushed these concerns from his mind, leaving the problem in the hands of a higher authority. It was time to act like the true soldier he is and focus on the importance of the mission, especially in terms of Russia's participation in the war on terror.

And, of course, not lose sight of the enormous payday for him and the others, should the mission succeed. The pay and promised bonus aside, the war on terror was remarkably one area where both the United States and Russia met on some common ground.

Despite what Americans felt about its cold war adversary, the Russian people still had a human side. And they understood the terrorist mentality. Maybe more so than the Americans. And maybe even more aware of the truly horrific consequences possible should these Islamic jihadists be allowed to perpetuate their radical fundamentalist behavior around the world.

Vasili motions for the other two comrades to kneel down with him on the beach. Forming a small circle, Zoyan yanks a small Maglite torch from a pocket and twists it to the on position illuminating the sand. Vasili pulls a folded piece of paper from his shirt pocket. Unfolded, it reveals a map now shone brightly by Zoyan's torch.

The map highlights a large area of the Gulf of Aden. Across the Gulf, towards the African continent, is Somalia, and directly to the west is Ethiopia. Vasili's finger pokes at the top of the map.

"Saudi Arabia..."

His finger moves slowly down, in a southerly direction, where it stops on a spot on the southern coast of Yemen identified on the map as Al Mukalla.

"We are here...Al Mukalla."

Chekhov grunts as if an unpleasant place. Not someplace he'd choose for a day at the beach.

Vasili continues. "It's where we start tonight."

He now slides his finger in a southerly direction down the Indian Ocean to a chain of Islands known as the Seychelles. And pokes his finger on an inconsequential island known as Silhouette.

"We load our cargo...then..."

Vasili's finger now moves along the map in a northwesterly direction to what looks like a deep-water straight that separates Yemen from Djibouti.

"From this point we sail into the Red Sea."

Chekhov says, "yeah. How long?"

Vasili takes a moment to quickly calculate.

"By Monday...0913 Zulu...1213 hours local Red Sea."

Zoyan shifts for a closer look at the map. Then says...

"Gimme time to inspect the engine of that boat. I'll get us better time into the straight."

Vasili holds a hard look on Zoyan. It's telling in the sense that this is Vasili's mission. And Zoyan will do what the mission leader says.

"No. We follow the pre-arranged time schedule. No exceptions."

Zoyan holds a hard look on Vasili. Then a look at Chekhov.

Chekhov takes a moment. Then..."Yeah. Then what?"

Vasili's finger moves on the map in a northerly direction into the Red Sea. It stops and he points to a place on the Egyptian coast marked Foul Bay.

"We arrive here...Tuesday...1249 Zulu."

Chekhov grunts. "Foul Bay...another shit hole, huh, my friend?"

Vasili glances over at Chekhov thinking it probably best not to start a confrontation with this thug. His time will come, for sure. But, no sooner does he dismiss Chekhov's contentious remarks when Zoyan's finger moves swiftly from Foul Bay to a spot up near the top of the map to a place identified as Israel.

Chekhov grins. "Yeah. Range to fuckin' target?"

On this Vasili develops a mask of strength and power, not unlike Vladimir Putin with compassion. He studies the Mafioso-type, hateful Chechnyan for a long moment. Then, with a trace of contempt Vasili says. "...Nine hundred kilometers."

Chekhov responds. "Da. Good. Good. Another ten hours to launch position Duba."

Vasili clicks the outer time navigation dial on his Rolex. Then takes a moment to compute the results.

"Da...Tuesday. 2345 Zulu. Five hundred fifty kilometers from the target...exactly one week from tonight."

Chekhov nods his approval, if it really matters in his mind, as Vasili folds the map and stands. The three Russians walk to the water's edge. Vasili turns and signals with his hand towards the tall saw grass area as if waving.

A moment before an Arab man – AMIN - in Kaftan head gear moves from the grassy area towards the water's edge. He drags a 9 foot Zodiac inflatable. On its transom, a small engine similar to what fishermen use while trolling quietly on a river. Amin is small in stature, bearded like most Arab men, fairly young. Perhaps in his twenties. With these guys it's always hard to tell. But for Chekhov, it's none of these things. It's what's under the Arabs clothing. Maybe a weapon. Chekhov's eyes carefully search the Arab.

Amin, of course, notices this and tries to avoid eye contact with the miserable Chechnyan. His look moves from the water's edge to Vasili, back and forth. It's Vasili who has hired Amin. And for a considerable fee. It's the only reason Amin is even here. If not for the money, he'd have nothing to do with these Russians. The job is quick, easy money for the poor camel jockey whose worldly possessions are limited to a camel and the clothes on his back.

And maybe the prospect of a bonus when he's able to sell the Zodiac. The small craft purchased by Vasili for the mission, but in Amin's name. More assurance that Amin will be able to sell it to one of the many rich fisherman in and around Al Mukalla. Ownership in someone else's name would bring immediate suspicion to Amin by the local authorities, most likely resulting in several body parts being painfully removed, without his permission, of course.

Amin and Zoyan launch the Zodiac into the water. All four climb aboard. Vasili at the bow; Chekhov and Zoyan amidships on the thwart. And Amin in the stern, his hand gripping the engine steering arm. The Zodiac drifts out about fifteen or twenty meters.

Vasili studies the surface. Then the shoreline.

Chekhov interrupts his thoughts. "Well?"

"Shut up, Chekhov."

The rebuke is sharp and quick. And Chekhov is pissed. Not at the rebuke. But at the fact the smelly camel jockey seated within arm's length heard his name. He grills a stare at Amin who now appears on the verge of a complete breakdown. Sweat forms beneath the Kaftan as his pleading eyes fall on Vasili who has turned his attention back out to sea for a long moment.

Vasili turns towards the stern. "Start the engine."

And with that, Amin pulls at the starter cord. The engine fires instantly, but remarkably quiet. For a moment, Amin seems to be relived. Likely because the engine did not fail him. He looks again towards Vasili who holds a GPS device in his hand.

Vasili raises his arm pointing slightly off the starboard bow.

"This way."

Amin adjusts the Zodiac's direction, his hand gripping the steering arm bearing his white knuckles. His eyes wide with fear as if at any moment the crazy Chechnyan will slit his throat. Body language Chekhov finds hard to resist.

"What's the matter? You don't like Russians?"

Amin manages a weak smile, although he has no idea what Chekhov has said. Once again he shifts his look to his perceived security blanket, Vasili who is intently focused on the GPS device.

Chekhov chuckles. Then pokes Zoyan in the ribs.

"I piss on your Quran."

Both Chekhov and Zoyan break into laughter.

From the bow. "Quiet. Both of you."

Chekhov and Zoyan exchange looks. Then both smile at Amin who is maybe taking an involuntary dump in his pants.

Chapter 2

On the Gulf of Aden
Wednesday, 0113 Zulu, 0413 Hrs. Local

Vasili monitors the GPS device in his hand then glancing at the waters' surface in several directions. Now he holds on a specific spot on the surface for a long moment. Then back to the GPS device.

"Stop!"

Amin has cut the engine. The Zodiac drifts gently on the sea as all hands are quiet. Vasili's mind registers slight concern, perhaps because of the darkness. But his training has taught him to rely emphatically on his instrument, the way a pilot does flying in bad weather despite the instinct to look out the windshield or trust his gut commonly referred to as "seat of the pants flying." A false sense of security that has led to many crashes. As a submariner, Vasili completely understands the need to rely on instruments. Which is why he's able to push the small concern out of his mind. Although, given the situation regarding his friend Lubin, a fellow ex-Naval officer, while knowing they're in the right spot, is Lubin still capable of fulfilling his end of the mission.

Vasili spins the chain and key as it winds around his index finger. Reversing the process. Then, re-starting it as his focus is all over the water's surface.

As a matter of fact, all three Russians scan the surface. Their expressions intense, maybe even a bit desperate. Chekhov's impatience is telling.

"I should've navigated that boat here – not that prick, Lubin."

Vasili takes a moment. "...maybe."

The only one not checking the surface is Amin. Perhaps because he's not aware of what is to happen next. He has assumed that the Russians were to be picked up by some vessel. Why would he be hired to ferry them out to sea like this, then return to shore, alone, if it were not the case? But for Amin, who now glances around at the surface of the water sees no vessel in sight. Although it is hard to distinguish the edge of the water from the horizon, at least he'd hear a ship if it were nearby.

He's totally confused. Maybe these Russians are complete idiots. They have come to the wrong place. But what if they blame him? He's just doing what he's been told. And being paid quite well for it. But paid well to do something perhaps dangerous and illegal. The more he thinks about it, the worse it gets. Poor Amin. If they're in the wrong place, the insane Chechnyan will go nuts. Maybe kill Amin and the other two in a fit of anger. He must pray to Allah for strength. That should do it. Yes. Pray to Allah. But don't let the Chechnyan see him. He gives it some more thought.

Then pisses in his pants.

From the bow, Vasili points directly off the starboard beam. The other three shift their view to an area about 20 meters to the west.

And it's here that the surface of the water breaks. And what can be seen first is the Sail; then two periscopes; a radio-sextant and several radar masts; all now breaking the surface slowly as water pours off the Bridge and down the Sail.

Then the bulk of a huge submarine gently floats to the surface. The only sound that of rushing water pouring from the subs' decks back into the Gulf of Aden.

The submarine is huge. A total of 154 meters in length; 18 meters on the beam.

Amin can't believe his eyes. He's never seen such a monster rise from the sea. He mouths "holy shit."

The scene in his mind is something similar to a match box toy car alongside a menacing Chevy Suburban.

Vasili swings towards the Arab. "Hurry up."

Amin fires up the engine and turns towards the port side of the submarine.

As they pull alongside the sub several people appear on the deck, coming up through a forward hatch. Two of the members of the greeting party are OFFICERS, and clearly Asian. North Korean officers to be exact. They view the shore party with some skepticism, though they become instantly all smiley face when a third man comes up through the hatch.

This is LUBIN, another Russian, but not as severe as Chekhov or Zoyan. More approachable, in a sense, like Vasili.

The introductions are miss- stepped, with out-of-sync nods and grunts. Quite noticeably the language barrier has created not only an uneasy atmosphere on deck, but an environment of miss trust and confusion as well, thanks to Chekhov's charming personality. He towers over the North Koreans with obvious contempt in his heart, if he has one.

Vasili has now turned suddenly towards the Zodiac and Amin. To his mild astonishment, Amin has pulled away, heading back to the Yemen shore. Vasili watches the Zodiac for an extended moment as it vanishes into the black of night. He actually wanted to thank Amin for his brave services. Wishing him luck, and to be careful not to say anything as they had discussed the day before. Vasili had a good feeling about Amin. He can read people quite well, a quality that many times had saved his life. He thought Amin to be an honest, reliable helper, which is why he gave him the opportunity for that extra bonus. The opportunity to sell the brand new Zodiac. No questions asked.

As Vasili stares off into the night, Chekhov slips behind him and to the side.

"I can still smell that bastard."

Vasili stays calm. But behind his back, Chekhov yanks a small device from a pocket. Not larger than a cell phone. From it, he pulls up an antenna. As if to make a call. Chekhov smirks.

"I think he may try to kill me someday."

Still focused on the vanishing Zodiac, Vasili says. "And his Allah might just reward him for it."

"Fuck you."

Chekhov presses a button on the device.

The explosion 100 meters away is thundering. It echoes violently across the water at warp speed, bouncing off the hull of the submarine. The North Koreans freak, quickly cowering for cover on the deck

A fireball billows 50 feet into the night sky. It illuminates the entire area.

The Zodiac, and Amin, have been blown back to the stone age in tiny flaming pieces that now start to fall into the sea.

Vasili turns sharply at Chekhov.

"You ass. That explosion will be seen by everyone within hundreds of miles. From the spy satellites thousands of miles up. "

Chekhov grins. "One less fuckin' Islamic asshole to worry about."

Vasili is steamed. The thought that wasting Chekhov here and now pings around his brain. But instead, he knows they need to get out of sight – quickly.

"Everyone below! Now! Now!"

And as everyone goes for the forward hatch, Vasili takes a heartbeat to look out towards the fiery remnants of the Zodiac. It's glow very much apparent. A glow that highlights the sub. And its 20 foot high Sail.

And the letters painted on its side. "CCCP."

Chapter 3

The White House, Washington, DC
Friday Afternoon, 1719 Hrs. Local

JACK CONNOLLY, that's me.

Often described by few as one very cool, extremely bright guy. Late thirties. Single. A babe magnet. And a Naval Officer. That's me. Running from the West Wing.

It's a happy run. Pleasant thoughts on my mind. It's not the White House, though. It's what lies ahead – about two and half hours down the road.

And I probably have some bizarre smile on my face that makes me look like someone not tightly wrapped.

Which is a bad thing around the White House.

It's Friday. The start of the Labor Day weekend despite the fact I have to work.

What probably doesn't compute here – at least to the average on-looker – is why I'm running from the West Wing entrance, away from the White House.

Now, yes, things are a bit nasty in the world today. Between the North Koreans and the Iranians spewing inflammatory and threatening rhetoric on a daily basis, our National Security apparatus is running constantly on overload. Something you'll quickly learn I'm acutely aware of these days.

I should point out that me running from the West Wing has no direct bearing on the serious nature of the truly electrifying and outstanding story you're about to read.

So, I'm running, despite the fact the place is crawling with hired guns – guys who wouldn't hesitate a moment to take-down a thirty something, good looking Irish-American dude in sharply pressed Navy whites beating the hell away from the place.

And carrying a large briefcase.

Since I was in my officers' uniform, they might think I was the guy who carries the infamous "football." You know that bag with the secret nuclear launch codes in case of a drastic emergency. It also contains the super-secret telephone number for the Reverend Billy Graham, just in case it's too late, where he can be reached either here on earth, or in paradise.

The "football" guy is never more than several feet from the President. I often wonder what happens when the President goes to bed. Does this guy just sit there, next to the sleeping President and First Lady?

I heard during the Clinton Administration he had to wear a blindfold and ear plugs at night.

Anyway, I have a lofty position here as a Deputy National Security Advisor to the President for assorted Navy stuff, and I'm usually in a business suit. That's how the guys in the trees and on the roof with guns know me.

Racial profiling aside, your average terrorist today has learned to blend in with the rest of us average workings stiffs. Like Naval officers running aimlessly on the White House grounds. Or members of the macho-male press corps standing like card-board cut-outs of Bill Hemmer holding a microphone trying to sound informed but wishing they could hook-up with anyone of those gorgeous women on FOX.

Despite my lack of a dark complexion, and sans the Kaftan head gear, I'm reasonably certain some pumped-up, eager to please law enforcement type perched on the roof of the White House has me in his rifle sights as I make a mad dash for my car.

Still, I was in somewhat of a hurry. I had an engagement at Camp Peary, near Williamsburg, Virginia.

My usual weekend Navy obligation that's become, shall we say, an obsession.

I'm on permanent reserve status – the operative word being "permanent" thanks to several Admirals out at Pearl Harbor who have a strange sense of humor. They assumed I'd be better off screwing up things at the White House rather than back on board a submarine which is, by the way, my true role in the U S Navy.

I'm a submariner.

At least in the White House you're reasonably insulated from any possibility of being responsible for an international catastrophe. Which brings me to an interesting question that's been plaguing me for the past year.

Why was I assigned Ollie North's old office?

Let's get back to the story.

As a result of an unfortunate incident at sea a short time ago - that's the term those Admirals used - incident - I was placed on reserve status as a Deputy NSA at the White House.

And, as I've mentioned, Colonel Oliver North's old office, which, by the way, is the size of my mother's shoe closet.

So, instead of being re-assigned to a submarine, where I really belong, I'm stuck here at the White House.

As a deputy.

Actually, I'm not in the White House, but in the OEOB, that ugly looking building next door that Dick Cheney tried to burn down when he was the Veep. It used to be the War Department before the Pentagon was built.

I'm learning so much in this job.

Anyway, to digress further, it still is the war department. Except the war is between the sorry sap in the Oval office and the five hundred and thirty-five bozos two miles up Pennsylvania Avenue on the Hill.

According to my boss, Ms. Eiko Narita, National Security Advisor to the President, I'm habitually late for early morning meetings where I have, to date, used the impossible Washington, DC traffic as an excuse.

Eiko never buys the traffic excuse.

Actually, as you'll find out, I don't think she likes me.

I do my weekend tour at Camp Peary in Williamsburg, Virginia, a top secret intelligence facility, secretly owned by the Navy, but secretly run by the CIA.

The whole place is one hell of a secret.

As a matter of fact, it's so secret, Admiral Peary, the first guy to trek off to the North Pole, and whose name adorns the Camps' letterhead, mess hall and latrines (heads), doesn't even know about it.

But, on the other hand, I heard he's dead.

At this point, you should know that the tour used to be just once a month. But I, being a true patriot, volunteered to change it to every weekend.

It's about two and a half-hours south of Washington, DC. Or like most of the crazed politico types in this town would say, "outside the blast zone."

Anyway, I'm Commander John Joseph Connolly, II – J.J. Connolly the "first" was my grandfather, a Navy hero in World War II.

Most people call me Jack.

My training took place as a midshipman at the Naval Academy. Like most things I had to do at Annapolis, I did just good enough to get by.

Except fraternizing with the female midshipmen.

I was the only guy at the Naval Academy who realized we might have a female commander-in-chief someday and good relations with the opposite sex never hurt.

At least not until Hillary came along.

I won't go there.

Now for me, attending the Naval Academy was mandatory. Both my father and grandfather attended. So it was never a matter of if, but when. That being when Dad could find a cooperating Congressman or Senator who would give me an appointment. And by this time Dad was already an Admiral.

But, some genius at the Pentagon – someone else with a sense of humor – decided to make my appointment automatic.

Grandpa was a destroyer Captain, then a fleet commander during WW II, "the big one" as he called it. Dad was a Navy pilot with more than one hundred fifty eight missions over North Vietnam.

During my forth year at the Naval Academy is when it all happened.

The Assistant Superintendent saw an autographed photo of Admiral Hyman Rickover, father of the modern American nuclear submarine fleet given to my Dad, hanging in my room. He must have thought I'd be a shoe-in for the submariner fleet.

That's when I knew.

But…Submarines? I'm claustrophobic.

Next thing I know, I'm in post-graduate school at some high tech, super-secret submarine training center, underground in the middle of nowhere, Connecticut.

It's still good to have connections.

Which is how I ended up at the White House.

Sort of.

I'll get into that shortly.

Bear with me.

Its gets better.

Really, it does!

Chapter 4

Southeast Virginia on Interstate 64
Friday Evening, 1922 Hrs. Local

I zip into the Williamsburg area, and getting close to the super-secret Camp Peary, I can't help but notice the rather large sign on the interstate that reads, "Camp Peary, next exit."

Well, so much for secrecy.

My guess is that someone in Washington, DC figured the average terrorist, now being sharply dressed like a U.S. Naval officer, may have a problem reading a map. So, that same someone decided to plant a sign right here.

Just in case.

Anyway, the bottom line is I'm just an average Naval officer, dedicated to honor, courage and service to my country. I say this because it sounds good. Reporting in for these monthly duty assignments away from the havoc that surrounds Washington, DC is like reporting in for play camp.

Except what goes on at this Camp is some serious shit.

The defense of our country might just depend on my small, but significant contribution here at Camp Peary. It's what drives my quest for advancement up the chain of command in the Navy.

Then…there's that one little benefit about this place I just happen to like.

Her name is Lieutenant j.g. Lauren Miller, USN.

Chapter 5

The White House, South Lawn
Friday Evening, 1927 Hrs. Local

DONALD GIORDAN looks Presidential as he walks from the White House onto the South lawn towards Marine One. If they made a movie about him, Michael Douglas would surely portray the role. Early sixties, handsome, terribly fit, and, of course, wealthy. It's always evident when someone is wealthy. Hard to miss.

Except if you're the lone exception. Like Warren Buffet. It's also a requirement for the job of President of the United States, a/k/a POTUS. Wealth attracts power.

Something that's badly needed, even by the President. Power gives the President the option of blaming someone else for his – or her – mistakes. Also as President you can lie – easily – without worrying about people not believing you. You're supposed to know right from wrong. And it's understood that you hopefully do.

Your decisions are officially questioned only by Congress. And who's going to believe them? The media is a whole other bag of worms.

And it's precisely what President Giordan had on his mind this evening. Lies. Who will be lying to whom? Who's going to find out who's lying to whom? Who's going to believe whom? Just one big mess of lies about to unfold. Which is why he has a smile on his face.

Coming off a successful first term, he's looking to jump into the re-election campaign on Tuesday against a Democratic opponent who's been handicapped by his own party. The fight at the Democratic National Convention was better than reality TV.

Party leaders holding true to their innate stupidity made the guy who did the best in the primaries bow down to a stronger political machine.

A machine that operates flawlessly on lies.

Which, by the way, may make them acutely qualified for the Oval Office.

The party line was clear. Forget all that talk about "experience." Tell the electorate what they want to hear. "It'll all be transparent – just trust me." Then, just do what you want when you get there.

Of, course, don't forget to check those over-night opinion polls first thing in the morning so you know what to say during the day.

But President Giordan didn't have those kinds of worries. He wasn't that kind of President. He relied on his instincts, his gut feel, that old stand-by known as street sense. Also, a lot of hard work. Never kind to special interest groups, or the powers that be in Washington.

The fact that the United States Senate operated on a seniority system meant very little to him. And Congressmen, who spent most of their time once elected running for re-election, thoroughly annoyed him.

His role was that of President of the people, defender of the constitution. With that in mind, his priority was fighting the war on terror.

And it was an ugly fight.

The toughest part?

Dealing with the civil libertarians and wimpy liberals in Congress. Wars, regardless of their shape, are not fought with pretty words or idle threats. President Giordan's experience in Vietnam brought that issue home clearly.

His stride out to Marine One was confident. In that Eisenhower-style waist jacket he loves to parade around in adorned with the presidential seal. He throws a couple of quick, sharp salutes to his adoring fans, the White House staff out to see the Boss off for the long weekend. Like the guy several yards away trimming the shrubs. The one in the permanent hunched position. The President is maybe thinking those Sharper Image shears he gave the guy for Christmas last year really are sharp. And so he needs to put on a friendly face for him. Single him out for a special wave. But the guy still doesn't smile, or wave. He just stares at the President.

Maybe the Chief of Staff needs to have one of those attitude adjustment talks with the guy. As soon as he puts those shears away, of course.

DREW CARDINELLI is the President's Chief of Staff, and a longtime friend from their days together drilling for oil in west Texas. Although neither man is from Texas, the feel of oil running through their fingers brought on visions of fame and fortune. The team clicked. All the way to the White House.

Cardinelli is kind of like the COO of The White House, Inc. And he's always just one step behind the President. As he is right now. Not unlike Prince Philip who's always one step behind Queen Elizabeth. She must have one good-looking ass.

Cardinelli is a no-nonsense type. Keenly aware of everything and everyone around him. He knows the players better than the players know themselves. And he thinks he's got the inside on the President. Unfortunately for Mister Cardinelli, the President plays everything a bit closer to the vest. Which explains why it's Giordan in the Oval Office, and not Cardinelli.

Drew pockets his cell phone, and steps closer to Giordan.

"Vice President Greene just called."

The only reaction from the moving President is his eyes. They shift, just slightly.

His stride remains intact. On a course for Marine One.

"And?"

"Said he forgot about a golf date with Senator Sykes. Won't be able to make the Labor Day picnic up at Camp David."

"Forgot?"

"Maybe he's finally feeling the effects of too many IED's going off near him during the Iraq war."

Cardinelli's tone suggests that the Vice President may just be a stand-in, like some Veep's of the past. Plus, it appears he just may not like the guy very much.

Cardinelli being an Ivy League educated business man, while Vice President Greene was a soldier, from the get-go, who worked his way up the chain of command to General in the Marine Corps.

No easy feat.

"Drew. He's a war hero. Let's not forget that. If I'd let him, he'd be back on the front lines – literally – leading the charge in this war on terror."

Knowing who's the boss, Cardinelli responds softly.

"Yes, sir."

The President takes a thoughtful moment.

"Sykes?"

"Yes, sir."

Cardinelli gets a little cocky.

"Not one of our favorites."

"What Democrat is?"

Cardinelli says nothing. But the smirk says it all.

There's a moment before the President stops and faces his Chief of Staff.

"Tell Vice President Greene he's excused. But if he loses to that horses ass, I'm gonna place his official portrait next to the one of Al Gore, a little lower."

The President holds on Cardinelli for a moment.

Then flashes a broad smile.

Turns and fast walks to the steps of Marine One.

Drew Cardinelli just loves this guy.

Chapter 6

Camp Peary Main Gate, Williamsburg, Virginia
Friday Evening, 1939 Hrs. Local

I slowed to a stop mainly because I didn't want to run-down the young Marine guard standing in the roadway with his hand in the air signaling me to stop. Something else they teach you at the Naval Academy.

Don't run down Marine guards.

Especially ones with guns.

It looks bad on your record.

Anyway, I, of course, know this kid, having become friends with him during each of my visits this past year in forced exile. And once again, he seems to have pulled Friday night duty, obviously low man on the totem pole, or unless he didn't eat his entire broccoli at chow.

I think his mother wrote a letter to the Marine Corps about his dislike for broccoli.

The only person I know of not required to eat broccoli is former President Bush # 1. He stood in the rose garden one day, pointing at the White House proclaiming "I'm the President. I don't have to eat broccoli."

Then he went and jumped out of an airplane. And parachuted into a broccoli patch.

He, of course, being a President immediately blamed it on some left wing liberal conspiracy made up of the elite news media, residents of Fire Island, NY, and Bill Maher.

So, my young Marine guard friend is standing there probably thinking about his buddies with the night off who went into town to pick-up chicks at William & Mary College.

I'm sure they're telling heroic war stories about Iraq or Afghanistan, and how they shot and killed lots of bad guys. Co-eds love this shit. The truth be known, most of these young Marines have only fired their weapons at a firing range, and only at targets that are supposed to look like terrorists. I've heard they now wrap towels around the fake heads.

So, still standing there staring me down is young Lance Corporal Jeffrey Mollerick, USMC. Looking all of about seventeen. I'm sure young Jeffrey lied about his age to get into the Marine Corps. I doubt he got his high school sweetheart pregnant, than ran from home in order not to face up to his responsibility. He's not that kind of Marine. What he is, though, is by the book.

Which is why I like to have fun with him every time I pull up to the main gate.

Rolling down my window, I coast to a stop.

"Jeffrey. How's it hanging?"

"Sir, may I see some ID, sir?"

Now young Jeffrey knows me. We're buds. But, you'd never know it every time I pull in here. He's just got to follow the rules. Me, on the other hand, I like to keep things fluid, as you know.

"I lost my ID, Jeffrey. I pulled over at a rest stop ten miles back and a bunch of guys named Bruce or Biff wearing cute Prada shoes jumped me. They took my ID."

"Sir?"

"I'd keep a sharp lookout for 'em if I were you."

Jeffrey needed a moment to compute. Which is okay because I'm reasonably patient.

"Sir. ID, please, sir."

Now it suddenly occurred to me that the way he's acting young Jeffrey must be having girlfriend issues. Otherwise, he'd play along.

I think.

I mention girlfriend because I know all about his girlfriend. Unfortunately for young Jeffrey should anyone else find out, he'd be immediately transferred to Iraq, standing guard over Saddam's gravesite...alone.

His girlfriend is Ensign Dana Davidson, USN. She's older, and, here's the problem, she's an officer. There's this thing in the military about that. So, it's a good idea that no one knows about it.

But I'm the only who knows. And young Jeffrey knows I'm a stand-up guy. Although, he is the one holding an M 16 at the moment. Since he's on this ID kick, I felt I needed to have a little more fun.

"Got an e-mail from Dana this week, Jeffrey. She's a little worried about, you know, the thing?"

I said "the thing" just in case someone with one of those ease-dropping devices was listening. I mean, this is a super-secret intelligence facility. I learned about saying "the thing" watching re-runs of The Sopranos.

"Sir, the thing, sir?"
Young Jeffrey has this annoying habit of starting and finishing everything he says with "sir." Probably a spin-off from the "don't ask, don't tell" policy formulated back in the Clinton "I didn't have sex with that woman" administration. "Sir" keeps everything neutral. Better than starting and finishing with, say, "honey bunch."

So I said. "Yeah. What I think is you'd better plan on boning her this weekend if you want it to stay cool. Ya know?"

At this point, young Jeffrey's face changed from powder white to beet red. At the same time I noticed his index finger move carefully to the trigger of his M 16. His head jerked in the direction of the Camp, which I instantly took as his okay for me to drive into Camp Peary.

I gave him a smile and quick salute, while driving through the main gate area. In my rear view mirror I noticed he was breathing heavily, kind of a huffing and puffing movement. I couldn't tell whether he was fantasizing about boning Ensign Davidson or really pissed at me.

The latter is likely.

I'm good at reading people.

Although, I did notice two other things.

One, he never checked my ID, and two, he didn't salute me, as is the custom between enlisted personnel and officers.

Interesting.

What could be bothering this kid?

More importantly.

I wonder if there is another way onto this base.

Chapter 7

Camp Peary Naval Reservation
a/k/a, Submarine Warfare Center
Monday, Labor Day, 0747 Zulu, 0147 Hrs. Local

It's not actually the submarine warfare center. It's the place where big shots, like me for example, pretend there's a war going on, and it's being fought with submarines.

Okay, that might be a stretch.

It's more like we engage in a pretend war strategy by pretending to guess what the bad guys are doing, or maybe thinking about doing. Then we come up with highly intelligent solutions to what we've pretended the bad guys are going to do, hopefully before they do it in a real-life situation.

It's called intelligence.

Which means, if you've somehow figured out this explanation, you're likely over-qualified for a job in the intelligence community.

It's close to two o'clock in the morning, and I'm beat. It doesn't help that the room I work in at this place, although filled with another eight or ten Navy personnel and CIA spooks, glows red.

Aircraft cockpit red.

It makes me sleepy.

Since I have an early start in the morning, an obligation to join the President and another fifty or so friends of his at Camp David for his annual Labor Day picnic, a little shut-eye would do just fine about now.

The room buzzes with a strange quiet. Everywhere you look there's equipment up the ass. High tech stuff you see only in the movies.

Lots of blinking LED lights.

Things like waveform analyzers. And audio spectrum filters.

All this shit dancing like Michael Jackson.

At least, before they planted the guy.

Speakers broadcast voices, quietly. But in a confusing mess of familiar and unfamiliar languages.

Like Russian, Farsi, Arabic, Chinese.

Despite my exhaustion, I'm focused on several charts and a few aerial photos. The charts illustrate various locations in the Indian Ocean and areas near the Persian Gulf. The photos are that of a submarine as it pulls from a harbor, presumably in North Korea. Then more photos of it submerging in the Sea of Japan.

My concentration on this new puzzle is suddenly broken by the sensation of a firm, well-formed female breast that is now planted against my shoulder blade.

Her soft, highly erotic voice grabs my attention, making the hairs on my neck stand up and salute.

"What's it like being in the Oval office?" She asks.

Now, I should mention at this point that the voice is that of the aforementioned Lieutenant j.g. Lauren Miller, USN. And the sound of her voice does more than just arouse even the palace Unix. Which probably explains why I really don't mind giving up some shut-eye, and working at two in the morning.

Without turning back at her, still focused on the charts and photos in hand, I answer.

"Scary."

I like to act nonchalant. You know, 'all in a day's work.' Give the impression that 'you don't wanna go there, babe.'

But she says. "I like scary."

"Then you'd love the guys in Brooks Brother's suits with guns the size of Volkswagens."

Just then she moves in a little tighter. With most of her knockout body against mine, she peers for a closer look at the charts and photos in my hand. She takes a moment to compute a careful, well-educated study of this potentially troubling situation. Exactly what I rely on her to do. Because, at the moment, I'm stumped.

She seductively says, "I get off duty at zero two hundred."

This is exactly why I get very little done here. And very little sleep, as well.

But don't tell the Navy brass.

"The President expects me for breakfast at Camp David, Lieutenant Miller. And the annual Labor Day barbecue."

"I'll make you breakfast, Jack. You know I'm good at making breakfast."

I give her a sideways glance that says it all: been there, done that.

So I quickly start shuffling through the charts and photos, mainly in an attempt to head-off a premature start of the launch sequence. She has that effect.

Pointing at one of the photos, I say "what else do you know about this, Lauren?"

"Russian submarine. North Koreans own it. They could be using it as a training boat."

I'm dumb-founded. "North Koreans own it? They can't afford to buy a pocket compass let alone a submarine."

She grabs some of the photos for a closer look.

"I've been on it for two weeks now. I thought I'd have it figured out before you got down here on Friday. But, now this new Intel tonight. Can't quite get the pieces together. Nothing makes any sense."

I pull some of the data off a stack on the counter in front of me. My mind is all over the place on this. Lauren is right. Nothing makes any sense.

A Russian sub. North Koreans operating it, possibly in the Indian Ocean. Heading for the Persian Gulf region, maybe.

And I can tell it's not one of the newer class of Russian subs. As a matter of fact it looks like one of their clunky cold war boats we use to chase around the North Atlantic.

I grunt. More like 'this is a mystery' grunt.

Lauren takes another moment. Then says. "The CIA Director, Mister Unger, has a red book on his desk. I had it delivered Friday. Everything we know so far."

I grunt again.

"I would've waited for you to give it a look. But he called."

"Simon Unger called you?"

She gives me a look as if she did something wrong.

I asked "what I mean is, he already knew about this sub?"

She thinks for a moment. Then, "actually, he said there was a piece of Intel that came through NSA headquarters at Fort Meade that mentioned the sub. He wanted to know whatever we had so he could add it to the daily brief for the President. And for the National Security Advisor. Your boss, Miss Narita."

I, of course, trust Lieutenant Miller's judgment without question. Despite being a gorgeous blonde, she's young. I think twenty-four. But, on the other hand, super-smart. Besides curvy and incredibly sexy. But I think you know that part.

What's wrong with this scene is Simon Unger calling for information. He doesn't call anyone. He has minions who call. Simon thinks everyone in Washington is an idiot and therefore not worthy of he calling them. So, I decided to simply file this piece of info in my little brain for future reference.

I said, "so, Miss Narita will have the Intel this morning. And this sub? It's Russian, for sure?

She responded, "retired Oscar Class sub. And yes. The charming Miss Eiko Narita."

"Who has a very sharp mind, Lauren."

"And tiny boobs. Like you once said." She added.

Not that I'm prejudice, but I believe my comments at the time related to oriental women in general. I don't remember. But, obviously, Lieutenant Miller remembers. She's good with remembering things I tell her during sex I hope she forgets, being caught up in the heat of the moment.

Which reminds me, I need to start undoing everything I've ever said to her about my family. Just in case our relationship gets serious. Which it seems to be getting. As soon as I tie-up some loose ends.

Like that Russian submarine commander she knows. I really need to get to the bottom of that situation first.

So, with a trace of melancholy, I ask, "still dating that Russian sub commander, what's his name?"

"You introduced us, Jack. In Geneva? Remember? And we're not dating!"

I certainly can't admit to that. I mean, remember? I'm not a fool. But I did attend a NATO summit in Geneva where the Russians were invited to observe.

Or, spy.

It depends on which way you swing.

Anyway, Lieutenant Miller was part of a top secret intelligence contingent that accompanied the SOD – that's military speak for Secretary of Defense.

Except, as one could imagine, Lieutenant Miller was no secret. Someone had suggested that we needed to put on our best face. So I suggested we take the lovely Miss Miller as an example of one of the many perks that are part of the U S Navy.

Just kidding.

Even the SOD was smitten. Unfortunately, the Russians had a lot of free time on their hands which led me to introduce Lauren to an acquaintance of mine, Commander Marat Ivanov, a Russian sub Captain who I'd met in a sauna one winter while stranded in Sweden.

I know what you're thinking. Weeks on end. Under water in a submarine. All male crew.

It's not like that.

Really.

Actually, I was in Sweden as a result of having to patch up a little problem with the Russians, and Commander Ivanov who, unwittingly, became the object of my little problem. But, more on that later.

Anyway, Marat Ivanov is a slick operator. Good looking in that Russian sort of way. Kind of a cross between Alec Baldwin and Josef Stalin.

He has Stalin's good looks and Baldwin's libido.

They hit it off. And I've been regretting it ever since.

She broke into my jealous thoughts, "I think he likes me, Jack."

"I still like you."

She stepped back a little…

"…oh? I thought it was a Navy thing."

"You mean a Naval Academy thing. The only woman ever to graduate first in her class. You keep reminding me. Remember?"

When I said Lauren was super-smart, I was not being completely honest. Super-smart does not quite get there. This woman is a genius. Her IQ is off the chart. And on a fast track to make Admiral before she's forty.

There's a tradition at the Naval Academy where each of the graduating forth year midshipmen get a chance to climb up the Herndon Monument in front of the superintendent's home, and place his or her cap on the top.

As a side note here, this monument looks like a giant penis.

I'd say something crudely inappropriate here about Lauren's quest at attacking this monument. But I respect her.

Really. I do.

Anyway, legend has it that the first graduating midshipman to do so will become the first to make Admiral from the class.

One problem.

The monument is greased.

So, to get there, one needs the help of his or her fellow midshipmen.

In the case of Lieutenant Miller, she had plenty of help. From what I've heard, an all-out battle erupted as to who would stand on whose shoulders to push Miss Miller up the monument.

It turns out the guy who had, let's say, the money position was Clay Robins, a good old boy from Virginia, and the wide receiver for the football team.

He had great hands. And his job was to use both hands to grip Miss Miller's tight ass, and push her up while being pushed himself by those below.

Needless to say, she got to the top and placed her cap on the pointed top.

And needless to say, Mister Robins was all smiles.

All the way up.

And all the way down.

Lauren confided in me not long ago that Mister Robins indeed had great hands. And a couple of great fingers that were in places they should not have been while on that monument.

Interrupting my thoughts, she asks. "So, that's it?"

"You do have a great body."

I'm quick on my feet, as you can tell. But, as most women I know will say, I listen to Howard Stern way too much. As disgusting and vile as he is, there is one lone subject – and only one - he's right about.

Men's minds drift between money and sex. And usually go nowhere else.

This male-gene defect has no effect on Lauren.

It's beneath her.

"Marat thinks so." She offers. "He's in the Middle East. On board the Barracuda. Heading into the Red Sea."

Now you could slice the tense silence that has now descended onto the conversation.

But she can't resist, "you remember that boat, right Jack?"

I can feel the blade penetrate my heart. The sting is ever present. As I turn to busy myself with whatever, I suddenly feel her breast poke into my arm. Her head peering over my shoulder.

And in that soft and sensual voice, "you like being a once a month weekend warrior down here?"

Still a bit stung, I turn back at her, "not really...orders!" Lauren pouts as only Lauren can pout. And the look disarms me. Again.

So, now I have to bring the conversation back to some level of civility as she has once again, turned the tables.

How does she do that?

"Well...it's...you know."

She jumps right in, "yeah...I know...I have pictures."

Now my breathing has been ratcheted up as I hold a stare on this gorgeous blonde, but quickly realizing the moment could easily spin out of control.

She has that effect.

But, you've already figured that one out.

So, back to the photos of the mystery submarine. And I'm still baffled. I need to get a handle on this situation because it clearly makes no sense to me. As they say, something's fishy in Denmark. In this case, the Persian Gulf.

My gut tells me there's nothing good about this Intel. And I need to lock into some better data.

Thinking out loud, I say.

"Only Russians know how to run these Boats. I wouldn't trust the North Koreans rowing my 8 foot dingy on the surface – "Porky" named for my Mom, by Dad, who has a bizarre sense of humor at times. They'd still manage to hit something."

I don't think Lauren heard me because she says, "you never talk about that incident at sea - the collision with the Barracuda?"

Okay.

Maybe she was listening.

But I want to keep her on the current problem. Not the one from my infamous past.

"I forgot about it." So there. Drop it. Okay?

I guess it's sometimes the way I say things, and not what I say that rubs her the wrong way.

She can't let go. Kind of like a tick that's got hold of a piece of your fleshy leg.

She starts in again. "Those Russians – "

I get eyeball to eyeball with her because I'd really rather not discuss this with her right now.

Or anyone else.

"I was cleared – it was an accident!"

End of story.

Thank you very much.

Good night and good luck.

I move quickly to a bank of computer screens and concentrate on an array of data that could be Greek, Arabic, or even Russian to me.

I'm pissed, and she knows it.

She plops down in front of a flat screen close by and bangs away at the keyboard.

And all of a sudden this computer junk I'm staring at gets blurred, going out of focus right before my eyes.

I can't help but think I'm slipping into one of those "not for prime time" moments in my life.

I jam my eyes shut, and…

…my mind travels to a point in time over one year ago, and to a place I know very well out in the middle of the Pacific Ocean…

Chapter 8

MEMORY HIT
Pearl Harbor Naval Station, Hawaii -- One Year Ago

I gaze to my left, looking out a window that frames a perfect view of the Fleet as the ships radiate in the sun on this perfect morning in paradise. I'm immune to the sounds around me at the moment in the room where I sit in full dress Navy whites. My mind and soul are out there, somewhere in the fleet getting ready to steam out to sea after several blissful weeks in Hawaii.

What an absolutely perfect place.

Heaven on earth in every respect.

The Japs were fools to try to destroy it.

At least part of it.

Maybe they should have just waited and did what the current roster of Japanese business zillionaires are doing, and just buy-up the place.

Then package it up in tidy little pieces, and re-sell it to us dumb Americans.

I can see the real estate signs all over the Islands promoting hotels, condos, town homes, senior retirement centers. Whatever!

"From those wonderful folks who gave you Pearl Harbor.

Sushi not included."

My concentration is abruptly broken by the voice of Admiral Linnan, the senior judicial officer here in Hawaii.

"Captain Connolly, please stand."

As I snap back to reality, I realize I'm not in paradise, but in a Navy court room.

It's large. Rectangular in shape with windows on one wall. The other walls in soft oak paneling give the feeling of a high class men's club. Which is presumably what the Navy brass thinks of themselves. At least most of them. Especially the ones with gleaming stars on their shoulders.

Don't tell my Dad I said that.

Anyway, there are three of them seated at a rectangular judges bench, elevated, of course, at the far end of the room, opposite the entrance.

The big kahuna, Admiral Linnan, has three stars.

The other two only one star each.

Slackers.

But they all enjoy the title "flag officer" which means they get driven around in fancy staff cars with a flag waving off the front end.

It's an ego thing.

There's also a court reporter, a rather severe looking woman in her forties, and not particularly attractive. Not a native Hawaiian, who are quiet pretty. But I recognize her from all those deposition meetings where they try to discover what really happened. It's called "discovery." Like when Columbus discovered America, but swore under penalty of perjury he was in Asia, or India. Which is why the following year he landed in the Caribbean – an area now known as the West Indies – but thought he was back in India. Which explains the name, West Indies. Which explains why "discovery" is a way for saying "let's really screw with these bastards."

That's generally a bad sign in a Navy court room.

I mean, to have a court reporter – that is, let's say, "woof, woof?" Well, you get the point here.

It means the big guys up front want the lowly guy – me – to stay focused on what they have to say and not on some hot babe in a short skirt typing out Morse code or whatever crap she's typing.

Now standing at attention, I brace myself.

Admiral Linnan starts.

"Captain Connolly. It is the conclusion of this panel that the collision between the USS Baton Rouge, a submarine under your command at the time, and a Russian submarine, the Barracuda, was an unavoidable accident."

I hear collision.

Then unavoidable accident.

Things are looking better, quickly.

I think.

Admiral Linnan glances to the one star on his right, a guy who, at the moment, looks meaner than a rattle snake. The next part must be his doing.

"However..."

Uh oh.

However?

Not good.

Admiral Linnan continues.

"...the fact that this incident resulted in the serious injury of six Russian sailors, including the Russian Minister of Naval Operations on board the Barracuda at the time, demands that this panel impose a certain measure of disciplinary action despite the profound apologies to the Russians issued by the President of the United States..."

Admiral Linnan takes a moment as if maybe trying to figure out who the President is.

Actually, he's referring to his crib notes which hopefully includes a note or two about my exemplary service thus far as a submariner.

In any event, I break a barely noticeable sweat as the Admiral continues.

"Effective immediately, Captain Connolly, your rank is lowered one grade to Commander. You are relived of active duty status, and will not be eligible for a sea command in the future, barring an unlikely dispensation from the Chief of Naval Operations."

So much for wishful thinking.

This has to be the doing of the one star rattle snake. Getting busted one rank probably means a cut in pay. Guess that means Dutch treat on dates.

Well. It could be worse. I could get tossed right out of the Navy. But that's a court martial. And with family in high places, the good old boys club is likely still alive and well.

At least I'm hopeful.

Which brings Admiral Linnan to his final decree.

He looks at both one stars on either side, as if this next part was no one's idea. At least no one on the panel. Their looks back confirm my suspicion.

"You are to report to Miss Eiko Narita, National Security Advisor to the President, and at the personal request of the President, will serve as Deputy National Security Advisor for Naval affairs at the White House."

Like I said, it's good to have family in high places.

Sometimes.

I wonder if this means I'll be looking after those rumored affairs between White House staffers and the interns.

Sounds challenging.

I note Admiral Linnan has now leaned forward. He looks pissed as he assumes a hard-ass, no nonsense posture.

Uh oh.

More bad news on the way…maybe.

I morph into that deer-in-the-headlights look when I think it's bad news on the way.

"The fact that your father, retired Admiral Chuck Connolly, flew combat missions with the President in Vietnam has probably saved your ass, Mister Connolly."

The Admiral takes a deep breath. Maybe he wants to smack me upside the head.

The rattle snake guy sure does. There's fire in his eyes. Then…

"These proceedings are closed."

As he says this, he gavels down hard on the table. And all three stand and leave the room through a secret door hidden in the wall behind the elevated judges' bench.

And I wait a moment before I exhale.

My eyes drift to the court reporter.

We lock eyes.

Her gaze is telling.

I clearly dodged a bullet.

Maybe even a torpedo.

And landed in the White House, of all places.

She stands, and takes a step towards me. She wants to say something but just can't find the words. Probably something compassionate, knowing what I've been through these last few weeks. She looks as if she possesses that motherly instinct to tell me that losing a grade, a pay cut, taken off sea duty, perhaps forever, and being sent into the lion's den, i.e. the White House, to not worry. As my Mom would say, "everything will be alright."

She softens, then says. "The White House, huh? Just what they need back there. Another smart ass."

She turns, and quickly leaves the room.

And here I thought she had a sense of humor.

"Commander…Commander Connolly?"

There's that sexy voice again. Which instantly snaps me back to…

Present Day & Time

And Camp Peary where Miss Miller has captured my attention as I slowly massage my temples.

She's fixed on several computer monitors, speaking to no one in particular...

"Holy cow! I should've caught this."

I wander over to her shaking the cob-webs from my recent brain journey and glance at the screens.

And say to her, "please don't swear – there's a guy from India visiting."

"Holy shit!"

I respond. "Thanks, that's better."

Lauren leans back. Arms folded. Still fixed on the screens.

"She surfaced six days ago – for maybe three – four minutes, tops. We've got a satellite intercept..."

She bangs away at the keyboard for a few moments.

Then, "twenty-two miles south by southwest of the Yemen coast..."

I pull a chair beside her and try to absorb the data on the screens, looking to get up to speed. Although with Lieutenant Miller, one needs a super-charged brain just to keep her in sight.

"Data from the USS Dallas has her..."

She whacks the screen with the palm of her hand. Not happy with something at the moment.

"Don't tell me that!"

I gently prod, "what?"

"The Dallas was ordered off the target." She exhales a sigh.

Now I'm on it. "Where?"

Without responding, she bangs away at her keyboard, working still a third screen to her left. Ambidextrous would not fully describe her stunning abilities at working three screens simultaneously, while absorbing complicated data all at the same time.

She's truly remarkable.

A one-of-a-kind piece of ass.

Now I'm turned on.

I think about saying to her "I wanna drop my draws and bury the salami." But I don't. It's probably the others in the room that would make it difficult at the moment.

I break a sweat and say...

"What are you doing now?"

With a trace of nonchalance, she says, "I'll hack into sub-surface com sync."

"You can do that?"

And she gives me one of those sideways glances that says "you gotta be kidding."

Then, "please..."

A moment while she bangs away on the keyboard – her head moving from screen to screen. Then..."looks like the Dallas is joining up with the Brits – Persian Gulf theater exercises – top secret. Don't know why. But they'll be close to the Iranian border."

I stare at the screens, having no clue what I'm looking at, but expressing several authoritative "yeahs..."

Then, I sit alongside Lauren, shoulder to shoulder, looking thoughtful and concerned as Mister Happy crawls back into his cave.

I ask. "Who called off the Dallas?"

Lauren takes a moment, then replies, "she's heading into the Red Sea."

By not answering my question I could tell she's deep inside this problem, the salient issues bouncing around her brain. A Russian sub - maybe - not on the official radar screens, moving about anonymously does raise some serious concerns. That's the problem with submarine warfare. There's always present a huge unknown. So the best strategy is to just follow the guy.

But in this case, someone pulled off our shadow.

Interesting.

At least with surface ships you're able to see them from other ships, airplanes and satellites.

Not with subs.

Tricky business.

And even more so when you add sonar to the equation. Listening to those sounds under water takes a very special talent. What you think may be an enemy sub could easily be a hump back whale that's…well…humping. That's why we've got the Anti-Sub Sonar guys on every sub. They walk around with these gigantic headphones on, not hearing anything said on the boat but can quickly zero in on any boat anywhere, then "ping" some bizarre sound right back at the rouge sub. Usually the Anti-Sub Sonar guys send "pings" that could be easily interpreted as rough sex in the Lincoln bedroom, a skill learned during training listening to secret tapes made by Barbara Streisand during the Clinton Administration .

I call them the ASS men.

As I am presently the senior officer on duty and a highly qualified submariner to boot, I felt obligated to chime in on Lt. Miller's assessment.

"Maybe - you could be wrong."

She shot back, "I'm never wrong."

Okay.

So much for training, experience, and let's not forget, connections. But, time to go with the flow - think out of the box, above the waist.

"Definitely Russians – no question in my mind. So, I think we gotta serious problem. Not just the Dallas being pulled-off by some intelligence hack at the Pentagon, but a nuclear capable boat heading into the Red Sea."

I'm on a roll.

She's probably very impressed.

I think some more.

"A mission of this nature – whatever it is – a lone rider – requires planning and funding. You don't just drop a twenty billion dollar boat off your dock and into the water outside your vacation cabin in North Korea and sail into the hottest spot on the planet. There's a much bigger picture here than what we see, Lauren."

I felt my warfare training senses gelling. Like my brain being wrapped in a Dr. Scholl's foot pad.

"North Koreans, Russians – perhaps Iranians – those are the guys with the green-backs – I'm not feeling much love here."

Lauren settles back. Arms folded and just stares at me for a very long time. Then, "fifteen minutes and you've got it all figured out? Certainly sure of yourself."

Yeah.

Right.

Get with the program, babe.

I think to myself.

I do feel something bad about this.

And I give her that look that tells her so.

Or maybe it tells her "no sex for you tonight, honey."

But before I can re-adjust my tough expression, realizing that the sex part – not the part involving the serious sub situation presently confronting us and the rest of human civilization – was near the top of my "to do list," she jumps in.

"I estimate in about 39 hours she'll be within range – a missile strike. Presuming she's armed."

Trying to make up for my tough stand…

48

"At what? A camel jockey in the Arabian desert?"

Not taking the bait, she replies...

"Somewhere in the Middle East – perhaps oil fields, refineries. Maybe a U.S. military base or two."

And time stops for both of us. It takes a heartbeat for the consequences to sink in. And other possibilities. It's likely the missiles on board that sub are nuclear tipped.

Powerful enough to wipe out a major metropolitan area.

I'm getting anxious fast.

My mind reeling with a short list of large metro areas that can be reached from the Red Sea.

"Sonofabitch. I wanna know who ordered off the Dallas – where is she now?"

I stand and pace for a moment. Then, I sit again, next to Lauren. My head in my hands. The dire consequences run through my brain. Situations like this are why we're here at Camp Peary.

Looking for these "out of the ordinary" events that pop up. Generally, we dispatch them quickly, efficiently, and most of all, quietly.

In most cases, if a real threat can be identified, with no one out there telling us why they are there, not communicating, acting in a very suspicious manner, then "zap," it's history.

Quietly. No questions asked. No answers given.

Like the man said to Tom Cruise, "we will disavow any knowledge of your mission, Jim."

I thought his name was Tom.

But to have something like what Lauren has been tracking, and then have the shadow ordered off by some unknown moron, makes me just a bit nervous. No, make that scared-shitless. And I'm good at this job. I'd hate to think how I'd feel if I knew more.

It reminds me of the intelligence officer who, when asked by some brainless Congressman, or maybe it was a Senator, to tell everything he knows, responded to the elected official "...if I told you everything, sir, you'd pack up your family and move to an island in the South Pacific...permanently."

Scary.

Once again, I ask Lauren "where is she now?" Lauren leans towards me. And I can't help but notice her blouse open enough to highlight her full, twenty-something breasts just inches away. She whispers, "about three hours away, sir." And now softer, and more sensual, "Camp David, I mean – sir – it's only a three hour drive to see the President....sir."

And I look into those seductive blue eyes and can only think to say.

"And the lovely Miss Eiko Narita?"

Chapter 9

Camp David, Maryland
Monday, Labor Day
1003 Zulu, 0403 Hrs. Local

EIKO NARITA stands at a handcrafted paned window.

Her smooth, slightly yellow/olive skin radiates a satin finish to her otherwise Oriental features.

Her natural beauty is subtly highlighted by the moonlight filtering through the double hung window in the rustic cabin. It conceals her youthful, stunning looks, as well as her small, yet perfect figure despite the fact she's not far from 50 years old.

Her gaze seems off into nowhere as her eyes stay fixed on the darkness outside. Not only is it dark, but there is literally nothing to look at.

Deep in the woods in a remote location in Northwest Maryland, and about 70 miles from Washington, DC, Camp David is the ultimate retreat.

Inaccessible to everyone, except the President and his invited guests, the Navy stewards who man the Camp, and the Secret Service who are never invited but always show up, Camp David gives the President a reason to escape into a quiet, serene world away from the media, the West Wing and the usual gang of idiots on the Hill.

It's a great place if you happen to not like anyone in Washington, DC which, for a President, usually runs in both directions.

President Eisenhower had it created for himself after things in D C got a little dicey during his administration. Lyndon Johnson, then the Senate Majority Leader, thought he was the President.

Although he ultimately got there, the result of a tragic incident in Dallas.

Having Johnson around town drove Eisenhower nuts.

Since he didn't like anyone very much, not just that blowhard from Texas, and was getting bored with the war games his military pals would develop on a daily basis – "Hey Ike, let's send Veep Nixon to Russia.

Then nuke 'em. Ha. Ha. Ha." - it's safe to say that apparently no one liked Nixon, even back then - Eisenhower needed a "happy place," or Mamie – his wife - was going to fling him off the Truman balcony, built at the White House during the Truman administration as a way of disposing Republicans after the brandy and cigars.

Having very few friends, he was hard pressed to give this new retreat an appropriate name.

After giving it some very introspective thought, he had it named after his young grandson, David Eisenhower.

In true Eisenhower military form he decided to screw the politicians who wanted to name it after a famous Navy Admiral – i.e., why it's a "Camp" and not a Fort (Army), which is telling unto itself as Eisenhower was the only 5 star General in the history of the U S Army.

Or name it – God forbid – after a respectable former Senator or Congressman (although he did comment to Lyndon Johnson suggesting that if he invited Veep Nixon to his ranch in Texas where just maybe the Veep would be "accidently" shot during a duck hunt – known in Texas as a Cheney shoot – he'd name the Camp after Johnson).

But in the end Eisenhower said…

"…the most suitable recognition should go to my 6 year old grandson, David."

It's good to be the President.

So thought Ms. Eiko Narita.

Perhaps the brightest star on the Washington, DC landscape, she has degrees from U C Berkeley, UCLA, not to mention a law degree from Harvard, and a PhD from Stanford.

And she had taught briefly at Stanford prior to being recruited by the President.

But Eiko harbors a truly painful emotional scar.

One not easily over-come despite her extensive education and remarkable climb to the top of the intelligence community, garnering more respect and admiration than any other National Security Advisor from previous administrations.

Including her hero and idol, Condelesa Rice.

Transfixed by the darkness outside her private cabin here at Camp David, unable to sleep, her mind wanders back in time to those days as a young girl in California listening to the endless stories her grandparents told.

Times spent in her home while her own parents worked long and hard hours to support her and her grandparents.

Stories of hard times for her elderly and frail grandparents. When they were rounded-up and placed in secure facilities known as internment camps during the second world war.

Camps that, for the most part, lacked even the bare necessities, a far cry from what most Americans took for granted as commensurate with basic human dignity.

Camps that turned a blind eye towards one group of Americans – men, women and, yes, children classified as Japanese-Americans.

Camps that were not at all camps in the sense that Camp David is a camp.

Prisons – not camps - that held decent, hardworking Americans. Forced to give up everything they had, and had worked for to provide for their families.

Eiko reflected on this quite often.

Perhaps way too often.

But even more so when she found herself here at Camp David. The thought of those stories gave her chills. It kept her from a good nights' sleep.

Something badly needed when you work directly for the President of the United States. Although her grandparents are long gone, the memories were still there.

Her only regret now was the disappointment she felt not being able to share her remarkable accomplishments with those two whom she loved deeply.

It was their struggle as immigrants, then as outcasts from the country and culture they freely accepted that has provided Eiko with the determination to make it all right again.

In her mind revenge may be sweet.

But pay-back is hell.

Chapter 10

Despite being a member of the United States military establishment since that first day I reported to the Naval Academy, I have never liked getting up before 9 or 10 in the morning. Before 6 in the morning just does not feel right. For one thing, it's dark. I mean, what can you do in the dark. Okay, some things, but not many. Then there's the problem of someone else sleeping not just in the same room, but in the same bed. Usually I end up waking that person because I'm not the most careful sleep-walker at 4 o'clock something in the morning. Particularly after getting less than two hours of sleep.

Which presents another problem. That is, having to stay awake the next 3 or so hours while driving up to Camp David. I'm thinking if I can make it to DC, maybe I can hitch a ride with someone for the final one hour leg. Actually, now that I think about it, the Veep, Seth Greene, owes me a ride in his chopper.

We were playing poker late one night in the OEOB – the Veep, I, his chief of staff, some nerdy bean counter from the White House budget office – they're all that way – and this gorgeous young intern, Jenny. She was maybe twenty-one, a student at Georgetown, and the daughter of some Governor. Maybe Michigan, or Montana – I don't remember. One those M states. The Veep was winning, of course, although the nerd from the budget office was determined to not let that happen. Little did he know that if he did end beating the Veep he'd be transferred to Guam, counting coconuts?

Anyway the Veep takes me aside and whispers, "let me win this next hand, Connolly – I wanna stick it the bean counter – he's looking to nail Jenny."

So was I, sir. But I couldn't tell him that, and then I'd be the one transferred to Guam. Or worse. I'd have to be Pelosi's assistant in charge of Botox treatments.

Before I could respond he said. "Make 'em look like a jackass, and you can have her. I'll set it up."

I'm getting to like the Veep more and more. My kind of guy. But I thought it best to play it cool.

"I don't know, sir. Maybe…if this works out can I get to use your chopper for, you know an emergency, or something." Actually what I had in mind was using his chopper to impress a date.

Date: "Okay, Jack. I'll eat wherever you want."

Me: "I'm taking you to dinner at Le Cirque in New York."

Date: "But we're in Washington…I think."

Me: "Not to worry. We'll just take the Veep's chopper."

Date: "Who's V P?"

Me: "The Vice President of the United States."

Date: "oh…OH…OH…OH"

Me: "Wait, that comes after dinner, when we're back at your place."

Maybe I need to stay away from the bimbos in this town.

Anyway, the Veep said okay, but he wanted proof.
Proof?
The guy is a typical Marine.

So, the next morning I strolled into his office in the OEOB and tossed a pair of pink lace panties onto his desk and said…

"I'll call you, big guy."

Actually, I didn't say that, but he got the message and knew that I'd be calling in the marker at some point in the near future.

The idea now is to sneak out without waking the lovely and sexy Lieutenant Miller who appears to be sleeping soundly – face down and buck naked. I mean after the work-out we had a little while ago, she should be exhausted. I know I am. But I've got about fifteen years on her.

And my neatly pressed uniform on.

And less than four hours to get to Camp David.

But I can't take my eyes off of that gorgeous butt.

...shit!

Chapter 11

Washington, DC
Monday, Labor Day
1215 Zulu, 0615 Hrs. Local

LARRY MITCHENER sits at his kitchen table. In a basic, no frills kitchen. His hands finger a coffee mug. It's off-white ceramic stenciled "I love my Dad." He takes in the sparse surroundings as if lost in a million memories. Or maybe just simply lost. Larry's eyes appear blood-shot, but it's unclear if it's from a lack of sleep, or something more.

As he stands to refill the coffee mug from a counter-top coffee maker, his gait and posture belie an African-American man perhaps in his eighties.

Truth be told, Larry celebrated his 48th birthday yesterday.

Alone.

Leaning against the counter, he takes several more sips of the black java, then meticulously rinses the cup in the adjacent sink, and places it into the dish rack. Each step carefully performed as if it had been done - alone - a million times before this time. A moment as he watches the remnants of water drip from the Rubbermaid pad down into the sink.

He then wipes the sink dry, carefully folding the towel onto a shining towel rack.

Larry takes a look through a curtain to the outside. He moves the fabric aside, checking the early morning sky.

As he holds a stare out onto the gently breaking daylight, his mind drifts back to how he got to this place and time.

A journey he takes at least several times a day.

A journey with lots of good and promising times along the way.

For Larry Mitchener it all started back home in Petersburg, Virginia where more the 30 years earlier his life became front page news. Despite the large percentage of African-Americans living in this small city south of Richmond, Larry transcended the racial divide that had made Petersburg an embarrassment to all of Virginia even after passage of the Civil Rights Act signed into law by President Johnson in the mid-sixties, and quickly became the towns' sports hero. A not so easy accomplishment in a town filled with the children, grandchildren and great grandchildren of slaves. A town that sits next to Colonial Heights, Virginia where Blacks and Jews were encouraged to live elsewhere up until just a few years ago.

And a town that is just a short drive from Chester, Virginia where its citizens proudly fly the Confederate – or Rebel – flag in the town square in place of the stars and stripes, even to this day.

Larry's accomplishments came from his spectacular performance on his High School football team. A performance that took him and his team to the state championships two straight years.

From out of the ashes of a miserable life in near poverty, Larry not only took full advantage of his athletic abilities, but was one who paid attention in the classroom, acquiring the education his parents and grandparents found hard, if not impossible to attain.

His great grandparents, slaves on the tobacco, then peanut farms, never saw the inside of a classroom.
The combination of brains and brawn won him several scholarship offers. And Larry wisely chose a school outside of Virginia, and in the North.

Princeton became his home for 4 years. And the school administration and alumni became his family away from Petersburg. Not for any reason other than his ability on the football field.

He could have anything and everything. And at times had to turn down certain "perks" knowing they were falling into the gray area of the NCAA rules. A decision that, at times, baffled alumni, hungry for notoriety at the expense of the rules, particularly the Wall Street lawyers and bankers who donated heavily to Princeton each year.

If there was anything his parents back home in Petersburg, Virginia had taught him, it was simply a man's character is built and sustained by his integrity, and nothing else. Recognizing that Wall Street and its inhabitants were anything but God-fearing, principled money changers, he held hard and fast to his principles as if they were the Lord's gospel.

His achievements were not just limited to the football field. He excelled in the classroom as well, absorbing everything he could, knowing his life after Princeton may easily be decided by the color of his skin. At least he'd be able to make a coherent and intelligent case for whatever abilities he possessed if he applied himself at Princeton.

With each and every class at Princeton, he absorbed not just the subject matter, but the over-arching lesson buried deep in the sub-text of how to fully learn what he needed to learn.

It was his early foundation in integrity that acted as a moral compass for Larry. And what better way to honor his parents with their basic guidance of him as a youngster then to move from college to law school.

Despite being drafted by the New York Jets of the NFC, he choose acceptance by the Harvard Law School.

For Larry, his connection with sports and his ability to get whatever he wanted using sports, placed him at a moral disadvantage from his point of view.

So, Harvard it was.

And it was.

Upon graduation, he found offers from the major New York and Washington, DC law firms to be attractive. The right pedigree that would help him move ahead quickly and make his family proud. Break the ties to poverty and slavery that bound his family to a history and way of life not addressed in the beliefs our country's forefathers had envisioned back in 1776.

However, he quickly learned that his reputation as a college football star – the star power it generated, the rejection of a pro career with style and grace, and being at the top of his class at Harvard – added up to the real attraction for these "white shoes" firms.

He was to be their token African-American super star. To be paraded in front of drooling prospective clients with deep pockets.

Larry would be the side show – the one who would get the big bucks into the tent.

All show – no play!

It was one of the more satisfying days of his life when he told them "…thanks, but no thanks."

He finally settled into a mid-level firm in Washington, DC. They did some corporate work. Largely insignificant cases that fell well below the radar in the District. Cases that involved clients on the fringes of the infamous Capital beltway. And some pro-bono work that involved community organizers and their efforts at helping the job-less and home-less.

He spent some part of each day waiting for that big break. A chance to reach out and catch the gold ring once again. But next, on his terms.

And then it came, as if an epiphany.

Larry would catch a pick-up game of hoop at a local high school two or three times a week. He quickly made friends with some of the fellas.

But one in particular would join Larry and a few others after most games for a beer at the near-by East Hills Tavern.

PETER MCGUIGAN was older than Larry – maybe by six or seven years.

Personable, but reserved.

Didn't say much, but offered opinions on most topics germane to Washington, DC. They were not way to the left, nor right. Just simple, plain spoken neutral and fair-minded observations.

Larry liked that.

Nothing pretentious.

Certainly nothing one would find in Washington, DC. Mcguigan had integrity and an open mind. Larry knew he was also an attorney, like most of the other guys who played in the pick-up game.

Not an unusual fact given they were in Washington, DC where many work the low road to discovery.

Kind of like living in Hollywood where everyone is a soon-to-be famous actor. Pimping for whoever is just temporary work. Just need to drop your drawers – or panties – every now and then.

Whether on a sound stage or in the White House.

Although Larry knew Mcguigan was with the Treasury Department, he wasn't sure in what capacity.

Not until Mcguigan asked Larry to dinner. At a quiet, out of the way place in Mclean, Virginia. Not all that far from the main entrance to the Central Intelligence Agency.

It was here that Larry's life took a new direction.

Mcguigan identified himself as a Secret Service agent.

He said to Larry. "There are special agents, Larry...then there are special agents.

And for the next twenty years Larry Mitchener, now Special Agent Larry Mitchener, worked for the United States Secret Service.

Not the usual every two year re-posting assignment, very little VIP protective detail assignments, but as a very unique and highly trained investigator.

He traveled the world investigating threats on U.S. government leaders, threats to our national security directly and indirectly related to those in high positions.

His work often dove-tailed with work performed by the FBI, giving Larry a broad scope of specialized experience. Working areas where quiet, behind the scenes criminal activities – the white collar kind – took place.

Most of his work was confidential and highly classified, the activities and results known only to highly placed individuals at the Secret Service and the FBI, and not ever including anyone at the Treasury or Justice Department, particularly political appointees.

God forbid they should tell the Justice Department everything, with subversive socialists, and other liberal hacks out to suck-up our liberties while playing God by wielding its power over these highly skilled, patriotic agencies.

Although he worked his way up to the level of Inspector, with a small, yet highly efficient team at his disposal, he grew weary of his very secretive unit's mission – "bring those behind the scenes of outlandish criminal behavior – those who used connections and well-financed legal teams – to justice."

Maybe it was the long hours away from his family – now a wife, Lou Anne, and two wonderful children – or the fact that most of the cases he had solved and wrapped up into neat little packages then sent off to a task force at the DOJ, but fell into the proverbial circular file, that started the downward spiral into hell.

We can't be sure.

But one thing is for sure.
Larry Mitchener is determined to get his life...
...his family...
...and his job back on track.

Chapter 12

U. S. Naval Observatory, Washington, DC
Monday, Labor Day
1230 Zulu, 0630 Hrs. Local

As dawn breaks through the gray/blue late summer sky it lights up the east front of the gray Naval Observatory building on the expansive grounds several miles up Massachusetts Avenue from downtown Washington, DC. The old building is a short punt from a huge Victorian-style structure on the grounds known as the Admiral's home.

Although, local scuttle butt has its current occupant pondering a possible name change more fitting for a former Marine Corps General. Based on stories that circulated this town during the time Al and Tipsy Gore occupied the home, it almost had its unofficial name changed to the "Green" House. Fortunately, those in power once again laughed off one of Al Gore's bone-headed ideas as a joke.

And so the name "Admirals Home" stuck.
It's a typical nineteenth-century home in the Queen Anne style as snobby Washingtonians would say, teeth firmly clenched together. It was built for the Superintendent of the United States Naval Observatory in 1893 on lands that had originally been owned and donated by Margaret and Cornelius Barber, wealthy Georgetown landowners, and perhaps influential lobbyists who were looking to have a naval ship named for them, but instead ending up having a chain of men's hair salon's – cleverly known as Barber Shops – named for them.

In 1929, the house became home to the U.S. Navy's Chief of Naval Operations, and was officially named "Admiral's House."

In 1974, the house was designated as the first official residence of the Vice President of the United States.

Since that time, seven Veep's have resided there with their families.

Entering the main foyer, a visitor is greeted by a Navy steward, and a sign that reads "Haircuts – No Charge."

However, it is well known that Dick Cheney was never allowed to run around the house with a pair of scissors in his hands.

Go figure!

Dew covers a vast expanse of lawn. It appears to twinkle in the sunlight. But, it then suddenly vanishes in a blink as sharper angled rays of sun strike the lawn as seconds tick by.

Four gleaming black Ford Crown Victoria's with tinted windows are parked near the front door to the Admirals home. But these are not your standard Secret Service issue vehicles. No SUV's that cleverly conceal an arsenal of massive fire-power, trained agents dressed in Kevlar fatigues ready to leap at anything or anybody, and enough communications equipment to rival any law enforcement agency in the world.

No, just four Crown Vic's.

And a small posse of casually dressed Secret Service Agents who wear Oakley or Ray ban sunglasses, and barely visible ear pieces.

And guns.

Really big guns that require special tailoring of ones clothes.

Several of these guys – and two women – nurse Starbucks coffee cups. Others simply stretch, yawn or scratch.

Another day – a holiday, no less – on a shit detail.

They stand at the entrance to the home of the Vice President of the United States.

Then, the sound of a two-way crackles somewhere near-by.

"Look sharp – Sandpiper is out in two."

The agents don't budge. Despite the announcement that the second most powerful guy in the free world is about to emerge from his current residence, the agents treat the announcement as if it were a bird chirping in the distance.

However, one agent takes a step or two, looking off in the distance. He's looking at a U.S. Marine Chopper parked on a grassy knoll about 50 yards from the Admiral's home. Its turbine engine wines – ready to rock.

The agent checks his watch. Then eyes another agent.

"You'd think the guy would have told the Corps not to send the bird over today. Ya know? Save a few bucks?"

The other agent – a more senior guy – steals a glance at the Marine Chopper. Then back to the junior agent...

"Not for Sandpiper. It's for some White House VIP."

The junior agent takes a moment to think about this. Then says...

"Yeah. I get it. Someone kissin' someone's ass."

Several of the guys chuckle in unison.

Chapter 13

On Massachusetts Avenue, Near 34th Street
Outside the Main Gate to the Admiral's Home
1234 Zulu, 0634 Hrs. Local

A scuffed blue and white Police unit pulls to a stop, blocking what little traffic – two vehicles - there is heading northwest, just short of the intersection. He jumps quickly from his unit, straightens his gun belt, and moves with some haste into the intersection. This guy's a greenhorn, fresh out of the academy. And seems to be more concerned about the two vehicles behind his blue and white unit then moving to halt any other traffic heading into the intersection from 34th street.

After a series of clearly bizarre hand signals that carry no meaning whatsoever to the two drivers waiting, he takes a moment to scan up Massachusetts Avenue and now notices another blue and white unit has blocked traffic heading southeast, about 500 feet from the scrubbed greenhorn cop.

That cop just leans on his unit, shaking his head at the newbie spinning around in the intersection, hands held up to stop traffic that is already stopped.

The young cop now shifts his attention the main gate and driveway leading up to the Admiral's home. It's flanked with two huge ships' anchors, reportedly off a retired aircraft carrier.

And as he just stares, looking for signs of activity, or simply signs of anything, the huge wrought iron gate swings open. Just as the gate clears the far side, with no room to spare, four Crown Victoria's suddenly appear, inches from each other, and at high speed.

They hang a left, and accelerate up Massachusetts Avenue, leaving some serious rubber, and vanish.

Just like that.

The newbie cop throws up a salute in the apparent confusing situation as the speeding vehicles fly past him. He, of course, is unsure which of the four vehicles carries the Veep. So, he simply salutes each vehicle.

Behind the smoke-glass tinted windows of each Crown Vic, Secret Service agents give him the finger.

Chapter 14

Intersection of Massachusetts and Wisconsin Avenue
1249 Zulu, 0649 Hrs. Local

And now the four car motorcade swings right onto Wisconsin, avoiding some serious collision possibilities as it nears the Washington Cathedral.

The few pedestrians out this early on a holiday pay no attention to the fast moving vehicles. It goes with the territory, as one might expect living in this part of the U.S.A.

Except for Larry Mitchener, who is standing in front of his apartment building, and who now burrows his forehead as he follows the Crown Vic's until they're out of sight. He then checks his watch.

Then casts another bewildered look up Wisconsin at the quickly vanishing vehicles.

Silently, under his breath, "shoot, what the hell…?"

As Larry searches his brain for a logical explanation…

"Hey, Larry! What's up, man?"

It's Larry's friend, Jack Connolly, our guy from Camp Peary, on his way to Camp David.

Jack bounds from Sid's deli with coffee and copies of the Washington Post, and Washington Times in hand.

These two guys are neighbors, and, more importantly, friends.

Chapter 15

Now here's my pal, Larry, staring up Wisconsin
Avenue as if he just missed a bus. And pointing as if there's
someone with him. Moreover, what's he doing out here on the
sidewalk this early in the morning? I thought his drinking
problem was behind him by now. We worked on it together
for several months. Now what's happened to the guy?

I get closer, "hey, Larry, you okay?"

Still pointing up Wisconsin, "who do ya figure at this
hour, Jack?"

I take a look at the almost out of sight motorcade.

"Crown Vic's? Metro PD? Can't be Feds. I mean, they
only go for the pricey rides, right?"

Larry just shrugs. Then…"hey Jack. Ya think I could
borrow your SUV? See it there in garage. Ya know, ya never
use it, and all."

Larry's car was re-possessed a few weeks back. And
when Lou Ann left him, and took the kids with her to New
York, the kids were already strapped-into the family van.
So, she took that, as well.

I take the SUV keys from my key chain, and toss them
to Larry.

"She might need some gas."

Larry thinks for a moment as he pulls out his wallet.

"Figured that already, Jack." As he fingers a twenty.

"Hey man, you're the best. Thanks."

I stroll a few yards to my 5 series Beemer parked at the
curb, "on my way to Camp David. The President's annual
Labor Day barbecue."

I turn and give him a big smile, "compliments of the taxpayers, you know."

Larry can't help but shake his head in disgust, "shoot, you White House guys burn my ass."

I jump into the Beemer. Crank up the 5.35 liter engine. Then lean out the window towards my friend.

"Sorry. Gotta go. Catching a lift in Sandpiper's chopper."

I give him a wave.

"Another boring day in the life of a White House staffer."

Larry just has say to me, "boring, my ass, Jack."

And I take off, heading for the Veep's residence just a few blocks away.

Chapter 16

Tenley Circle
Washington, DC
1259 Zulu, 0659 Hrs. Local

The four car motorcade, all black and shiny Crown Victoria's, flies around Tenley Circle scaring pigeons near-by into flight who quickly vanish into the early morning mist. The motorcade picks up Wisconsin Avenue on the far side of the Circle, and now crosses out of the District of Columbia shortly after they bear left onto River Road, traveling just west of Chevy Chase and Somerset where the scenery changes instantaneously as it is now in...

Montgomery County, Maryland
1300 Zulu, 0700 Hrs. Local

...and several hundred feet short of the infamous Beltway/I-495 entrance ramp. And it's here that the rear two cars of the motorcade break right onto Burdette Road, and slow to a glide.

The Two Lead Crown Vic's...

...continue northwest at high speed on River Road. Off in the distance to the southwest, less than three miles away, yet clearly visible poking through tops of oaks, maples and poplars, is the unassuming, yet mysterious roof of the Central Intelligence Agency.

Antennas and satellite dishes point ominously at the heavens.

On Burdette Road
The Two Rear Crown Vic's...

...limp down Burdette Road as if checking the high-end homes in the fancy neighborhood, home to wealthy Congressional leaders, senior government officials, White House senior staffers, and those really wealthy Federal decision makers, lobbyists.

Except those, of course, currently residing in Federal prison along with swell guys like Bernie Madoff and all the former Governors of Illinois.

On the left, a golf course hidden beyond large trees, and a chain link fence topped with two racks of barbed wire. Local lore has it that the barbed wire serves as a deterrent - i.e., to trap players looking for a quick escape - those golfers who play with the high and mighty of Washington, DC, but lie about their handicaps. Suddenly having a great round and a high handicap doesn't sit well with the usual lying and cheating power brokers of DC.

Entrance to Congressional Country Club

In the meantime, the two lead Crown Vic's waste no time. They now hang a left, through an entrance gate of someplace that immediately looks exclusive.

It has the air and calm of waspy snobbery, too many Jags and Mercedes in the tucked away parking field, and hunched-over, well-aged African-American landscapers. One would never hear Spanish spoken at this place, that's for sure.

The small, discreet sign at the entrance reads Congressional Country Club.

Near Burning Tree Country Club

On the other hand, our two rear Crown Vic's pass a well-worn sign at an unobtrusive entrance gate.

It reads Burning Tree Country Club.

Private.

Congressional Country Club

At the Congressional Country Club our two lead Crown Vic's come to a stop at the bag drop.

From the two vehicles four Secret Service men exit as a golf pro, and let's ID this guy as TONY, steps up to the vehicle and looks in, then moves to the next vehicle and carefully examines the interior is well.

Then Tony, looking a little befuddled, turns to one of the Secret Service men and asks "hey, where's the Veep?" There's an awkward beet here, somewhere below the surface, it's quite deceptive.

Two of the Secret Service men exchange glances one not knowing what the other will want to say in the situation. The agent that appears to be the man in charge turns back to Tony and says quite emphatically "the Veep will be along shortly."

And that's that. Now, everyone just stands around looking at each other.

Chapter 17

Burning Tree Country Club
1305 Zulu, 0705 Hrs. Local

All is very quiet as we find ourselves at the number one
tee box.

SENATOR JOE SYKES, a guy somewhere in his 40s,
and looks a little bit older, pockets his cell phone, takes a puff
on his Monte Christo cigar, and steps to a guy named BOBBY,
an aging golf pro.

Bobby, adjusting his bifocals, squints at the tee-time
sheet in his hand. A moment passes.

"Listen Bobby. Why don't you just go on in. I'm just
waitin' on a couple of fellas from the staff. No one really
important today."

Bobby glances up at Sykes, then back down at his tee
time sheet, then back up to the senator and says,

"slowest Labor Day I've seen in the month of Texas
Sunday's, Senator."

Sykes has a gentle smile for Bobby. Takes a look around
himself at the quiet, peaceful environment, and comments
softly, "yeah, you got that right, Bobby."

With that, Bobby wanders off back towards the
clubhouse.

As Sykes carefully watches him move away.

His smile vanishes. And he develops a deceptive, then
concerned expression.

For those who know Sykes, it is quite obvious he is a
politician's politician. A man with many, many secrets below
the surface. Nor is he easily fooled. He plays the game well,
much to the disappointment of even his fellow colleagues in
the Senate.

So it is no surprise that this man may have a very secretive agenda which involves not just lying to the starter, Bobby, but also attempting to manipulate anything and everything in his environment.

He is simply a man to be watched and feared.

Chapter 18

Congressional Country Club
1311 Zulu, 0711 Hrs. Local

At the Congressional Country Club bag drop, Tony, the starter, trots over towards a Secret Service agent standing casually alongside the car.

Tony hesitates a moment looking over the Secret Service agent carefully not knowing exactly how to approach this guy in the sunglasses, wearing an ear piece, and who appears to be quite indifferent to Tony, puts on a somewhat happy face.

He says "say, I got a full till today chief. Is the Veep gonna be long, you think?"

Slowly the Secret Service agent turns towards Tony and gives him a pissed look through his sunglasses. He holds that look for a long moment.

Then sites casually down the long driveway, ignoring Tony.

Tony waits a moment, looking over at the other agents, not knowing how to break the ice.

Although he does begin to wonder why the Service never did a thorough security check several days ago as is the customary procedure. He's been in this town long enough to know the ins and outs of dealing with high profile politicians.

He takes a new tack.

"Listen. You guys gonna fill me in on what the hell's going on? Or do I place a call to the Veep's Chief of Staff, who just happens to be a member?"

This gets the lead agent's attention.

The lead agent takes a few steps at Tony, towering over him by several inches, and in his face.

Another agent moves from behind.

Tony can feel the guy breathing down his neck.

Maybe he made a bad call here.

Tony breaks a sweat.

The lead Agent takes an eternity to simply stare at Tony. Then, a glance at his partner behind the former amateur golf pro.

A sharp glance at Tony...

"Go ahead. Make that call."

Chapter 19

Larry Mitchener's Apartment
1314 Zulu, 0714 Hrs. Local

It's a neatly furnished, modest apartment.

It has the look of a new bachelor.

Clearly absent is the use of color and stylish fabrics. Not exactly a bachelors pad but a place to crash, and modest might be an overstatement. It is certainly clean.

And everything seems to be in its place and very well organized. Its occupant must be a methodical, careful person.

Someone who strives for perfection to the point of being almost anal.

Larry Mitchener comes through the front door. Even though it's quite early in the morning Larry looks as if he still needs another full night's rest. He closes the door carefully, and sends home the dead bolt, turning to notice the answering machine on the entrance hall table.

Staring now for a long moment at the answering machine he notices the red message light flashing.

This surprises him as just less than one half hour ago there were no messages. He checks the time on his wristwatch and frowns again for a long moment then back to the answering machine.

Larry punches the play button and hears the new message beep.

The machine says "new message at 7:08 AM."

Then followed by a condescending voice of obviously someone very important.

"Agent Mitchener? This is director Mcguigan. I need you at Homeland Security. My office. ASAP."

There's a long pause here as Larry waits for the message to continue, at the same time he checks his watch once again.

"We've got a serious situation."

There's a loud beep.

It's a moment before Larry hits the stop button.

He stands there staring at the answering machine.

"Shoot."

Chapter 20

United States Marine Chopper - a/k/a Marine Two
Somewhere over the Potomac River
1317 Zulu, 0717 Hrs. Local

The Marine chopper normally identified as Marine two, roars along a flight path just 500 feet above the Potomac River. Usually accompanied by another chopper, this aircraft is traveling solo.

At least that's what they tell me. Why there is not another chopper flying alongside for extra added protection I don't know. Perhaps the Veep himself is using the chopper, but then again I was told he's supposed to be playing golf somewhere in DC. So my take on this situation is that if there were a very well trained yet mentally challenged terrorist hiding along the river banks of the Potomac River holding a bazooka on his shoulder he'll look up and probably say "hey where is the other chopper?" Then after giving it some very serious thought would then conclude that since there is no second chopper, the chopper I'm flying in does not carry the Vice President of the United States. So, therefore I feel perfectly safe flying with just one chopper, and me being in that one chopper.

Or so I keep telling myself that to make me feel much more comfortable. It's simply a matter of basic common sense. But then again why are the Marine officers on this aircraft armed?

And why are they flying so low?

And carefully looking left and right.

Maybe they're looking for a terrorist with a bazooka on his shoulder.

I gotta stop thinking like this.

Maybe I'll make a call on the satellite phone on the bulkhead here in front of me. I'm sure the Veep won't mind. He probably doesn't check the bills from the phone company. In all likelihood he just turns them over to some low-level lackey in the general accounting office who would not dare question the vice president's telephone bills.

Since this is probably a secure telephone, I'll need to punch in a lot of numbers. This is to get through the near impossible security firewall that exists from this chopper to Camp Peary where I think I'll check in on the lovely and talented Lieut. Miller.

As the phone on the other end rings I take a look out to the right side and notice a well-manicured golf course. And I wonder if that's where Veep Greene is going to get in a round of golf with a couple of big dogs from Capitol Hill. And I also wonder what's on his mind. Who is he going to beat up today, and for what. He's one tough cookie that Veep and I would hate to be on the golf course with him today.

Who knows what could happen.

I hear the receiver on the other end lifted, and then just some soft breathing.

"Lieut. Miller. Did I wake you?"

Lieut. Lauren Miller, her naked body barely covered by a pastel blue sheet, shifts the telephone handset to her other ear, and seductively says...

"Three times, Commander."

I can barely contain myself, even on the telephone several hundred miles away she knows how to get me going. My thoughts race like crazy from everything that happened in the past five or six hours not including the drive up to Washington DC where she was constantly on my mind. I've got to get back to the topic at hand. I gotta get myself focused and ask her an important question.

Right now, my mind is pudding.

I take a deep breath.

Okay, get it together, Jack.

"Lauren, make contact with Admiral Max Hasslinger, at the Pentagon. See what he knows about the Russian sub."

Max is a good friend and an expert on submarine warfare. And at one time my boss. Someone who can think clearly, and be trusted. A hard combination to find in Washington, DC. Now he's got some lofty job at the Pentagon, where his aides do everything for him, except think, after serving almost 25 years on a nuclear sub, the last 6 years as Captain. And now we need him to think about this potential renegade submarine in the hands of North Koreans. I hope he still likes me.

" Right. Admiral Hasslinger."

Sitting up and holding the pastel sheet up high she thinks carefully, trying to get sharply focused on the matter at hand.

"I've been giving this some thought, Jack. It can't be a training mission. They'd have to call ahead to get through the Suez Canal. You know they're all kinds of fees and paperwork, which they didn't do. I checked earlier while trying to plot a possible course."

Thinking about that, I know she's right. She's on top of this. But as the commanding officer I have to say,

"I already know that, Lauren. But what I'm thinking is there's no way those bird-brain North Koreans can find their way back to Korea after dropping off their "cargo" near Yemen. Which is presumably what they did."

"Okay, Jack, I'll e-mail all the data we have to Admiral Hasslinger right now."

"Right. Do that. So what I'm thinking is someone else is on that boat."

She says, with conviction, "Russians. Russians have got to be on that boat as hired guns. Not just navigating."

She cuts off my thoughts and jumps in to say. "Unless they are heading towards the Suez Canal. I mean, into the Red Sea. That puts them close – ballistic missile range close - to some sensitive places like, say, Israel without having to go through the Canal."

"Right."

And I can't think of anything more alarming at the moment. Obviously, if this particular scenario is truly viable then we've got a responsibility to send this data up the line. However, my gut tells me that does not include the CIA Director, Mister Unger. Better to let the President, or Eiko, give him that piece of analysis. And I'm still going with my best instincts here.

"Just tell the Admiral Hasslinger what we've been up to, okay?"

And with that question Lauren plops back down onto her pillow and develops a very comforting smile, her free hand moving slowly under the sheets.

"Shall I tell him everything, Commander?"

A heartbeat before I go completely rigid. I swallow hard. And after a moment I start looking quickly around the interior of the chopper. Wondering if anybody has just heard our conversation. Then it suddenly dawns on me the NSA over there at Fort Meade in Maryland, probably have not only heard everything we just said but have been carefully recording this conversation.

I break a sweat.

I manage to get a voice, and say into the phone...

"Clear."

And quickly replace the handset on the bulkhead.

Chapter 21

The 154 meter Oscar Class Russian submarine, Bear Oscar Kim Jong, whips along at 30 knots. Its torpedo-shape cuts through the deep blue-black water. A total of 12 hatches, six hatches on each side of the huge Sail just ahead of mid-ships, cover 24 missile tubes. The menacing submarine shows some serious signs of wear and tear on its outer hull.

On-board the Bear Oscar Kim Jong
Officers' Quarters

The expressionless Russian, Vasili, spins a chain and key around his finger. Chekhov, showing signs of anger and possible boiling rage – a nut job, without a doubt - chain smokes nearby.

The accompanying cough is most likely going to kill him. At least Vasili and perhaps others certainly hope so. And for all intents and purposes, not soon enough!

Chekhov stands and paces around the very cramped quarters and says...

"I'll receive the order of Lenin for this fuckin' mission, Vasili. Then I'll ram it up Putin's ass."

Vasili can only stare at this idiot; then takes a moment, and says...

"It's just not you, my friend."

Chekhov spins at Vasili, "fuck the others, fuck the Jews."

Vasili is quick to respond...

"And the money, Chekhov?"

Chapter 22

Burning Tree Country Club
1356 Zulu, 0756 Hrs. Local

In the quiet of the early morning two golf carts pull to the number four tee box. In the first golf cart, Senator Sykes. His driver is Secret Service agent PHIL WITTE, top-notch, earpiece plugged in. They slide out. And amble over towards the tee. As both Sykes, and Secret Service Agent Witte, take in the near perfect day for a round of golf a second golf cart pulls up to the tee box.

In the second golf cart, the passenger is…

SETH GREENE.

Age 53, and known to the Secret Service as Sandpiper. Seth Greene is the Vice President of the United States. He's gray, but not with age. Tall, tough, and he smiles a lot. But at first glance this guy is one mean looking bastard. A United States Marine that you would never want to mess with. As a matter of fact most in and around Washington DC believe that Greene thinks of himself first as a Marine, and then as vice president. As a Marine, Greene was always the first off the boat when engaged in an amphibious landing. His large frame would hit the sandy beaches full bore, smashing anything his way with his size twelve boot, including those innocent little birds known as sandpipers. This fact, that became legend, gave the Secret Service a reason to assign Greene the code name "Sandpiper."

God-help anyone joining Greene on the golf course with the clear intention of beating the Veep at a round the golf.

At the helm of the second golf cart is…

Secret Service agent DON WIERDA.

He fingers his earpiece, and scans in all directions. Wierda, typical of all Secret Service agents, stays loose, but alert. A consummate pro at protecting the Veep.

As Veep Greene walks towards the tee at number four, Sykes turns at Don Wierda and winks. Then at the Veep, Sykes says...

"Titleist four, Mr. Vice President?"

The Veep either didn't hear that or as is perhaps the case, he chose to ignore the Senators' condescending comment. Greene plants his ball. Then he takes a moment to carefully study the perfectly mowed grass down the fairway. Then, without losing a beat Greene whacks his ball off the tee. And the ball is up and, - uh oh - makes a hard hook to the left. A very hard left and into the dense outer perimeter woods. Greene slams his driver into the grass tee box and says, at the top of his lungs, "son of a bitch!"

As Greene slams his club once again, Sykes chuckles as he walks over and tees up his ball. Still with a smile on his face, Sykes needlessly has to say to no one in particular...

"As my young deputy chief of staff likes to say, this is going to be one bitchin' day..." -

"Just hit the freakin' ball, Nancy!"

That was Greene.

Things are going downhill fast for the Veep.

Then, WHACK!

Senator Sykes' ball flies high and long – pretty –

Tiger Woods pretty.

Sykes leans to grab his tee from the grass, and finds the right amount of politically correct sarcasm to lodge at the Veep.

"I don't screw like a Republican either...sir."

Greene can only glare as he huffs off down the fairway, not waiting for Witte, or a ride in the golf cart. The Senator's smile widens. Meaning the two Agents, "you guys are taking notes, right?"

They give Sykes a hard stare.

Moments Later on the No. 4 Fairway

The two golf carts are now side by side – about mid-way down the 385 yard hole.

Sykes points off to his left, about 10 yards up.

"That's mine."

Seth Greene moves from the cart, new club in hand, followed by Agent Wierda. As he fast walks towards the wooded perimeter, he says over his shoulder,

"Hit up, Joe. We'll be in the woods."

Sykes watches the Veep for a long moment. Shrugs. Then jumps from the cart and addresses his ball. But before he hits away, he takes another look over his shoulder at the disappearing Veep who is now camouflaged by the massive under-brush of the perimeter, purposely allowed to grow out of control.

Privacy is a big deal for the members of Burning Tree.

Senator Sykes looks over at Secret Service Agent, Phil Witte.

"I told 'em to drop a new ball. In the spirit of bi-partisan cooperation, even here on the golf course, I said no penalty, of course. We Democrats are like that, you know, Phil?"

He takes a puff on his Monte Christo cigar. Blows smoke into the thin air.

"Cheap bastard!"

He turns and fires away at the number 4 green as Secret Service Agent Phil Witte holds a concerned stare at the perimeter woods and the spot where the Veep, and Witte's partner, Agent Don Wierda, have now vanished.

Chapter 23

I'm quickly jolted back to reality with the sound of the Marine Chopper turbines changing pitch, and winding down. Sounds are right up there for a submariner, alongside eating and sex. On board a submarine 150 feet below the surface, you get used to the constant hum that permeates the entire boat. Any change in that sound usually means trouble.

I have a friend, Toby, a former sub commander whose wife goes nuts now that he's retired and sleeping at home every night. It seems that Toby's wife, Sally, whom he lovingly refers to as "cement head," put a new HVAC system in the house while Toby was out chasing Russian subs around the South Pacific. The problem is this system can be heard - just barely - cycling on and off throughout the night. Toby can hear it. As a matter of fact, he can probably feel it. And the change wakes him every hour or so.

Sally has suggested that he sleep in another room. At a cocktail party with them several months ago I offered my take on the situation. After hearing of this problem, and perhaps with one too many martini's, I suggested to Sally, that while lying there next to her husband, to consider that Toby had spent way too many nights in a submarine, surrounded by an all-male crew, and was simply trying to re-claim his guy side.

And she should strike while the iron is hot.

So to speak.

They haven't spoken to me since.

Maybe it came out wrong.

When I arrived at the White House last year I was told to cut down on the drinking.

Which I did.

Which I think has made me dim-witted, but with an enhanced libido.

Go figure.

We finally set down on the Helicopter pad at Camp David. During the brief ride, I changed into my civvies as I know the President prefers the atmosphere to be strictly casual at this place. No stress. No tension. No cell phones. No work. No babes. And probably no sex. I can't speak to that as I wasn't here during the Clinton administration. Which is why I was not allowed to ask the lovely and charming Miss Miller to join me. Although, the last time I took her along for a boon-daggle she got all chummy with that Russian sub guy, what's his name.

Once the forward hatch is opened, I move from my seat to the steps. I quickly notice my boss, Miss Eiko Narita, waiting at the edge of the pad. Despite her not quite 5 foot, 100 pound frame, she stands out. Actually from this short distance one could easily mistake her for a grade school kid. However, I would strongly advise that one should never suggest such with Eiko.

I think she knows some of that martial arts crap.

I bound down the steps and stroll over towards Eiko saying with a 'happy to see your boss' smile, "are you my official welcome?"

She just rolls her eyes, not answering me. But I do notice she has developed a very concerned, distant look. I know that look. It means this will likely be a working barbeque, despite the big guys' – a/k/a the Prez – rule about stress-free events.

She turns towards the main cabin, uphill about 50 yards, indicating for me to step in line alongside her for the walk. Clearly to be out of ear-shot from the small ground crew and the Marines standing-by. Sure don't want those leather necks to know what goes on.

They're probably under orders to report everything to Sandpiper – a/k/a the Veep, and former Marine big shot. Isn't Washington, DC fun. Everything's a secret. Except everybody knows everything. It all comes down to the spin.

With that in mind, I take the opportunity to hand Eiko a large white envelope with red stripes, and marked Top Secret.

"You need to eye this A-SAP."

And don't tell anybody. Right.

She takes the envelop without even a glance, nor showing any interest in what it might contain. When you're the top National Security dog to the President, or someone in a very important position with access to Top Secret information, I guess nothing will alarm you. Or should. Unless, of course, you're Al Gore, in which case you need to find the closest tree to hug while yelling, "I need a massage therapist."

I felt the need to bring her up to speed on the order of the day. Which is, fun.

Pointing at the top secret envelop I say, "we've learned that Ahmadinejad can't seem to find condoms that are small enough. He says the ones Hugo Chavez sent him keep falling off."

Nothing.

Okay. Something is on her mind. Must be serious. Maybe something I did. Or said. Not that I'm paranoid. But working in the White House makes you say stuff you don't really mean.

Well, okay. Maybe you do.

Sometimes.

Like when Joe Biden said to Obama, referring to the new Obama-care law, "this is a big fuckin' deal." Did he mean it was a big deal? Or, did he mean that they're fuckin' the American people? Hard to know when it comes from Joe.

Quietly, Eiko says, "Jack. Anything strange happen in the Seychelles Islands lately?"

Now that was out of nowhere. The Seychelles Islands? I think I know where they are. Somewhere east of Africa. In the Indian Ocean. I once zipped by the place, chasing one of my Russian pals in a game of tag, you're it. Submariners play this game with sonar.

"Ping. You're it, bastard American capitalist."

"Right, Ivan. Let's nuke 'em, Biff!"

But back to the business at hand.

I respond to Eiko, "the what?"

"Good." She says, then scoots ahead of me.

Chapter 24

Burning Tree Country Club
The No. 4 Green
1408 Zulu, 0808 Hrs. Local

Senator Joe Sykes and Secret Service Agent Phil Witte pull up to the green in the cart. Sykes leaps out, "will you look at that lie. Am I good or what."

But Witte is focused on the area almost 200 yards back and at the wooded perimeter as Sykes steps to his ball only 6 yards from the hole. He picks it up, not marking it, of course, and turns towards to Witte with a big smile. "Phil, this is gonna be my lucky day."

Witte slips from the cart, still zeroed in on that spot down range. And the empty golf cart that sits on the edge of the wooded area.

"Where the hell are they?"

Witte fingers his ear piece, listening for a sound. Any sound.

Nothing.

He jumps back into his cart. Makes a sharp 180, digging up some expensive turf in the process. And makes a bee-line for the Veep's empty golf cart.

Sykes looks up.

Then shouts, "hey, Phil. What's up?"

By this time, Witte has come to a speeding stop at the Veep's golf cart. He moves to it, quickly.

Looks. Then walks several yards to the edge of the thick, wooded area, and stops. Looking closely at the full foliage and compact under-brush, he scans, very slowly, left to right, looking for any movement, listening for any sound.

Nothing.

From a pocket inside his wind-breaker he yanks a small black device. Something not much larger than a cigarette lighter and, speaking with deliberate clarity, he says, "Sandpiper leader, you there, sand – ..."

He stops as suddenly as he had started, spinning at warp speed in the direction of the Veep's golf cart. Then, muttering to himself, "what the...?"

Witte races the short distance back to the Veep's golf cart. Standing over it, he scans it carefully.

Then, once again, into the small black device, "Sandpiper lead -..."

He stops his broadcast at the sound of an echo – the echo being his own voice as it comes from inside the cart. He leans in, and from under the ball-carrier, he reaches into a cubby, yanking out a small transmitter wired to an ear piece.

Witte doesn't miss a beat. He moves like a machine, the product of his intense, well-disciplined training, and years on the job protecting the powers that be in this town.

From his rear pocket, he grabs a unique two-way radio that fits nicely into his large hand. A cool, deliberate expression takes shape on his face.

"Red dog! Red dog! Red dog!"

Chapter 25

Central Intelligence Agency
Langley, Va. Headquarters
1413 Zulu, 0813 Hrs. Local

TODD GITELSON is a young, nerdy looking guy.
Maybe mid-twenties. The cocky smirk and "I don't give a
shit" attitude, not commonplace at the CIA, permeates every
fiber of his being. He never feels the need to let anyone know
he was perhaps the youngest student ever to graduate from
MIT, and with honors. People should simply know that fact
about him. Nor does he boast about his ability with computers
and a variety of electronic devices. If you don't know Todd
Gitelson, then "fuck 'em." How he landed at the CIA, and in
the position he currently holds, is somewhat of a mystery
around "the Company." There's speculation that he's
somehow related to its Director, Simon Unger. But people in
the know usually don't speculate about the Director.
Especially if you value your job. The Director is very
protective of lots of things, and certain people. And Todd
Gitelson is one of those "special" few.

Gitelson sits at a large desk in a small, cramped office
somewhere in the bowels of the Agency. As a matter of fact,
his work space is off-limits to everyone. On very specific
orders from the Director.

Gitelson faces an array of flat computer screens.
Multiple voices can be heard crackling as they stream through
various speakers haphazardly placed around the room.
Different pitched voices coming from the speakers. Some
speaking in normal, everyday tones. Others speaking with
some degree of urgency.

Gitelson swivels aimlessly in his chair, thinking. Something he does quite frequently. And not about money or women. He's usually thinking about ways to circumvent the norm in the country's security communications apparatus. How to fool those bird-brains up on Capitol Hill, part of the various over-sight committees, who refer to themselves as "watchdogs." Dogs, yes. And the only thing they watch over are their lofty positions, and, of course, their PAC bank accounts. Money they're permitted to take when they leave public service.

Suddenly, his head jerks to the left. His eyes glued to a specific speaker. It's a heartbeat before he reaches for the replay button on the console if front of him on his desk. It gets pressed, then a knob gets cranked-up.

From a speaker, "Red dog! Red dog! Red dog!"

Jolted from his chair, as if shocked with a gazillion volts, he's up and out the door of his office.

Chapter 26

Burning Tree Country Club
Main Clubhouse, Rear Patio Area
1416 Zulu, 0816 Hrs. Local

The eerie silence is deafening.

Although, it's the quiet that's the norm at this exclusive Country Club at this hour of the morning.

The silence is suddenly broken by the thunderous roar of two spit polished black Ford Crown Victoria's that tear towards the rear from the front portico where they have jumped the handcrafted stone curbing, crushing pieces of the rare stone to dust.

Several miniature Japanese ornamental trees are flattened.

They fly by the pro shop, ripping up flower beds and beautifully trimmed native American shrubs brought in from the far corners of the continental United States.

The cars rip across the golf cart parking apron.

About a half dozen custom made and very expensive golf carts get wiped out, slammed against a wall of concrete.

As the Crown Vic's go airborne onto the number one fairway, their speed has accelerated to near Mach I.

The lead Crown Vic swerves more towards the center of the fairway, a straight-a-way to the far end.

The open path, which is down range from the clubhouse, now has its manicured grass shred to mulch.

The Crown Vic takes a more definitive lead.

Chapter 27

CIA
Office of the Director (DCI), Simon Unger
1422 Zulu, 0822 Hrs. Local

SIMON UNGER looks older than his professed 55 years. It's probably the shaved head. A grooming decision he made with the intention of looking devious and threatening. Clearly an ego trait. Fortunately for Director Unger he didn't need the change in appearance, made many years earlier, because he is devious and threatening. Which is perhaps the reason he has ended up as Director of the CIA. Not a job for thin-skinned, wimpy liberals from, say, San Francisco, whose idea of a good time is drinking Cosmopolitans and discussing different ways to stuff roll-up socks into your tighty whities. The kind of people Unger has privately criticized in no uncertain terms. In public, he keeps his opinions to himself, fearful of intrusions by the press, another group he could do without.

Of course, for Simon Unger, he makes sure his looks and body language are misleading. What he thinks never makes it to the surface, playing his cards close to the vest. Except in private.

He sits in his comfortable desk chair, behind an over-sized intimidating desk, eyes glued to the front page of the Washington Post. A Monte Christo cigar jammed into tight lips. His breathing not at all discernible. Whatever is on that front page does not seem to bother him. At least, not yet. After a moment, he drops the paper to his lap. And another moment as he searches his brain for a devious thought. The Post headline captures his interest once again. This time he's more focused, having run through an assortment of scenarios, most dealing with ruining some citizen's life.

It reads, "Vice President Greene Demands Over-haul of CIA."

Unger grunts. A kind of disgusted grunt. But one that is wrapped in revenge.

It is not until he looks again at the sub-headline that he begins to boil, his complexion going from its usual ashen to beet red.

"DCI Simon Unger May Be Out."

This time the paper gets tossed to the floor as he spins in his chair now drilling a stare to the surrounding thick wooded area just 30 yards from his bullet-proof, tinted office window. Unger schemes, thinking of a fictional character, Cat Shannon, from the novel, Dogs of War, who, at the end of the story, simply walks into a thick wooded area, not unlike the one Unger now looks at, never to be seen again.

"Director Unger...Mister Gitelson?" That's Joyce Kersey, Unger's admin. A middle aged, attractive widow and long-time employee of the CIA.

Before she can finish announcing the unexpected visitor, Todd Gitelson has already moved in behind Joyce, positioning himself in front of the Director's desk. Unger takes a moment to regain his mask of power as Joyce takes the same moment to make herself scarce. He turns looking up at Gitelson, not happy with the intrusion. But knowing if it's this guy then it must be something urgent.

"Just came across." Gitelson hands Unger his legal pad. The Director takes a moment as he studies the message, carefully thinking about its significance.

Gitelson can't wait. "They changed frequencies again. That's twice this week. And it's only Monday." Gitelson shrugs, looking for the Director to help make some sense of this piece of news. Unger grunts softly. Then stands and drifts towards his window.

His back to Gitelson, he develops a wry smile while holding a fix on that thick wooded area. His mind runs through multiple options, from an assortment of options he has contemplated for several weeks, but only those specific few that have suddenly moved to the front of his brain, the result of this new information.

Gitelson is still a bit antsy, "so, whatdaya think happened?"

Unger appears to have ignored his young assistant as he takes in the exclusive view to the outside. Relaxing his shoulders, he takes a deep breath, his lungs expanding with a new wave of confidence and satisfaction.

"I want to know when President Giordan leaves Camp David. And who he calls."

He quickly turns at Gitelson, drilling him a hard, no bull shit stare.

Gitelson freezes for a nano second. Then,

"Yes, sir."

He bolts from the Director's office.

Chapter 28

Camp David, Maryland
1435 Zulu, 0835 Hrs. Local

I can hear Marine One as its turbines roar about 75 yards away from the main cottage here at Camp David. The level of excitement and anxiety is quickly reaching the explosive stage. Given the news about the Veep, the President seems more than anxious. He's beside himself. Understandably, of course. Vice Presidents just don't vanish at the drop of a hat. But for this President, it's a bigger political picture because of the up-coming election just two months away.

Early in Obama's presidency, good old Veep Joe Biden was doing some swearing in duty when he joked about Chief Justice Roberts' blunder at the inauguration. Although Obama tried an *"a-bra-kadabra"* it didn't work. Joe managed to still be there. Obama couldn't make him vanish.

Looking out the window, I notice that one of the Marine choppers has lifted off, making a bee-line to the southeast. Certainly, it will join Marine One, once we're airborne.

I say we because the President has ordered both myself and Eiko Narita to return to the White House with him on Marine One. I would normally think this to be really cool. But today, the big guy is pissed. Which may very well be an understatement.

Speak of the devil, he appears from an adjacent room, walking quickly, and very determined, with another order...

"Let's go! Now!"

He's out the door, and we follow right behind him. There're six of us. The President, Eiko, yours truly, and three guys wearing ear pieces, all carrying serious looking weapons, in full view, of course.

Must be Secret Service. I'm very observant.

The President wears his signature Eisenhower-style waist jacket ablaze with the Presidential seal. And continues to bark orders to those around him while his hard gaze is fixed on Marine One, 50 yards away.

"Eiko! Bring in your National Security team. Don't tell 'em why just yet. But let them know it's a code red, and I'll be there."

Eiko nods her affirmation of the order, her eyes glued to the ground.

"And nothing – I mean nothing – to the press!" Under his breath, the President mumbles some colorful description of the White House press corps, a group he, and every other President since Washington has had issues with. For some reason, those guys are just not all that friendly. Except WH press corps alum, Helen Thomas who's quite the charmer, especially when the Israeli's are in town. She's been around since Lincoln or Grant, I'm not sure which one, and, although having a firm grip of some ones' nuts, she still managed to get herself booted.

I feel the need to jump in here, "they'll be all over us like a new suit, sir."

The President responds, "just be careful what you say, Jack!"

I just can't resist, given my skills at reading people "you *are* making a hasty retreat back to the White House, sir."

"This is not a retreat, Jack. I'm limited to what I can do, or even find out here at Camp David."

I pause for a nano second. "Yes, sir." This place really is isolated. No wonder Presidents love it here. Very private. Secluded. The President can do whatever he wants. I wonder if Hillary ever came up here.

The President sighs heavily, then says, to no one in particular, "the Vice President vanishes one day before we kick-off the re-election campaign...Jesus Christ, what's next?"

I can't but think what his reaction will be when he learns of the renegade sub snooping around the Persian Gulf region.

I have confidence in his ability to put political priorities on the back-burner when some hot international incident pops up in his face.

Which it is about to do as soon as Eiko gives him the really bad news. Vice President Greene may be expendable. But certainly not our friends in the Middle East.

Anyway, if Greene truly did vanish and is not playing the re-election sympathy card for the nation at large, i.e. let's stay focused on poor President Giordan who has lost his Veep on a golf course, and not concern ourselves with the Democratic ticket made up of a far left minority candidate and a bone-headed former liberal member of Congress, then he's simply brazen enough to shoot his way out of any dangerous situation.

And I mean shoot! Greene can make Marshall Dillon look like Tiny Tim on roofees.

But, I need to follow the party line. So I chime in...

"Right. Bad timing, sir."

"You have any more smart-ass remarks, Jack?"

Lucky for me Eiko jumps in, "the DCI called to confirm tomorrows' eight AM brief, sir. I'm gonna blow him off."

The President stops on a dime, and gets right in Eikos' face. His blood pressure just took a leap up. Way up.

"Simon Unger called to confirm a meeting?"

There's a really long pause here.

"That bastard never calls. Something's fishy. I wanna see him today."

Eiko firmly responds, with pleasure, "yes, sir."

The President fast walks ahead, passes a sharply dressed, saluting Marine, and leaps up the short forward hatch steps, and onto Marine One.

Eiko and I head for the rear hatch door, guarded by another sharply dressed Marine who holds a salute. I think for moment, then glance at Eikos somber expression. Again, I think she needs some cheering-up. We head up the short steps.

"I guess the barbecue is off."

Chapter 29

Larry Mitchener's Apartment - Off Wisconsin Ave.,
Washington, D C
1442 Zulu, 0842 Hrs. Local

Larry Mitchener still has trouble getting used to the
quiet. Sometimes it's so bad, the silence becomes deafening.
He drains a cup of coffee, seated at the kitchen table. His gaze
shifts to the three empty chairs around the table. His focus is
intense. His mind now in free-fall for a long emotional
moment. After a moment, he gets up and places the empty
ceramic coffee cup, one that reads, "World's Greatest Dad,"
into the dishwasher as if an unfamiliar task. For a long
moment he studies the dishwasher, looking for a clue as to
how to get it closed properly, then on for a wash cycle. He
gives up, sighing over the process, and thinking to himself
he'll have to deal with it later.

Grabbing his suit jacket, he slings it over his arm as he
adjusts his tie and shirt collar. While doing this, he walks
slowly into the entrance foyer. Putting on his jacket, he checks
his appearance in the foyer mirror. The suit and tie pass
muster, barely. But it's the blood-shot eyes that give him a
start. He thinks to himself, it is what it is.

From a small table under the mirror he removes a
holstered SIG SAUER 357 magnum. He gives it a nervous, yet
painstaking study. Then a deep breath as the weapon gets
clipped to his belt.

Off the table top he lifts his credentials – a/k/a creds –
and another pained look takes hold as he reads softly to
himself, Secret Service Agent Larry Mitchener.

Another deep breath and he hits the door, and is gone.

Chapter 30

On Board Marine One
Enroute from Camp David to Washington, DC
A Distance of about 70 Miles
1444 Zulu, 0844 Hrs. Local

The President sits quietly in the forward cabin, seat 1A, the one exclusively reserved for him.

Its cushion and seat contour re-designed for his weight and six foot, two frame. One of the many quirks afforded the Commander-in-Chief.

The seat cushion used by the last guy had way too many beer farts imbedded in its fabric. He's thinking, hard. Not knowing what could happen next. Although what has happened with regard to the Vice President is quite serious, he runs through a mental laundry list of possible consequences.

President Giordan's ability to sort through complex issues before coming to a conclusion is a quality widely respected by the White House staff. However, there are times when he chooses not to bring everyone up to speed, keeping some aspects of his triage process to himself.

Sometimes even going as far as writing his own statements to the press without the benefit of the press secretary and his staff giving it a glance before going public.

President Giordan has always felt that the words he speaks should be his words. From the heart. With heart-felt integrity.

He has studied the ways of his hero and long-time friend, Ronald Reagan. It's Giordan's way of honoring one of the greatest presidents in the past 100 years, alongside FDR.

Giordan snaps back to the present moment by turning towards the aft section of the chopper. He sees Eiko on the satellite phone, and Jack sound asleep. He can only speculate why Jack Connolly is sleeping so soundly despite the racket that Marine One makes, even inside the cabin. Giordan wonders about her, and how she handles Jack. Fortunately, she's not a White House intern, or one of those Congressional aides who are so fond of White House staffers. The President has rules about such behavior. Restoring moral decorum to the White House has been a priority since "W" took office in January of 2001.

The President leans further towards the aft area, saying rather loudly, "Jack!"

Is this a bad dream, or am I really sleeping next to a guy? Doesn't sound like Lauren. I better have a look. So I peek with one eye and see the President waving for me to join him forward. Just when Lauren was suggesting another trip around the world. I do need to catch up on some shut-eye. And soon.

I'm up, and I amble carefully to a seat next to the President. Once buckled in I give my undivided attention to the Boss, who appears to be lost in some unpleasant thought as he stares out a starboard window. Then, quickly turning to me, he says,

"I'm worried about Simon Unger."

Okay. That's out of left field.

"Shouldn't we be worried about the Vice President, sir?"

The President holds a long stare back out the window.

Then back to me, he says, "I don't want him involved. Simon Unger is inclined to run the CIA with a free hand. He hates the over-sight people up on the Hill. And rarely acknowledges his boss, the Director of National Intelligence."

He pauses, giving his current, but brief performance review of the CIA Director further thought.

Looking straight at me, he says, "whatever you do, don't ever trust the guy."

Fortunately for President Giordan, he didn't appoint Unger. That was the guy before Giordan, a Democrat, and community organizer. So, it'll be easy to dump the guy at some point. Unless, in what is generally acceptable political behavior, he plans to keep Unger so he can dump the bad crap on him, then give him the boot.

I see the President getting himself tangled up in some sort of Unger issue. So I decide it's time to get him focused on a real issue of significant importance.

"Sir, we had a potential Middle East security situation surface at Camp Peary. Lieutenant Miller and I..."

"Jack. Let's just say Simon is a problem."

I don't think he's listening. Unger has him tied up in knots for some unknown reason. As I'm about to repeat what I almost finished saying, he looks back at me with a somewhat jovial expression, "you behaving yourself with her, Jack?"

Okay. So he does know about Lauren. Like I said, Camp Peary is just one big secret. Unless you're the President.

"Not any more than I can help, sir. She's a real credit to the Navy. Smart, intuitive, unmatched by most intelligence people I've served with this past year. Gosh, has it been a year already?"

"But you still wanna get back out to sea."

I can't tell if that was a question or a statement. In either case, the President can make that wish come true. However, right now I'm not so sure how far to push the envelope. He is one of Dad's best pals, but deep down, like any President, deeply afraid of the military. I don't wanna put him into a spot between a rock and hard place.

But, hey, I'm above doing the right thing in this spot for myself.

"A dispensation from the Chief of Naval Operations...or his boss (I mentally wink)...will do it."

"I understand, Jack. I understand your desire. Help me work through this mess."

By mess I think he means the currently missing Veep. Who somehow, because of his "missing" status, involves the CIA Director, Mister Unger.

As I've said, I'm good at reading people. I watch the President as he has once again shifted his worried gaze to the outside. Looking past him to the ground myself, we both lock onto a golf course surrounded by a thick, wooded forest.

Chapter 31

Burning Tree Country Club
Thick, Wooded Forest Area
1456 Zulu, 0856 Hrs. Local

Secret Service Agent Phil Witte walks briskly towards a chain link fence topped with a double rack of barbed wire. He's accompanied by two other Agents.

Younger, and hungry for some action. At the fence there is an upended wooden crate. It stands about two feet off the ground, and leans against the fence.

Witte gets down on one knee. His hand moves above an area of the ground just behind the box. He takes a moment, looking at the ground, then through the chain link fence to the other side.

He stands, and says…

"…box was chucked over from the other side. Indentations in the ground show that. I'm certain."

One of the Agents with Witte adds…

"…you don't take someone over a double racked barbed wire fence forcibly."

"Yeah."

For Agent Witte, this is certainly a head scratcher. The three men are just dumb-founded and speechless.

But for Phil Witte, an experienced Agent, he knows the best approach is to keep it simple, for the moment.

"Wierda and the Veep wanted to go."

About 40 yards behind the Secret Service Agents, and on the fairway, Senator Sykes holds a stare on the wooded area. He also holds a cell phone to his ear.

"Yes, we do need to talk, Simon."

Chapter 32

Homeland Security
Office of the Director of the Secret Service
1513 Zulu, 0913 Hrs. Local

LARRY MICHENER sits rigid in what is otherwise a comfortable arm chair that faces the Directors huge desk. His expression is tight as a drum.

His focus is on the Director, PETER MCGUIGAN, a fortyish, sly character with a mind like a sponge. Mcguigan is more a patriot than a typical agent assigned to a protective detail. Nor does the fact that he's a lawyer get in the way of his patriotism like most of his "acquaintances" at the Justice Department.

Peter Mcguigan channels his energy and smarts at what's best for his country. To the point that, at times, while his strategy makes sense, his tactics are perhaps miss-guided.

Regardless of what those in the circles of power in Washington, DC think, his one and only allegiance is to his friend, the President, Donald Giordan. Not even to the Secretary of Homeland Security, a former Governor whose appointment to the cabinet was out of support for the Presidents' election bid, the need for a woman in the cabinet, and someone from a state that is dominated by the opposite party, and not for her required ability to handle national security issues.

However, for Larry none of these issues are at the forefront at the moment. What's on Larry's mind is the crises of the day.

The Vice President of the United States has vanished.

Not assassinated, kidnapped or gone mentally off the reservation.

But vanished?

At least as far as anyone knows thus far. But for Larry, it's a bit mysterious. Just the way the Director described what he knows, and how the Service is handling the matter. Larry understands the need to not alarm the country until all the facts are known. But it appears this matter is being held close to the vest. An in-house problem that needs complete secrecy. Maybe the Service needs to save face, if, in fact, the problem is the Secret Service. Maybe Mcguigan needs to get a handle on all the facts before going public. Or maybe, just maybe, there's a bigger picture. Something more sinister. Larry can't make it out. He knows the Veep is one tough guy. Not that well liked. But respected for his bravado and hard-charging work ethic. A character trait not at all appreciated by those working up on Capitol Hill. Veep Greene has never been one for spine-less politicians on the tax-payers dole.

So Larry sits waiting for more. Waiting for anything, for that matter. So far, it all seems a little too bizarre. Very hush, hush. But Larry knows his friend, and boss, is giving him a shot at getting back in the game, full time. Thinking about it, this may just be the opening he's been waiting for these past several months. No, make that praying for.

"You'll work with your friend, Jack Connolly, at the White House. The President will ask him to follow the same procedure I've outlined for you. None of this is for publication or even discussion with anyone yet. And you'll report to me on whatever you learn at any hour of the day or night. Mister Connolly, for some reason, has the trust of the President. I see him as an outsider. But that may be a good thing right now."

Larry stares straight ahead. "Yes, sir."

"That includes no contact with other agents unless I or the President so instructs. I've set up a tight investigative team for the moment – just in case – we need to point to something should the press get wind of this the next several hours."

Larry is taken a bit off guard here. Another mystery procedure.

"But, what about the detail? The ones who were with the Veep when he vanished?"

Mcguigan rocks slowly in his chair, holding a look to the outside.

"They're being de-briefed as we speak. I'll see to it that you and Mister Connolly get a copy of that report. But, let me stress again. It's not to be shared with anyone, Larry. Am I clear?

Larry takes a deep breath. "Vanished? I don't get it."

Before Larry can continue his thought, Mcguigan, needing to deflect his agents' obvious quest for the truth, jumps in.

"We go way back, Larry. You were a top agent. The best of the best. I think you still have it."

"Something's fishy, Pete." Larry loosens up, gaining some of that "I know better" confidence he once had. "The Vice President of the United States is too well protected to simply vanish."

With that, Larry holds a tight stare on Mcguigan while leaning forward in his chair.

Mcguigan's eyes dart away. He stands and paces towards a window. Taking a moment to look down on the DC traffic, he sorts through a laundry list of prepared responses to Larry's comments. Items he has already thought of prior to calling his friend in for this chat. Mcguigan is smart enough to know that Larry Mitchener is no fool. But also clever enough to know how to manipulate a man in a weakened state.

But for Mcguigan he has been tasked with a mission, directly from the President. And he needs an agent like Larry Mitchener to run through the back channels of this incident. Someone, while on the edge, who will be able to filter through every milepost and spot, not just explanations, but perhaps issues that may impact the political implications for the President.

Larry is a man desperate for his life to swing back, away from the dark side. Sometimes the situation calls for a less sensitive approach. It helps bring clarity to the "personal" situation. A tactic employed by men and women in power. Those who hold someone's mental state in the palm of their hands.

Still staring out the window, and still not able to make eye contact with Larry, "you're off the bottle? Sober?

Stung, Larry grits his teeth hard as his eyes dart over at the Director's back.

"Yes…sir!"

Knowing that Larry is likely quite pissed, he keeps the pressure on.

"Any word from Lou Ann?"

Larry grips the arms of the chair. His knuckles turn a ghostly white, the blood circulation now cut off. "Took my kids. Went home to her folks in New York."

Mcguigan takes an extra-long moment. Then turns, now making eye contact with Larry.

"You will do this our way, correct, Agent Mitchener?"

Chapter 33

SIMON UNGER focuses intently to the wooded perimeter outside of his 7th floor office suite. He feels in control. Not at all burdened by the questions that will come at him these next few hours, or even over the next day or so. Nothing Unger does is last minute, or in the absence of careful planning. He has a few heroes from history. Not many. But several whose clever explanations of their actions or accomplishments generally shut down nay-Sayers, stopping them dead in their tracks. When it comes to planning a complicated, life-threatening mission, Unger falls back on one such pronouncement made over 80 years ago by Colonel Charles Lindbergh. When the press dubbed him "lucky Lindy" for making it across the Atlantic from New York to Paris in a single engine aircraft, a feat most initially thought to be foolish and impossible, he became distraught at the thought he was merely just lucky. He knew better. And made it clear in every press interview that it was far from luck.

It was careful planning.

Simon Unger has always adopted that approach. He also knows how to lie. Play dumb when the circumstance presents itself. But more importantly, and very much a part of the planning stage, he knows what questions to expect. And what answers to give.

In a low key, monotone, still facing the outside, he says, "I don't know what you're taking about, Senator."

Walking through a plume of thick cigar smoke, Senator Joe Sykes moves closer to the Director. And he wants answers as he comes to slow boil, " I'm talking about Vice President Seth Greene. Is this your mess, Simon?"

Unger moves past the important Senator, a man who chairs a powerful committee on the Hill who could, with the snap of his fingers, bring hell raining down on the CIA Director. He casually takes his seat behind the massive desk and carefully rearranges several papers on his desk almost as if he didn't hear Sykes.

Then, after a moment, and not making eye contact with the Senator, "you're asking me a direct question?"

Sykes responds sharply, "yes."

"I thought you were never going to do that, Joe."

Sykes takes a moment to move to the far side, further away from Unger. Thinking how to jolt Unger into a more responsive mood.

Sykes says, "better me than the White House, Simon."

Unger leans back, and develops a sly, almost satisfied, yet thin smile, and now faces Sykes, "I have no intention of availing President Giordan a re-election victory." Looking more content than normal, "his poll numbers are way down. And it's likely that blow-hard Greene will bring them down further between now and election day."

Sykes tries a counselor approach, hoping to jar Unger, get him to open up a bit more, "you under-estimate his motives. He didn't get to be rich and powerful on his good looks, Simon. I've always felt he holds too many cards close to his vest. Trumping his opponents when they least expect it."

Unger weighs his words with a hint of caution, "I think the President is suppressing something in order to get re-elected. But, you know that's just a hunch."

Sykes chuckles, saying. "And you'd like to keep your job another four years."

Unger takes along moment to size-up Sykes. He's never trusted the Senator. And for Unger it is a matter of trust. In the high stakes game known as the war on terror, letting politicians make the rules, then referee the match is foolishly dangerous.

He'll play along, of course. Over-sight from the Hill, while very much there, is nothing more than a pimple on an elephant. Or in the case of a Democrat in the White House, a pimple on a jackass.

The CIA Director has certain responsibilities as outlined in the CIA charter. What they can and cannot do. All in the interest of protecting Americans from unfriendly forces outside of our borders. However, the high tech world has brought the enemy inside our borders. And to not recognize that is misguided.

So, for Simon Unger the battle lines are clear. He will do what is necessary to protect this great country, and its citizens. 9/11 changed the United States forever. And to allow politicians like Sykes, or even the President to draw their own battle lines without regard to the potential consequences of showing our hand to the enemy is simply reckless.

The country needs true patriots who can clearly judge the threats, from both within and without, and take the steps needed to strike, and strike with conviction. And make sure everyone of our enemies knows. As Ronald Reagan said many times before and during his Presidency, "peace, but with strength. "Simon Unger has anointed himself the one capable of re-enforcing that strength.

Chapter 34

Walking through the West Wing is kind of a surreal experience. I mean walking in this place, through these hallways, on this carpet, beats at your subconscious, creating a fantastic imagery of some of the things that go on in here, very much an incongruous juxtaposition of the expected subject matter we, as Americans, believe happens here.

Like the decision to take-over whole industries to protect the employees, a/k/a, unions; invade a weak country in order to try out a cool new weapon, but really because they possess something else that's cool, like, say oil; or having your admin pencil in Monica for some face time.

I'm simple minded. And therefore believe that, if these walls could speak, I'd hear conversations that could be construed as either issues that may determine the fate of all Americans, or perhaps a skit from Saturday Night Live.

It's a fine line that only politicians can draw, and know how to move in order to keep us regular folks fat, dumb and happy.

Anyway, I've got to see the big guy because of a call a few minutes ago. In Eikos absence – she's in with him now in the Oval Office - I get the important calls.

Like when the Domino's Pizza guy can't find the White House.

Pizza Guy: "Hey, dude, like, where are ya?"

Me: "The White House. 1600 Pennsylvania Avenue...dude."

Pizza Guy: "Is it like, a white house, man?"

So much for our public school system.

Here I am outside the Oval Office. To give you some idea how important the President is he has three female admins. Two of whom I'm convinced are Secret Service Agents in drag. The other is some old broad who's been here since the Eisenhower administration. And is the official gate-keeper, i.e., the one who says who gets into the Oval Office, and who doesn't. I've heard that back in the day she would seek sexual favors for the privilege of getting into the Oval. Then Clinton came along, took one look at her and had a secret entrance to the Oval Office constructed…just for himself.

Obama changed the process. He had a large cardboard cut-out of fellow Chicago resident and pal, Louis Farrakhan placed at the entrance to the Oval Office to scare off unwanted visitors, and other evil spirits. Now you know why Obama gave little red clip-on bow ties to visitors. I heard they read "made in Yemen."

Granny motions for me to halt. Looks me over, head to toe – I'm not sure what she's thinking. As a matter of fact, I don't want to know what she's thinking, if you catch my drift. Then she points to a chair, obviously where she wants me to sit and wait. I happily comply, giving her a wink and a smile.

She gives me the finger.

The Oval Office

It's rare for President Giordan to be so emotional. But one on one with a member of his staff, whose motivations are perhaps suspect, gets in his craw. At the moment, he's not all that happy with his National Security Advisor, Eiko Narita. They both stand, separated by the President's desk. On a normal day the pressures of his office are enormous to say the least. Today, the pressure meter dial has gone passed the red zone and off the meter.

The President takes a moment to regain his composure. Then grabs a sharp look at Eiko.

"Eiko. I did want you on the ticket as the Veep candidate. But it wasn't entirely up to me. You know that, dammit!"

She's not very happy with that, responding, "then why is that bastard, Seth Greene on the ticket?" Then adding, sarcastically, "handpicked by the American Jewish lobby, I suppose."

She paces, clearly furious, "who's in charge here?"

The President turns for a look out onto the south lawn searching for some solace, if not from Eiko then from his own inner self, a moment felt by every person that has ever occupied the Oval Office. This place can be the loneliness 400 square feet on the planet, despite its occupant being surrounded by 150 staffers within the immediate confines of the West Wing.

He says softly, but with confidence, "the Vice President will succeed."

Eiko takes the conversation a notch up, looking, not so much to force the President's hand, but to be sure he's thought through every contingency.

"And if he doesn't?"

The President can just stare. He doesn't want to go there. Not right now. It's too early in the mission to let doubts lead to second guessing. As he moves back to his desk, standing, shuffling through several documents that need his signature, there's a knock at the door.

As the president looks up, the door swings open, and standing there is Jack Connolly. I stop at the threshold, mainly because Eiko has just given me one of those looks. The one that says, "oh, shit, not him again." She then turns her back to me, pacing to the far side of the office.

I figure I had better say something because the President's expression is turning from deep, focused thought to "oh, shit, not him again."

I say with authority and confidence, "excuse me, Mister President."

I wait again because usually at this point he would say "come on in, Jack. Good to see you. Have a seat."

Instead, it's the silent treatment.

So, I continue, from the threshold, "Israeli ambassador is on his way over –"

The President abruptly breaks his silence, "Margolies?"

I walk slowly towards his desk, saying, "yes, sir. Just got the call. He was very serious. And short with me. But then again he usually is."

The President glances over at Eiko, saying "I smell a rat."

Then back to me, he says, "get rid of him."

I take half a second, then, "I tried –"

Eiko jumps in, "we have Admiral Hasslinger –"

The President is back on the move, cutting her off, "I'm one President they won't lead around by the nose. Do I look like Clinton?"

Still on the move, he bolts for the head, slamming the door in the process.

Now I'm alone with Eiko, so I take the opportunity to address our other issue du jour, "Eiko, has the President seen – "and, once again, I'm cut off.

"I read it, Jack."

I fill her in further on my over-sight, "I've got Lieutenant Miller all over it."

She just can't let me finish, "it's nothing."

"We're talking about a renegade submarine, Eiko. Possibly armed and manned with a crew who may know how to use the weapons' system on board."

She gets in my face, "you're not an Intel officer, Jack. I'll deal with it."

This matter goes beyond simple Intel information. In my view, it requires a look at the bigger Naval picture. And certainly from my perspective. You don't just drive a submarine thousands of miles from home, and into a hot war zone looking for a spot to picnic with the fellas. A submarine mission requires months of intelligent and expert planning. And lots of money. None of which the North Koreans have.

I stand firm, looking right at her, "I'm a Naval submariner-"

"- who's been relived of active sea duty, Mister Connolly. I'll deal with it."

With that, she bolts from the Oval Office.

I'm pissed. Her reaction is not only infuriating, it's odd.

I grab the handset off the President's desk. Punch in a number. And wait for an answer as I fume.

On the other end, Lauren answers, "Lieutenant Miller."

"Lieutenant! Pull all your data together on the Bear Oscar. Put it on a disk. And get your cute butt up here. Pronto! Use the NSA chopper."

There's a slight delay before she says, very seductively, of course, "I've been waiting for your call, Commander. Will I be spending the night?" My mind bounces off all ends of the universe. I grip the President's desk for support. And try to get my breathing under control. No doubt this call is being recorded by an array of devices both here at the White House, and over at the NSA in Maryland.

And probably at spook central, a/k/a, the CIA.

So I cleverly say, "ahh...change of plans. See you later."

And I hang up, thinking she's going to be the death of me yet. On many fronts.

With the President still in the head, I wonder if I should wait. And take a shot at discussing the Bear Oscar Intel with him or not. I suppose it would be a serious breach of protocol if I do. And Eiko, who already doesn't like me very much, would have a cow. Since my career as a grown up is already on thin ice, and I'm desperate to get back to sea, I choose to exit the Oval Office - - quickly.

As I reach for the door knob, I hear the President, "Jack, hold up."

I turn, and face him coming towards me from the head, "yes, sir. Just on my way to head off Ambassador Margolies."

He says, "no, no. Let Eiko handle the bastard. He's probably coming over because something serious has happened, and he needs our help. You know the drill. The Israelis have been taking advantage like this since the Reagan years. We're getting good at lip service."

I can't help but say. "Maybe he knows where the Veep is."

"Jack. We're not to say anything to anybody. Am I clear?"

"Yes, sir."

"We need to get our arms around this issue. Then we'll put it out there."

Issue?

Did he say issue?

I need a more genteel line of work.

"Jack. I promise. We'll get into this. Give me a few hours."

With that, he gives me "the look." The one that says "leave!"

Chapter 35

On Board the Bear Oscar Kim Jong
Beneath the Red Sea, East of Ethiopia
1610 Zulu, 1910 Hrs. Local
1010 Hrs. in Washington, DC

The control room, located slightly forward and just below the Sail, topsides, is alive with subdued, but nervous chatter. However, it's far from a modern, updated control room. Most of the equipment looks well used. Computer screens flicker, not holding their images very well. The steering as well as the bow and stern planes controls are worn to the nub. Leather upholstery that once adorned the swivel chairs has frayed to the layers of cotton and rusty springs.

And then there's this constant dripping sound. Water dripping onto metal surfaces. And not just in one or two places. But throughout the control room. If not brought under control, one would think this boat will eventually sink on its own, without the benefit of further flooding the ballast tanks, replacing the small amount of neutralizing air with additional water.

If one is standing in this control room it would be immediately apparent that something quiet strange is taking place. That being the controls manned by Koreans. North Koreans to be exact. And not experienced sailors. But young men, fresh out of secondary school. Sent by their dear leader on a mission from which they may never return. Never mind the endless years it takes a U.S. Navy sailor to be selected and elevated to the ranks of a "submariner." And then there's the training. Followed by the weeding-out process where only one in twenty-five make it to sea.

A closer look indicates that these young men look like fish out of water. And clueless. Color-filled displays line the upper racks of the control room. Although the data that should feed continuous information is sporadic at best. Certainly making it more difficult for this young, ill-trained crew to interpret with any degree of knowledge. At the "Conn" is a young North Korean officer. He stands ridged masking a lack of familiarity with his command. His eyes dart nervously around the confined space looking for clues that may tell him what next to do. Several other North Korean officers are hunched over navigation charts at an under-lit table at the center of the control room. They mumble softly, both to themselves and to no one in particular in the hopes of perhaps some divine intervention. One officer holds a translation dictionary in his hand which clearly is adding more confusion to the situation. Sweat forms on their brows, afraid to poke their heads up and ask for some guidance. Any guidance, for that matter.

As this scene plays out, Vasili, spinning a chain and key around his index finger, parades into the control room. He is followed by the charming Chekhov and his side-kick, Zoyan. All three Russians take in the activity with mild delight.

Chekhov mutters under his breath, "amateurs."

Zoyan now moves to a position behind a young North Korean whose sweaty hands grip the bow planes' control. The young sailor feels the closeness of the Russian and starts to tremble, more sweat dripping off his forehead. Zoyan smiles with delight.

Vasili approaches the officer in charge.

"Captain Kim!"

The North Korean snaps his heels together, "sir," holding a sickening stare on Vasili.

Vasili takes a moment before asking, "our position, Captain?"

The North Korean officer suddenly looks like the last kid standing in a spelling bee contest. And he doesn't know the answer. Fear has gripped every fiber of his small body. He's thinking that this Russian will jam him into a torpedo tube, and jettison him to the promised land. Or, wherever.

Vasili calmly motions the officer to follow him towards the navigation charts, where the several other officers quickly back away. When the Captain is at his side, Vasili points.

"Here!"

Vasili's finger indicates a spot just east of the Dahlak Archipelago in the very southern portion of the Red Sea. Although the Red Sea starts to widen at this point, the deep water channel is somewhat narrow. So Vasili is careful to pay close attention to the route he plans to take as the channel is usually occupied by large vessels, both merchant and military. Staying at a concealed depth will require an experts' knowledge of these waters and the navigation hazards that they may confront. Which is why Chekhov was chosen for this mission, but still very much against the mission leader, Vasili. Chekhov's experience as a navigator at this point is irreplaceable. For this reason, Vasili has chosen to maintain his cool in Chekhov's company. At least for now.

Vasili turns and makes eye contact with the Captain, saying " give the order to steer three five three degrees for the next..." Vasili turns towards Chekhov, giving him a determined look, that is asking for him to finish the order.

Chekhov smiles, knowing full well his importance to this mission, and without him the whole thing may go down the tubes, "four hours, twelve minutes, and nineteen seconds starting..." Chekhov takes a long moment to study his watch.

Then says, "now!"

The North Korean pivots immediately, shouting the order, as if in command of this boat. The crew instantly responds.

Vasili continues, "and take us down to four hundred feet, Captain, and engage flank speed."

The Captain repeats the order, and the bow and aft planes officers respond.

Chekhov steps hard at the Captain.

Now in his face, says, "and don't hit anything, you stupid slope-head bastard!"

This cracks-up Zoyan, but generates a stern look from Vasili who takes a moment, then turns and leaves the control room quickly.

Chapter 36

Outside, between the West Wing and the OEOB
1630 Zulu, 1030 Hrs. Local

I fly through the door the serves as the guest entrance to the West Wing. Fortunately, the Marine guards that man the door 24/7 saw me coming and opened it before I tore it off its hinges. I'm not particularly happy at the moment. Probably because the President, by yanking my chain, is stringing me along some path towards bizarre-ville. Of course, this is Washington, DC where most everything takes on a bizarre persona. But I just can't get my arms around this way of doing things. It's counter-intuitive, to use a big word. Although, I'm not sure what it means.

It's times like these that you need, say, an honest journalist to bring clarity to the picture being sketched out by some of the most powerful people in the country, if not the world. I'm a pretty simple guy. It's a matter of common sense.

Okay, the Veep vanishes.

A pretty important guy.

Okay, maybe not pretty. But you muster together the law enforcement community, and you start looking. And you tell everyone.

"Help us find the Veep. He's needed at the White House. We're just really worried."

Then you put out a description. Some vital statistics. Maybe a photo or two. Throw in a quick clip of the sobbing wife. Surrounded by the kids and grandkids.

As I'm thinking while walking towards the OEOB, I catch a glimpse of a journalist I just happen to know coming my way from the media pad. I speed up my pace. I hope he's not looking for me. I don't like journalists. They ask questions. Usually the questions you don't want to answer.

Never the ones you would love to talk about.

Like, "Jack, is it true you're a stud?" Now I'm assuming that the question is being asked by one of those hot babes at FOX.

Then, from behind me, a raspy, accented voice, "Mister Connolly, got a minute? Tom Delgado, Washington Post."

Without stopping, I turn for a look see. And, sure enough, I see Tom Delgado, whom I know, of course, doing a half trot from the media pad. He kind of looks like a girl with no athletic ability, trying to run. Tom sort of reminds me of Geraldo Rivera on a good day. But slicker.

I say, "we know each other, Tom. White House correspondents dinner? Last April? You introduced me to...what was her name?"

"April?"

I'm stumped. "April? I thought it was something like Cynthia...ahh...something with an S? Berkshire Mountains? Massachusetts?"

He frowns, then says, "last April? I'm not connecting."

That's okay. Because the woman he introduced me to was his date, and I frankly don't think he wanted anything to do with her. So he tried to pass her off on me. After a couple of drinks, I knew why. Someone who had clearly escaped from the funny farm.

Tom continues. "Anyway, someone on Burdette Road – it borders the Burning Tree Country Club, you know, - says four men jumped the fence at about eight this morning. Any comment?"

I ask. "Were they breaking in?"

Tom tactfully avoids my key question, and says, "the same witness said one of 'em was the Vice President, Seth Greene."

I can think fast on my feet. Even when I'm moving, like right now, in the direction of the staff door to the OEOB, where reporters are not allowed, or is it not welcome.

I respond, "he wouldn't jump a fence, Tom. That's why he's got a big-ass limo."

Tom still right at my heels, says, "reports are that the President rushed back to the White House from Camp David. Is there something about the Vice President that caused him to return here so quickly?"

I give him the party line, as instructed by the boss. "The President has a re-election campaign on his agenda. It kicks off tomorrow. As a matter of fact, your newspaper has been making a big deal about it. Front page stuff. Bold headlines. Lots of pictures. I'll grab you a copy, and send it out with a staffer."

As I dart into the OEOB, leaving Tom standing several feet from the "staffers only" door, looking up at a rather tall uniformed Secret Service guy, I hear him ask, "is that with or without the Vice President?"

OEOB Office Corridors

"Son of a bitch!" That's all I can think to say, out loud, at the moment. This is going to be tough. If the Washington Post suspects something fishy, then it's likely the rest of Washington, DC will as well. Except, of course, those 535 bird-brains up on Capitol Hill who are so used to the smell of dead fish, they'd have to wait for the story to appear, unvarnished, fair and balanced like the scales of justice (sic) on FOX. Or biased, tainted and fictionalized on MSNBC, while they blame George W. Bush, who is still hiding out in Texas. Don't tell his biggest fan up on the Hill, the Botox Queen.

I feel like I'm on high octane right now. Although I don't notice, staffers are moving for cover against the walls for fear of me knocking them over. Steamed, I keep my head down.

I mumble, "Jesus Christ."

Without looking up, I know I'm heading for my office. If I look up I may run into someone I know. Then I'll have to stop. Tell him or her about my weekend at Camp Peary. Well, not everything. I'll keep it clean, at least to Washington, DC standards. You never know about people in this place. When they leave, the first thing they do is write a book. As I slip into my office the first thing I hear is a little girls' voice from behind. I, of course, know that voice. And because she's usually so quiet, it's perhaps possible she's been right behind me since entering the OEOB.

KRISTEN SANDERS is my admin. She's young, maybe twenty-two, and shapely. Not to mention cute. I'm not sure how she got this job, but having the opportunity to observe her, listen to her side of personal, yet weird phone conversations, and other kinky behavior the past year, my guess is that it's the result of some lofty political connection. But somehow she seems to know everything, and most of the time before it even happens. Maybe she's psychic. Actually, I think it's one of those "strange bed fellows" situations.

I hear her say, "so, Jack, maybe you know where the Veep is."

So much for secrecy. If she knows the Veep has gone off the reservation, then who else?

I do an about face, and slam the door to my office. Without a word to Kristen, I sit at my desk, head in hands.

She stares down at me for a moment. Then adds, "it's like hide and seek with that guy."

I guess I need to keep her in some kind of loop on this story. I know I can trust her not going rouge with any information that is even the slightest bit sensitive. At least I hope I can.

I respond, "he vanished. Playing golf."

Her mouth drops, then she says, "vanished? Like pouf?"

"Like with Agent Don Wierda," I answer.

She develops a very sly smile. Shakes her head while folding her arms. Then says with a twinge of sarcasm, which she gets from me...

"the gay Secret Service guy?"

I pop up, "gay? Where'd you hear that?"

"Heddy."

I lean back, and brace myself for another bizarre revelation by asking...

"Your friend? Heddy Downs? That Heddy?"

One quality I appreciate about Kristen is her sense of self confidence. When she tells me something it's without any doubt in her mind the fact. She simply knows. And that's it.

"She tells me everything. I don't say anything, of course. You know that, right, Jack? Like, my job and, ya know?" She looks for some confirmation from me that I can trust her. I nod, while thinking this story is going to spin right into the hands of the opposite party. Not good for the re-election campaign plan.

Kristen leans in towards me, and over the 3-foot detail model of an attack submarine, the USS Baton Rouge. I can't help but notice the cleavage.

She says, "he'll show. Just like the Secret Service to keep hiding the guy. Like, it's Dick Cheney all over again. Maybe some terrorist threat thing. They gotta stick 'em in a bunker somewhere. You know, like that place in Virginia? Near Charlottesville?"

I don't think she's supposed to know about that. But, come to think about it, the Washington Post has likely done a weekend travel feature on the spot. With photos.

Kristen stands, still leaning in, and still, her cleavage captures my undivided attention. She begins to almost seductively finger the model of my former submarine.

"So, can I, like, I need to borrow your car, you know, I gotta pick-up Heddy."

I should have known there was an agenda with this young girl. But I'm sometimes too shallow to pick-up on the obvious hints.

"At the moment, it's at the Veep's home. Admirals House? Had to leave it when I caught a ride in his chopper."

She resets. Takes a moment. Frowns. "Oh."

Then, with her usual air of confidence says, "I'll have hot Rod Ballard drive me over. He owes me a big one."

I calmly say, "okay." And toss her my keys.

As she turns to leave, she says, "you know why they call him hot Rod?"

"No. And I don't want to know. I'm not that way."

Kristen can only smile, then gives me a wink. But before she leaves she unravels several scrapes of paper pulled from a pocket and says, "you have a message." After a moment, "oh, yeah. You have a black dude waiting to see you, Jack."

As I stand and collect some papers, I inform her, "I'm expected in the Map Room."

Still reading her unreadable note, she adds, "a Secret Service Agent. Let's see if I have a name."

This gets my immediate attention, "am I in trouble?"

"Well, Jack, I'm over eighteen." As she walks out the door, "but I can't speak for the others."

Chapter 37

The West Wing
In the Map Room
Near the Oval Office
1714 Zulu, 1114 Hrs. Local

The atmosphere is tense. One could slice the air. It's clear that no one presently seated in this room wants to be here. It's usually like this when the Israeli ambassador drops in for little chat. The fact that we spend more on foreign aid to Israel than any other country in the world never seems to hit home with the Israelis. At last count, Congress has appropriated about four billion bucks to these guys each year. Much of it in the form of military hardware. Defense officials over at the Pentagon jokingly refer to Israel as a "test site." They like to say that "if the gun works there, then will buy more and issue it to our guys."

I've always thought of this policy as a bit hypocritical. We tell the Saudis', who are drowning in oil, much of it we need, not to worry about the weapons we give to Israel. Because they have to ask permission from us to use them. Otherwise, they won't work.

The Saudis' usually respond by saying they're still pissed at us and the British for not letting Lawrence of Arabia include Palestine as part of their new Kingdom. We, of course, cleverly reply that was before the Saudis' discovered oil underneath all that hot sand. Had we known about the oil, their Kingdom would be known today as a premier American beach resort and nudist colony. They don't think that's very funny. I would suggest they watch the movie again. Sir Lawrence Olivier is terrific.

Although the Saudi King feels the actor - Sir Alec Guinness - who portrayed his grandfather, Fasil Saud, was miscast.

Everyone's a critic. Who'd they think was a better choice? Sidney Greenstreet? Or maybe Mel Gibson? Actually, he was only in elementary school bashing Nuns with all kinds of colorful expletives when the studio made that flick.

Anyway, the Israelis are quite adept at using our oil relationship with the Saudis to keep their hand out. As if they had rigamortis.

I happen to have landed a seat right next to the Israeli ambassador, Gideon Margolies. He's a soft spoken guy, but a tough Israeli Irgun. A tribe known for its fierce battle tactics. A kind of "take no prisoners" approach to everything they do, including diplomacy.

The President and Eiko sit across the table. And just stare.

Seated at the far side of the President is Admiral Max Hasslinger. He's the chief of Defense Intelligence. Usually quite skeptical of everything not military. But more importantly, he just loathes intelligence amateurs. Like me.

The atmosphere is tense, even strained. Margolies nods to no one in particular, but smiles thinly at the group. I'm thinking he's already congratulated himself on scoring yet another meeting with the President on short notice. It's the thin smile that gives him away.

It also pisses-off the President who's clearly short on the formalities at the moment.

"Well?"

Margolies clears his throat. Folds his hands as if praying. Which might be a good idea right now.

"Certain former Iraqi officials – part of Saddam's inner circle who eluded you in 2004 –"

Somehow I think Margolies liked saying that last part. As if it would never have happened had the Israelis been in Baghdad at the time. It's all in the tone.

Bastard.

He continues, "...have developed a collaboration with certain individuals in lofty positions in Iran. Stolen oil money, of course. These same individuals – whom we believe to have been summarily executed by the Iranians once they turned over their plan and money to Ahmadinejad – had already completed part of Saddam's plan with a third party, the North Koreans – "

The President jumps in, "Saddam's dead. What's so urgent?"

Margolies smiles again, giving the President his due. Then, continues...

"The Iranians and their terrorists' friends have set up shop in the Seychelles – on an island known as Silhouette."

The Seychelles? Interesting, I think as I shoot Eiko a look. She avoids eye contact with me knowing full well just several hours ago, up at Camp David, she had asked me about that very same remote dot on a map.

Very interesting, as a matter of fact.

As I give this some more thought, mainly a thought that includes the question that I ask myself, "am I being played here by my boss?", Margolies takes a map from his briefcase. He says, pointing at that very small dot on his map, "...rather remote, isolated in the Indian Ocean about five hundred miles – "

The President interrupts again, "I know where the Seychelles are, Mister Ambassador."

Again, Margolies gives the President a thin smile as he presses on.

"The local government has leased Silhouette – an island of only twenty-two square miles, give or take – to certain government officials in Yemen. Who, some months ago, sub-leased it to the North Koreans?"

We all sit in dumb-founded silence, waiting for Margolies to drop another shoe.

Although, I suspect that somewhere in the daily intelligence brief the President gets, this information was mentioned. However, given further thought to this possibility, it's likely the Israelis found this out, but didn't bother to tell us. I can hear the conversation now:

CIA: "Why didn't you guys tell us?"

Mossed: "Oh. Did we forget again? So sorry. We must have been busy building more settlements in the occupied zones with your money."

Bastards.

Margolies continues, saying, "We're certain local government officials in the Seychelles, including from the Prime Minister on down, were unaware of this agreement. Except us, of course."

Of course.

The President jumps in again, "where's this going?"

"Mister President, these – shall we say terrorists – have loaded two nuclear warheads onto an old Russian submarine. Warheads obtained through a network of shady arms dealers working inside Russia."

Now that got my attention as I bolt up straight in my chair. It also explains the missing two weeks when the shadow was pulled off, that Lauren uncovered not knowing where the submarine she found has been since it left the Sea of Japan, then re-appeared off the coast of Yemen, then vanished...again.

The bigger question is, however, why was our shadow pulled off? And who gave that order?

Again, if we, in fact had a shadow on that sub, it would have likely been included in the President's daily intelligence brief.

I hope.

The President leans in, pointedly at Margolies, and says, "is there more?"

"Perhaps I should add, Mister President, that this particular submarine is formally a Russian military asset. The North Koreans purchased it – with Iranian money, of course – a fact we learned after two weeks at breaking codes – and, let's say, some healthy interrogations. We have also learned that the North Koreans have hired some very nasty Russians to run this boat."

I can't sit still. I'm fidgeting like a little kid who needs to pee. What Margolies is telling us seems to dove-tail nicely with what our intelligence apparatus is telling us good guys at Camp Peary. Like me. Which is a clever way of giving the very gorgeous Lt. Lauren Miller credit for breaking this story. I need to remember to give her a compliment. A sexy one, of course.

Anyway, I'm getting quite anxious. I have to ask Margolies several questions or else I really am going to pee in my shorts.

"Russian sub-mariners, sir?"

He moves his look over to me. A look that says "brilliant question, Commander." At least that's my take on his look.

"Chechnyans, to be precise, Mister Connolly."

To the President, "we desire that you respect our position, Mister President."

I jump back in, but not before I notice out of the corner of my eye that the President looks about to say something. Since this is somewhat serious, at least from my experience as a former nuclear sub commander presently in rehab at the White House before returning to sea, hopefully – I'm the eternal optimist – I just have to ask, "did you say nuclear warheads, sir?"

"Jack!"

That was the President. And he's not happy that I jumped in.

"Sir?" I say with the up most level of respect. But I, at least, got my concern on the table. Sub commanders can fire those things, and no one would ever know who, or where.

Scary, huh?

The President gets eye ball to eye ball with Ambassador Margolies, and pronounces..."now, I'm giving you a warning, sir, (i.e., asshole), Israel will not take unilateral action without confirming to me, unequivocally, that Israel is the target."

Pissed, Margolies sits back and stares down the President for a moment before saying, "threatening is not like you, sir (i.e., jack-off)."

"No. That's correct. I don't threaten, Mister Ambassador."

The President takes a moment to let his blood pressure drop a thousand points. Then, "thank you for dropping by. Always a pleasure to see you."

Now Gideon Margolies is no dummy. With that condescending smile still present he, I presume, reads the situation clearly. He gathers his little map of the Southern Indian Ocean, as well as his papers, stuffing them into his briefcase. He stands. Nods respectfully at the President and Eiko. But not to me or Admiral Hasslinger.

And leaves the room.

Without a word.

Not even, "thanks for the coffee and donut."

Bastard.

The President sits quietly, thinking. Eiko watches him carefully looking for the right moment to say something. Sometimes it's hard to tell. Saying the wrong thing at the wrong time could get you exiled to someplace really dreadful.

Like the Interior Department, counting Elk at Yellowstone National Park. With no calculator, having to use your fingers and toes. During the winter season.

But I'm not a patient guy. I like to say what's on my mind. Usually at the wrong time, as you probably now know. So, I figure the best thing to do is to get the conversation going.

"That submarine came across our data at Camp Peary this morning."

That seemed to have jolted Eiko for some reason, because, as usual, she didn't let me finish, by offering...

"We'll keep an eye on it, sir."

Neither Admiral Hasslinger, not to be undone by the NSA girl (that's his take on Eiko) nor the amateur intelligence dunce (i.e., me) chimes in with his highly experienced carefully thought out point of view...

"That sonofabitch is blowing smoke up your ass, Mister President."

The President turns his attention towards me, ignoring the much smarter people in the room.

"What are you saying, Jack?"

I'm on. Finally.

"The sub – we've identified it as a Russian Oscar Class sub – it surfaced near Yemen, in the Gulf of Aden, six days ago, Mister President."

The President gives some thought to this. My guess is he's more pissed about having been told about this issue by the Israelis than the Defense Intelligence Agency or, more likely, the NSA.

Which may explain why Eiko seems a bit pre-occupied.

The President finally asks...

"How long have we known about it?"

Admiral Hasslinger attempts to soften the sting in the President's question.

"We tagged it as a training boat when it left the Sea of Japan. Then, we lost contact with it in the South China Sea. We didn't think a training boat needed constant surveillance. At least until it came into view again – sonar contact – in the Indian Ocean. Heading for the Persian Gulf region."

"And then, Admiral?"

"We put the Dallas on its ass."

Hasslinger's statement drips with authority and confidence. Which leads me to ask, pointedly, "who pulled the Dallas off?"

This upsets Hasslinger. Whether he knows who, or even knows the Dallas was, if fact, pulled off, is up in the air at the moment. In any event, Hasslinger has been caught off guard.

"Admiral?" That's the President.

But I can't wait.

"More importantly, was it in the Seychelles?"

Eiko has finally come back from her mental trip and counters my question by saying, "speculation, Jack. We know it's a training boat. Let's not get wrapped up in speculation. It's not something professional intel people do."

Thanks for the heads-up, Eiko.

She turns to Admiral Hasslinger, "I'll have Mister Connolly get you a copy of the Camp Peary data. Then you should give the President a more professional assessment of the situation after your people match up the salient facts."

Staring at Eiko, Admiral Hasslinger appears to be going through a mental replay of Pearl harbor – the 1941 version. And a lengthy list of methods of punishment for those who attacked the U.S.

As he stews, I give him the opportunity to bring his blood pressure down a thousand points by saying, "those nukes could be targeted at Israel, sir. Clearly, it's why Margolies was here."

The President asks. "How can we confirm that?"

"We can't," I say.

Eiko adds. "Which rips Margolies' information to pieces. We have no reason to believe that sub is a threat. Who cares that the Dallas was pulled off. We'll let the Israelis think about this some more. Jumping because they say jump is not our policy."

The President jumps up, "find that god dammed submarine!"

Steamed, he bolts from the map room.

Admiral Hasslinger is also on his feet, giving Eiko a rather distasteful look, he hits the door and is gone.

I'm not sure meetings in the White House are supposed to end like this one just did. Generally, everyone stands when the Prez stands. They would all kiss and make-up for any naughty words, nasty looks, or finger pointing, including "the finger", that may have been intentionally or mentally exchanged. Then leave. Rumor has it that ever since Rahm Emanuel was here as Chief of Staff, decorum and civility left the White House for safer hides, yet to return.

I can't help but think about how this mornings' priorities are shaking out. The President wants to know where that pesky Russian Oscar class sub is that may possibly be armed with a couple of nukes.

Yet on the other hand, the Veep, Seth Greene, appears to have vanished into thin air. Tough to do for a guy his size.

Who is also the loudest blow-hard around.

This is not shaping up to be a good day for the White House, and in particular, the President. And we're reaching the point where something will have to be said to the press corps. On both matters. Some already suspect the Veep to be missing. And we can, of course, count on the Israelis to leek information on that renegade sub that is possibly heading for their shores. It's a delicate balance, i.e., what to say to the press.

Maybe one of Obama's former Secretaries of Spin will make an encore appearance to deliver a convoluted, yet partisan assessment of events thus far this morning, capping his little announcement, cloaked heavily with his usual brand of bull shit, to include an arrogant statement blaming the whole mess on George W.

Then check the palm of his hand to make sure he doesn't forget to pick-up eggs, butter and a couple of joints for his nightly dip in the hot tub. He's still looking to ease the pain from being bitch-whipped by The Madame Speaker.

The day's going to be tough sledding. Maybe the President has thought about this and has come up with a diversion strategy.

As Eiko heads for the door, I say...

"Eiko, maybe the President will reschedule the Labor Day picnic for the Rose Garden. Whatdaya think?"

She mumbles something.

I say, "what's that?"

But, she's already left the room.

Okay.

Now, did she say "move on."

Or was that...

"Moron."

Interesting.

Chapter 38

Central Intelligence Agency
DCI Unger's Office
1723 Zulu, 1123 Hrs. Local

SIMON UNGER has been pacing in his spacious office. Alone.

Thinking.

The wheels turning, pulling clever thoughts, deceptive thoughts into a cohesive, yet devilish plan. Unger prides himself on his impressive ability at creating complicated plans.

Plans that would take the amateur Intel officer months to unravel. Experienced personnel, somewhat less time. But still, a lengthy slice of time to figure out what he's up to these days. A cushion of time he is most comfortable with, given the various pieces of a puzzle he is creating.

And the end result which would trump any negative assessment that would ultimately be drawn by the Intel analysts.

Those employees whose careers and livelihoods are in his hands.

Bottom line?

At the end of the day, Simon Unger will ride in on the proverbial white horse. Claim victory over the inept politicians. And declare himself savior of the nation. The only true hero in the war on terror.

No one will give a second thought to the bodies left in the wake of the developing mission.

Thus far, the plan has not run into any bumps in the road. His influence and power over the security apparatus of the United States, including the military, while without bounds, would strike the average government official not in the "security loop" as perhaps frightening on the surface. But Unger has developed an almost cult following amongst the folks at both the CIA and Homeland Security. When the heat gets turned up, most feel comfortable sleeping at night, relying on that often heard comment, "not to worry, Simon will handle the problem." A position of trust and authority that has taken years to earn. Starting back in the Clinton administration, when he could smooth talk the smoothest talker ever to occupy the Oval Office. If Clinton lived by the lie, it was Simon Unger who wrote the text book. Not a phony or an opportunist like Clinton, but a truly brilliant man who just happens to have a few wires crossed in his brain.

He sits down hard in his over-sized executive chair, and spins to a position in front of the LED screen of his computer. He takes a moment to steal a glance at the perimeter trees and foliage outside his window, thinking how quiet and peaceful this view portends. If the general public knew what turmoil around the globe and frightening issues surrounding this turmoil is dealt with inside these walls, they'd all move to a remote island in the South Pacific.

He has booted-up his secure e-mail screen, and starts to bang away at the keyboard:

"Nick – our friends have moved closer to the target – ETA Tuesday – 2300 hours Zulu – confirm rendezvous with the Jackel. Dick."

Unger studies the screen for an extra-long heartbeat. Then moves the mouse pointer to send.
"Click."

He leans back and closes his eyes as he thinks about his "friends" – a thought that makes him chuckle – and how he was able to move their journey along, unfettered. Having the Dallas pulled off that submarine was easier than ordering a Grande latte at Starbucks.

Chapter 39

PRESIDENT GIORDAN is clearly pissed. He holds a tough stare out the 2 inch thick bullet-proof window where he stands behind his massive desk. The view is to the south lawn. A place usually filled with accouterments that are part of the pomp and ceremony of the office of the President of the United States. Today, it's quiet. Serene. With the exception of a few hunched-over landscapers, hourly grounds keepers who wouldn't know that Labor Day is an official holiday to be spent with friends and family barbequing. And if they did, it's unlikely they would be anyplace else but here. Any job for a minority in and around Washington, DC is a god-send.

Eiko Narita just stares at her boss. She, too, is pissed. But for a range of other reasons. Right now she needs to bring the President back to the mission at hand. Time is crucial. And the sooner they get their arms and heads around these rapidly developing issues, the sooner his focus can be moved back onto the re-election campaign.

"It's not an abortion, sir. And it's not falling apart. I don't wanna hear that from you."

She moves closer to the far side of his desk trying to catch a glimpse of his facial expression. She's worried that he might call-off the mission. Months of planning, based on valuable intelligence reports have put a new emphasis on the war of terror.

Al Qaeda, having no luck left on the Pakistani-Afghan border, and a diminishing presence on the Arabian Peninsula, thanks, finally, to the efforts of the Saudis, has built training camps and other support facilities in the Seychelles.

Who would have thought a remote, out of sight, out of mind chain of Islands would come into play. Only through the extensive and brilliant efforts of the United States military in the Persian Gulf region, has Al Qaeda been forced to run for cover. Although their move from the war zone was slowed down once George W left office, the U.S. military commanders kept pressure on the White House, despite its liberal bent on war, and successfully pushed the bad guys into a corner. The military commanders, and the SOD, were not about to let a new commander-in-chief betray us.

The President is still tense. He speaks softly, with a hint of resignation in his voice...

"Seth Greene is on his way to jump terrorists who are probably not even there."

"We know there are plenty still there. And the bunkers they've built. Weapons, explosives, other crap that can be used to kill us. We've got them in a box."

She moves to his side of the desk, and continues...

"Margolies could be dead wrong – I mean about the intent here."

He turns at her, up close and personal, "what if Margolies is right? They loaded two of those stolen nukes on a submarine, and have escaped, Eiko. You have a plan B?"

Eiko moves back to the far side, and paces. Thinking.

"Well?" Now the President is angry.

She gives more thought to the issues on the table. Then...

"We'll invade the Island, blow it to fuckin' Uranus. Find that sub, and deep six it. The Veep is there to claim victory over the terrorists."

The President says, "I don't want anything to happen to the Veep."

She's still pacing. And not listening to him.

"Then we tell the American public we out-smarted the terrorists. Explain everything we've learned the past several months. The actions we've taken. And why, finally, once again, the war on terror is working."

She stops short, and faces her boss to finish...

But he has to ask, "what about the Veep? He's already in serious danger, yet nothing's happened."

With a wave of her hand, "G I Joe – ex Marine shit. He's like Ollie North, but smarter. Always lookin' for trouble. It's his culture, and everyone in America knows it. You can award him the medal of honor – if he gets his ass shot."

She leans back, arms folded, and smiles...

"Your pole numbers will leap off the page – mission accomplished."

Chapter 40

Here I am gazing up at the sky. It appears that I'm contemplating cloud formations, which is a sure-fire sign of some mental impairment. But actually I'm thinking. And waiting. I know Eiko should be heading this way. And I just need to get some clarification. Like, "what the hell's going on?" The Marine guards at the entrance to the West Wing haven't noticed me yet. Otherwise they would have radioed the Secret Service to mosey on out and have a chat with me. Asking something like, "have you finally lost your mind, Mister Connolly?" I guess that's the way I look. Because some low level staffer just walked by, not saying a word to me. But wanting quickly to get to wherever she's going. Usually the cute ones nod or smile, or say "hi, Jack. Wanna screw?" I made up that last part.

I spot Eiko coming from the West Wing doorway. I slip in next to her despite the fact she seems to pretend I'm not there. Or here.

Before I get to say anything, she says, "all we've got on the radar screen is a North Korean training boat, Jack."

I add, "Margolies said nothing about it leaving the Seychelles. But if we know it left, then so do the Israelis."

Eiko thinks for a minute. Then, "Putin put those Chechnyans on that sub. He gave us iron-clad assurances."

I stop dead in my tracks. My brain has just shifted into over-drive.

"What? So we knew about the sub ahead of time?"

Eiko has stopped and turned towards me. And she just looks. As if looking to deflect my question. Which now pisses me off big time. I count to ten, while thinking what to say next. If she really believes it's a training boat, operating under the guidance of Putin, not especially a trust-worthy guy, then why would the Israelis want us to go down another road. Like blow that sub out of the water. I think Eiko is smart. But the Israelis, who are always suspicious, given their rocky history, often come up with interesting pieces of intelligence, albeit by some rather unorthodox means. And are usually mostly right at the end of the day.

I say, "so what about Margolies? I'm still inclined to buy into his problem about Israel being some kind of target."

Eiko checks the area close-in as if there may be ease-droppers listening in. I feel like saying that eighty-something black dude trimming the azalea bushes on the south lawn reads lips. Levity sometimes brings more focus. But not now.

She says, softly, "unrelated, Jack. It's nothing, trust me."

On your word as a politician?

She continues, "Israel works miss-information as a matter of routine. And Margolies doesn't have a dialogue with Putin."

"No one has a dialogue with Putin. Not even his wife. Okay, maybe his mistress."

She sighs, then continues, "they want us to react, take the lead down a dark alley, clear the land mines so they can storm in and look like hot shit."

She gives me a hard-ass stare.

Then adds, "fuck 'em."

I can only look around the area. I'm trying desperately to compute everything I know, and how it fits into what I don't know, but suspect.

I ask, pointedly, "is the Veep in trouble? Somehow I think he fits into this problem."

Without answering, she turns and heads for the OEOB door.

"Eiko?"

She looks over her shoulder, saying, "this has nothing to do with the Veep."

Chapter 41

The Pentagon
Covert Operations Center
1737 Zulu, 1137 Hrs. Local

ADMIRAL HASSLINGER bursts through the door having taken the fastest staff car ride from the White House to the Pentagon in the history of automobile travel. He studies the vast array of computer and LED monitors that cover two walls and every desk top and work station in this darkened environment. Not to mention the big screen displays that cover a third wall with real time video feeds from God knows where in the world. Most appear to be Middle Eastern, judging from the desert back-drops on the screens. A platoon of uniformed personnel, some at stations, and others in motion around the tight space, are packed into the room. Despite a senior flag officer entering the room, those here stay put, focused on their screens, while listening to audio feeds in their respective ear buds.

The atmosphere is as tight as a drum. The personnel are charged. What's happening here right now is not a drill. But the real deal. Hasslinger surveys several screens, and then says to no one in particular, "give me the current status on Air Force Two."

From the far side of the room, about fifteen feet from the Admiral, a young Army 1st lieutenant speaks over his shoulder...

"Scheduled re-fueling stop at tango foxtrot one hour, twelve minutes, sir. Nineteen forty nine hours, Zulu, sir."

Admiral Hasslinger contemplates the information, computing several tactical scenarios in his head. Including the time it would take for an assault force, already staged and ready to roll, to be given its orders to move.

Also, the ramifications of adding air and sea support should the situation spiral out of control. His biggest fear at the moment is the decision to take aggressive offensive or defensive action, depending on the circumstances at ground zero, is in the hands of a select group of White House personnel, including that "NSA girl." The thought, at first worries him, and then angers him. Amateurs. This mission, while political in scope, is primed for disaster, and should be run as a military mission.

Admiral Hasslinger will be ready.

Just in case.

A middle-aged staffer, female, with the rank of a Navy Lieutenant Commander, slips in next to the Admiral. And hands him a single page document.

She holds back a nano second. Then says. "Just came in from Admiral Keyes on board the USS Ronald W. Reagan, sir,"

Hasslinger takes a moment to read it twice. Hands it back to her. She stands at ease behind and to his left awaiting instructions.

After a heartbeat, he says, still focused on the big screens, "when Air Force Two reaches its re-fueling point, let 'em know he's go for X-ray one niner..."

He turns to give her that look of authority flag officers give to junior officers under their command...

"...the Seychelles Archipelago."

Chapter 42

The Seychelles Archipelago
Beau Vallon Seaside Bungalows
1741 Zulu, 2141 Hrs. Seychelles Local Time
1141 Hrs. In Washington, DC

NICK is not his real name.

As a matter of fact, no one knows his real name. Nor are the names on his various passports his real name. Not that it's important. It's a fact better left unsaid. A CIA operative for about twenty years. He's in his late thirties. Cagy. Impenetrable. And perhaps frightfully dangerous. His missions come with a proviso: payment in advance to a numbered Swiss bank account. And not one of the big, well known Swiss banks. But one whose policy of discretion really means "discretion" unlike the big boys of late who are willingly giving up names of depositors to authorities in the United States.

Not Nick's bank. His banker knows better. And his banker plans on sleeping nights. Not worrying about his life, nor that of his immediate family.

Nick studies his laptop screen, frowning at the short message from Dick. He grunts, as if he already knows what's happening. As far as confirming contact with *le Jackel*, well, if he determines that Dick should know this he will tell him. If not, then let Dick stew. Nick is not one to communicate when it's not necessary. He has his orders, and they will be followed. With or without Dick. He is the ultimate independent contractor. The man who was the first to defy an executive order issued by then President Bill Clinton stating that no member of the covert intelligence community was to cause harm nor execute a foreign national in high political office on behalf of the United States in the interest of gathering intelligence.

Bull shit. That was Nick's response. He knows better. Those we have identified as our enemies can only be treated one way. With a one way ticket to paradise. Let them survive and their rhetoric and philosophy will multiply amongst the brethren. Especially the radical Islamists. What's wrong with our leaders? Don't they see the incongruity of their policies? Political correctness has strayed well beyond basic common sense. Nick has become incensed and gravely disappointed with the leadership in Washington. Being out here in the field has opened his eyes to an assortment of issues. America is not what it used to be. Thanks to the leaders – if any exist – in Washington.

And it's this current mental state of mind that lead Nick to accept this newest assignment. His end, once completed, will send shock waves through the establishment. Exposing the faults that permeate the new thinking in Washington, "let's talk to the bad guys. Maybe they'll understand us better." Talk is cheap. Which is why it never got us anywhere. President Wilson tried it back in 1917. It didn't work. And he ended up sending troops to Europe, engaging the U.S. in a devastating confrontation known as World War I.

Nixon just *had* to talk to the North Vietnamese in Paris when the military guys said "…just let us win this war. We know how to do it, Mister President. We have the hardware."

Then the biggest fiasco of all. Jimmy Carter letting the Iranians take over our embassy in Teheran. "If only I could talk to those fellas we can work out our differences." Ahmadinejad, a young student radical at the time, and one of those responsible for holding the Americans for over 400 days, left a photo of Jimmy Carter hanging in the U.S. embassy just so he could give it the finger every time he walked past.

So much for talk.

Nick now stands and walks the short distance across a high gloss oak floor to a double patio door. On the other side a wrap-around patio that has views of the Indian Ocean and the tropical rain forest, thick foliage of green that gets soaked for twenty minutes each day at about four PM. A semi darkness has set in, this Island being just south of the equator with longer days. In forty-five minutes it'll be completely dark.

Nick steps out onto the patio. He takes in a lung-full of the clean ocean air. It's pungent salt flavor mixes perfectly with the floral fragrance gently flowing from the forest complements of an off shore breeze, typical at this hour. On the patio a full moon illuminates this tropical paradise. Heaven on earth. Yet little known to the vacationing public around the world, including the U.S., except those snobby Brits who would never tell anyone of this incredible find.

The nocturnal noises of night creatures high in the hills above the bungalow remind one that he is not alone in this remote, luxurious hide-a-way in paradise.

And perhaps not really alone as a figure moves from the thick foliage towards the bungalow. He's slow and careful, taking each step as if the landscape is littered with land mines.

Nick, startled and on high alert, reaches quickly under his loose fitting shirt and draws a 9mm Beretta, holding it close to his leg, and out of sight from the approaching figure. He flips the safety up, running a check list through his head. He did clean the weapon just this afternoon. And replaced any spent cartridge with new, hollow-tipped live ammunition. The kind that will quickly remove an appendage like an arm or a leg at 20 yards.

There's this strange, weird silence for an eternity as Nick's eyes adjust to the rapidly developing darkness of the night.

Then, a low, throaty, French-accented voice is heard, speaking English.

"Monsieur Nick?"

Nick takes a moment as he zeros in on a middle aged, well-built man who has emerged from the shadows and the foliage. He's a dangerous looking dude who has clearly seen a scrape or two in his roughly 40 plus odd years. He wears a beret, tilted carefully to the side of his round head, and covering jet-black hair. Hair that is matched in color with a thin, mysterious looking mustache. The man stops, and just stares in Nicks' direction. Then takes a wooden match stick from behind an ear, and strikes it on a metal chair haphazardly placed in the sand, below the deck.

As he lights up a cigarette, the flame dances, and finally reveals the profile of a hard face. Two days of stubble. And the real clincher, an ugly scar that stretches from just below his left ear-lobe, running across his neck, ending just below his right ear-lobe. Obviously stitched by someone with no medical experience. Not even a seamstress, for that matter.

This is the JACKEL.

And not the Jackel found in that novel of the same name, portrayed in the film version by the great British actor, Edward Fox. No, this guy is the real deal. A disturbed man in his mid-forties. And known to be feared on at least three continents since being recently, shall we say, *furloughed* from a French prison. A place that would make Devils Island look like Disney World. A place where the authorities are still finding bodies that somehow went missing right after the Jackel went missing. The Jackel takes a long pull on his filter-less cigarette, slowly releasing the smoke into the night air before he says…

"Bon soir, mon ami."

Nick, bringing his nerves under control while slipping the Beretta back into his waist band, says. "Ever think to call ahead? I could've shot you."

The Jackel chuckles softly, as if that would've happened.

In the Jackel's mind, Nick would have had to yank an eight inch knife blade from his heart well before he had an opportunity to raise the weapon and shoot.

The Jackel lets it pass, and gets to the mission at hand.

"You have the weapon, no?"

Nick gives the Jackel a once over, assessing the hired gun standing about six feet from him, off the deck, and in the sand.

He knows this guy comes highly recommended by those in the dark world of assassins and mercenaries. People with questionable ties to those that even the terrorists fear. People whose only known identity is a numbered bank account in some remote corner of the universe. Not even the internet is capable of tracing these folks.

Not long ago, Nick attempted to trace a questionable contact through the internet with the help of some "friends" at Langley, i.e. CIA headquarters. He gave up after working his way back through twelve different servers spread around eight different countries, ending up with a blank screen.

Nick moves to the deck railing, pointing out beyond the Jackel, and saying, "you can try it at sunrise…on the beach…you know, those shitty little birds-

"The Jackel interrupts…

"Sandpipers, no?"

Chapter 43

The OEOB
Office of the National Security Advisor,
Ms. Eiko Narita
1746 Zulu, 1146 Hrs. Local

Since I don't buy any of the crap Eiko has been giving me the last few hours, I have barged into her office. As usual, she's ignoring me. So, I figure I'll just stand here, looking out her window at the West Wing. And wondering what my next move should be without really pissing her off, something I'm prone to do. But the fact of the matter is that I'm being played. There's a bigger picture out there. And I'm not in the loop. Now I know how it feels to be a Democrat on the Hill, and have Nancy Pelosi not let you into the inner circle. But claim to be your voice on the Hill. Not that I'd want to be in her inner circle.

Women in power.

They can be such bitches.

This is one of those times I'm glad to be a non-conformist. And just say what's on my mind. And brace myself for whatever comes flying back.

"Somehow the Veep's preference for playing hooky is related to this mess."

Eiko, who up to this point has been totally distracted with her e-mail screen, suddenly perks up and says.

"What mess?"

Here we go again. It's like la la land, and nothing's happened. Maybe I'm just paranoid. But the Veep's missing. There's a renegade sub out there in the Indian Ocean, possibly armed with a couple of nukes. With Russians on board, no less. And she wants to know what mess! But you already know all that. And I'm hoping it's everyone else who's gone over the edge.

Except, of course, the lovely and talented Lauren Miller, who, at the moment, is sorely missed.

Eiko bangs away at her keyboard, while saying, "look, Jack – I'm stumped as well. It's all very bizarre. And it makes no sense. The fuckin' guy's a loose cannon."

So she's stumped. Okay. But I'm worried about lots of people. Now I've just added her to that list. The NSA to the President needs to be on top of every single situation involving National Security. And, therefore, have several fundamental tactical solutions in the hopper. Being stumped is not one that I would necessarily include. Let the general public be stumped over the fact that the guy who's second in line to the Presidency is AWOL. Not good. Moreover, the issue of that pesky Russian sub is also a matter of National Security. Probably somewhere at the red level, or better.

"Eiko. Russian submarines don't take pleasure cruises. At least not the ones I've met up with while out in the deep blue sea on patrol."

With her back to me, she waves it off, saying, "Margolies is likely wrong."

"And were you, this morning, at Camp David? Remember? You asked me about the Seychelles?"

Bing!

She whips around. And as she is spinning in her chair, ready to leap at my jugular, I make a quick get-away. Out the door, and down the hallway.

Chapter 44

The Oval Office
1752 Zulu, 1152 Hrs. Local

I watch as the President paces behind his black leather executive desk chair. He just had to get a new chair when he moved into the Oval. One of the old ones he could have had, particularly a nice one left behind by Obama. Another one that had too many beer farts in the seat cushion. He's thinking. He's also clearly disturbed at my latest piece of breaking news. He stops and looks right at me.

"The Washington Post, huh?"

"Yes, sir. Tom Delgado is the reporter in question here. Says he has a source. An eyewitness. Who just happened to be out on Burdette Road when the Veep leaped over the fence." I take a deep breath, trying to soften the blow. "Probably know one I know. Fancy neighborhood. Rich lobbyists."

The President grunts, then moves to a far wall, about three feet from a pair of brass clocks. He squares his jaw. Thinking. Although it's hard to tell, but I think he's focused on something tucked away, well hidden in his gray matter. It's the silence that gives it away. Usually he has something to say quickly.

Those brass clocks are placed side by side on the wall. They're 5 inches in diameter. And shaped like ships wheels. With eight spokes. Eight day jeweled ships bell clocks.

Brass markers under each clock ID the time zone.

On the left, Zulu. The right, Local.

"These clocks, Jack, were a gift from the air wing on the USS Enterprise, CVN 65, from my tour during the Vietnam War."

"Yes, sir."

Alongside the clocks are several photos taken on the Enterprise during that time. The President stares at one in particular. A young squadron leader, the President, on the flight deck of the huge aircraft carrier. He stands alongside another young Navy pilot. In the background is an A6E Intruder. The photo is dated October 11, 1969. I, of course, recognize the other guy. It's my dad. And one cannot help but notice his extraordinary good looks, wavy dirty blonde hair, and muscular build. It's no wonder people I meet who know him usually comment on how I'm "a chip off the old block." At least I think that's what they say.

The President fidgets. It's the little things like a hand on his tie knot, fingers that he runs through his hair, a deep breath, and then a long exhale. Something clearly on his mind. And it's not just the office of the President of the United States. There are bigger issues at play here today.

"Your dad looks good in this photo, Jack. A real hot-shot pilot..." He seems to mumble to himself as if reliving some old memory.

Then, "seventeen fifty four Zulu..."

"Sir?"

"Sonofabitch, Jack...I need to push the clock."

The President swings back towards his desk, punches a button on his telephone console. I can't see which button, but before I ask what's up...

"Yes, Mister President."

A woman's voice from the console has answered. Towards the speaker, he relays his instructions to the woman on the other end.

"Call the press corps to the briefing room, please, Helen."

From the console, "yes, sir." Then, a disconnect.

I step in closer to his desk and ask. "Push the clock, sir?"

The President, head down, shuffles papers on his desk as if looking for something. Still moving the papers around, he asks. "How old was he? When he made Admiral?"

I just have to stare having no idea what he's talking about. He snaps up, looking me right in the eye and says.

"Your dad. How old was he?"

What the hell kind of question is that? I really don't want to answer that one since, from what I can recall, he was pretty close to my current age. And I'm just a Commander. Down recently from Captain thanks to a few hard asses out at Pearl harbor. And perhaps heading further down the chain of command if I don't answer the boss. Which is in the opposite direction most all officers move in the chain of command. Those who don't move up are usually the ones given the boot out of the Navy, or into the brig.

"I don't know."

The President takes a moment to think.

Then, "...forty-two, I think. Yeah. Forty-two years old. Youngest Admiral in the Navy at the time."

Thank you very much. I needed to hear that. Especially from the commander-in-chief. The one who generally nominates a guy for that first star. So I give the big guy a stiff, pissed-off shrug. His look darts to the floor, probably because he knows I'm pissed, or he intended to piss me off.

"That gives you a few years, huh Jack?

He gathers some papers and makes a bee-line for the door, while saying. "Think you can live up to your Dad's legacy?

He's out the door. And I can only just stare.

For some reason I'm still focused on the door, but I'm trying to remember the telephone number for that truck driver's school plastered on the tail of a truck under a sign that read "Drivers Wanted."

Chapter 45

Members of the White House press corps are quickly moving into the room to take their assigned seats. There's a bee-hive kind of activity with the press corps on edge and murmurs that buzz around the room, well above the whisper stage, and not at all the norm for this place.

I had followed the President to this part of the West Wing. He now stands just outside the press room giving the members of the press corps time to find their seats and get settled. I scan the room looking for Tom Delgado of the Washington Post not knowing where his assigned seat is at the moment. As I catch a glimpse of Tom sliding into row three, seat five, not prime real estate but close enough given the liberal bent the Post takes when writing about President Giordan, the President materializes from the staff doorway.

He leaps onto the small stage, looking grim.

The group stands.

I'm keenly aware that the President will be extemporaneous. But I'm also confident he'll come clean with the press. In this town you must be, or else it's doomsday for your career. And since he's running for a second term, the re-election campaign to officially start tomorrow, he will need to be totally honest with reporters, especially those who control the 24/7 cable world.

He begins, politely, but firmly in control of the event.

"Please. Be seated. Thank you. I have a brief announcement."

He takes a deep breath, making eye contact with those in rows one and two.

"You may have heard a rumor that the Vice President – my friend, Seth Greene – has suddenly vanished."

He pauses. And I take note of the faces in the crowd. Most reveal that look of confirmation. Tell us more, please.

"Nothing could be further from the truth. As a matter of fact, I spoke with him just moments ago."

What? Okay, maybe before I jumped into the Oval he did speak with the Veep. But he would have told me. Right? No. Maybe not. Things are quickly getting better.

"He is well and secure. This miss-conception spun out of control this morning as a result of two, unrelated incidents. One, the Veep had a golf date with friends at the Congressional Country Club for which he did not show."

So he bagged the Congressional date for a date at Burning Tree, right?

"The second, and perhaps more absurd rumor involves several residents who live near Burning Tree Country Club having seen four men jump a fence – one jumper being identified as the Veep."

The President breaks into a wide smile, and chuckles just enough for the audio devices to pick up the reaction.

"The actual events of this morning involving Vice President Greene are the fact that he was rushed to a secure location, leaving his official residence at approximately six thirty-five this morning.

"The details of how he left are secure and only known to the Secret Service. His last minute departure was the result of several very specific threats that surfaced very early this morning.

"However, I promise you, and the American people, he will be joining me on the campaign trail later this week."

I notice the President take a step back from the podium, his head down as if in silent prayer.

He brings his head back up, and I now note a stone-cold demeanor has replaced the serious, yet approachable expression of just seconds ago.

"This is a very difficult incident for you all to understand given the level of protection the Vice President enjoys."

As the President stops to give his next statement more thought, I drill a look in his direction.

And wonder what he means by "incident."

Alongside the Potomac River
The Virginia Side
On the George Washington Parkway

A Lincoln Town car glides smoothly down the Parkway towards the 14th Street bridge that will take it into the District of Columbia. It's followed by a black SUV with tinted windows. It's view across the River is that of toney Georgetown, with the University sitting high on a hill overlooking the river-front commercial district.

Seated in the back seat is Simon Unger, Director of the Central Intelligence Agency, a/k/a, the DCI. He takes in the pleasant view. Up ahead and across the river from Roosevelt Island is the John F. Kennedy Center. He takes a look. He scowls, then gives off an audible snort. His head swivels back to the radio speaker embedded in the seat- back in front of him. And drawn to the voice of President Giordan as he continues to deliver his statement to the press in the White House press room.

"But not impossible given the threat of terrorism that surrounds us each day."

Unger grabs a copy of the Washington Post, scanning the back page ads.

"Protection that, should our intelligence gathering apparatus ever rise to a new level of expertise – something I will personally work hard to continue to achieve if given the opportunity to serve a second term as your President – and be commensurate with the Vice President's recent proposal for an over-haul of the Central Intelligence Agency – may not be altogether necessary in the weeks and months to come…"

Unger lowers the newspaper and glares at the speakers.

The West Wing
Press Briefing Room

I can't help but notice that the President seems to be more firm and confident in what he is having to say to the country, and the world at large, for that matter. However, what bothers me is not knowing the answer to this nagging question pinging around my little brain. Is he being completely honest, or is this just a political stunt in order to kick-off the re-election campaign with a bang, so to speak?

I lock eyes with Tom Delgado of the Washington Post.

He shrugs, not knowing where all this is going, but looking to me for some direction. So, I find it necessary to return the shrug, but this time with a wink.

That should keep him guessing.

The President continues, "…unfortunately, we live with terror threats every day. But, I promise you, as your President, we will find and destroy these terrorists and their bases of operation. On that front, we are very, very close despite foolish policies of the previous Democratic administration who let words get in the way of action."

At this point, the President stops and looks out over the press corps appearing very CEO-like as cameras click away at a maddening pace.

At the same time, Eiko rushes in, and slips next to me against the side wall, a place where the press secretary runners-up usually stand, and asks in a charged, yet low voice.

"What the hell is he doing? Did you tell him to do this, Jack?"

I take this opportunity to completely ignore her as the President finishes.

"Thank you, all. And may God bless America."

The President bolts from the podium.

Getting within six feet of me and Eiko, he gives me a wink. To which I respond by thinking, "oh, shit."

The press corps continues to shout, "Mister President, Mister President."

Then some bone-head in the back yells, "is Greene dead?"

I'm almost certain that every broadcast and cable network picked-up that question, which will undoubtedly be the lead-in at MSNBC later tonight.

But not appear at all on FOX. Katie Couric, if still with CBS, would have probably e-mailed her viewers - it was a small list - with a question. "Who's Seth Greene?"

Isn't news reporting fun?

It's certainly no longer professional.

But, hey, what the hell? If they paid me fifteen gazillion bucks a year, I'd say whatever those left-wing radical bosses want me to say.

Chapter 46

I love these pictures here on the wall of my office. When I get into a funk I just stand here and stare at them. Pictures of submarines. Several attack subs, Los Angeles Class, my favorites. Because it's these subs that are the reason Americans can sleep at night. I used to command one, the USS Baton Rouge. There are no less than twenty four of these babies scattered around the globe, underwater. They're in strategic places, and there are only two big dogs at the Pentagon who know where these guys are patrolling.

All of these submarines carry no less than twenty-four nuclear armed missiles. And should any of the bad guys, a/k/a, the axis of evil, get out of line, and do something stupid, then on orders from the President of the United States it would take only about ten minutes and these bad guys, and the countries they lead, are toast.

Everything else, the million-man army of troops, - army and marine corps - the planes, the surface ships, and ordinance on the ground around the world, the spy satellites, it's all for show, folks. It's these nuclear attack submarines. That's why most of us in the know, know. And why we sleep at night.

And here's the kicker.

We've provided detail information on our plans to the bad guys - should they get out of line - around the globe, including most of our allies as well.

Except, of course, the location of these subs.

Checkmate.

So, now you know where I'd like to be. Certainly not here. Maybe someday I'll get back to sea. I think the President did say it would happen. Although he seems to be a little miffed with me at the moment. Not to mention my immediate boss, Eiko Narita, who hates me.

I know I have an employment contract here at the White House. Someday I plan to read it to see how the hell I can get out of here. But for the moment I need to keep the leader of the free world happy with my opinions. It seems the less I say the more I feel the President likes me. Maybe if I shut up altogether, I'll get appointed ambassador someplace. Hopefully, some warm climate where the lovely Lauren Miller and I can lie on the beach, naked.

Suddenly, I feel someone looking over my shoulder.

"I'm a bettin' man, Jack. I'd bet I'm the only agent on this case."

I hear my friend, Larry Mitchener, but I'm not listening. I'm still on a sub photo.

"Twenty-six years at this crap. I'm damn good, man. Damn good, Jack."

"Less than four years," I say. "I'll be forty-two years old in less than four years."

"Say what, Jack?"

I turn and now face Larry.

"That's all I have. Less than four years."

Larry gives me one of those looks – "get a grip, man,"

"Larry, he calls a serious national security breach an incident. Not to mention he's lying. And he wants to be re-elected?"

Larry shuffles around the office.

He's thinking about a number of things.

Pulling puzzle pieces out of thin air.

Something he's quiet adept at doing.

A few years back, before the drinking, he would be several chapters ahead of whoever was briefing him on whatever subject. How he keeps it altogether in his head is way beyond me.

And I'm getting a good feeling that he hasn't lost that unique quality. Because right now, we need it.

He stops and turns at me, "we're lookin' at a conspiracy. Right here. Inside the White House, Jack."

"And my boss, the lovely Eiko Narita, may have a thought on that, Larry. I'm sure you can't wait to meet her."

"And check out those tiny boobs?"

That was Lieutenant j.g. Lauren Miller who just happened to slip into my office, unannounced. She's good at shocking entrances. And a sight for sore eyes, as they – whoever they are – say.

I give her a pleasant smile, then a glance at my watch and wonder what Navy chopper pilot has some promised favor heading his way as a result of her getting up to Washington DC from Camp Peary in record time. But more importantly, I'll have to remember to ask her what exactly is the favor she promised. I doubt she'll tell me. Or maybe just say she promised the guy a happy meal at McDonalds.

I know what you're thinking.

I give her a wink, and throw another idea at Larry, "maybe you need to have a little chat with Senator Sykes as well."

Lauren perks up, and I can see the wheels now turning. She grabs a note book from her purse. Scans a few pages. Then says, "I already have something there. Pulled it off the Sprint data network. Sykes made several cell phone calls starting at eight forty seven this morning. He made three calls…"

"Lauren! By the way, this is Secret Service Agent Larry Mitchener."

I'm slow with introduction protocol, which I find suddenly necessary, given what Lauren just said.

"He's a federal law enforcement officer. He'll probably arrest you for computer hacking, or, whatever."

She ignores my warning, turning to Larry, and adds...

"one call to a reporter..."

"Thomas Delgado of the Washington Post."

Chapter 47

The Oval Office
1826 Zulu, 1226 Hrs. Local

The President leans aggressively on his desk, between the chair and the desk drilling a look of contempt at Simon Unger, casually seated on the other side. His blood pressure is rising quickly, noticeable by the change in his complexion that has gone from a light tan to beet red. The flared nostrils move in and out as he mentally counts to ten.

"In view of developments this morning, Mister President, I assume you'd like the full attention of the Agency from here on out."

"No. I think not, Simon. But thank you anyway."

Unger, sensing his boss has more to say, continues.

"Very discreetly, of course."

"No!"

The President's firm response causes Unger's expression to change perceptibly to one of annoyance, and disgust. He watches the President move to the ships bell clocks thinking to himself of the tight time frame now in place surrounding the events he has put into motion. He smiles thinly feeling comfortable that his plan will be glitch free. Unlike the plan being carried out by the leader of the free world. A man who has every conceivable resource at his fingers tips. But not the will–power to do the right thing. He is, by all accounts, a simple politician. Whose focus today is doing the right thing in order to get re-elected.

Fools these politicians. They live by the polls and the words that bring millions of dollars into their coffers. If only they would spend the time required on what really matters to the American people. Their safety and security. Able to reap the benefits and rewards of living in a free democratic republic.

Politicians. Simply bumps in the road for people like Simon Unger. He knows better. And will act when and where it is necessary in the interest of preserving values that all Americans worship.

His focus is dead on. And so must the President's be at this moment.

"I'm alarmed about certain intelligence regarding the Seychelles, Mister President."

President Giordan turns slowly at the DCI, and softly says, "such as?"

"Israeli intelligence, once again, sir, has fallen prey to their own paranoia."

"So what's the good news, Simon?"

Unger sits back slightly, crossing his legs, more confident, "the current status of your re-election campaign, sir."

The President moves closer to Unger, "I see no connection, Simon."

What has always bugged the President about this guy is his ability to cleverly connect issues, giving everything the degree of importance required to send staffers chasing red herrings. Somewhere there is an agenda that is only known to Simon Unger.

"Simon. I see no connection whatsoever."

Unger can only just smile to himself. Once again he's got the President on the ropes. And in such a situation, will need to rely on his advice.

"I only stand to offer advice, Mister President. Only from a National Security angle, of course."

The President takes it up a notch, "and I'm ordering you to stay out of this matter. Am I clear on this point, Mister Director?"

A heartbeat.

"Is that final, sir?"

"It's final."

Unger slowly rises from the chair. He buttons the middle button of his tailor made gray suit jacket. And stiffens his upper body, looking President Giordan straight in the eye, "then, I believe we have covered everything.

Unger turns, and strolls to the door. He opens the door gently, passing through, and carefully closes same.

Only a small click is heard.

Chapter 48

President Giordan is on his cell phone. Sounds like a family matter. I walk alongside, being granted another several minutes of his time. Which is telling in itself. I never get this much time with the boss. But today is different. For some reason he feels the need to keep me closer than ever.

What's that saying so often quoted? The one Michael Corleone said? "Keep your friends close, but your enemies closer."

I'm not sure I want to think about. *Forgetta 'bout it!*

He snaps his cell phone shut. And for a long moment he's silent. Then he says, "my daughter. She saw the press conference. In her second year at Bryn Mar, you know."

"Yes, sir."

I refrain from adding a post-script to my days at the Naval Academy when we had weekend leave one April. And a couple of my pals and I visited one of the women's dorms at Bryn Mar, spending the weekend in, well, several beds.

Uninvited.

"She says I'm full of shit."

I need to make him feel wanted. So I add, "that place is a hot spot for wacky liberal policy. I heard they've got Nancy Pelosi scheduled to sing Christmas carols at the "Bring-a-Bitch" holiday party in December."

"She's a registered democrat."

"I know…sir."

The President takes a small bottle from his pocket. He applies a nasal spray to his nostrils.

"Rhinocort. My sinuses. It's a steroid. You know that?"

"I think there's more, Mister President."

"I'm sorry, Jack? What's that?"

"You said incident. An incident, Mister President."

"Yes I did, Jack. As opposed to a National Security event."

"So, let me get this straight. An incident is better than a National Security event. But worse than lying."

"Jack. I'm not in a drug-induced stupor."

"Actually, sir, your health is not my concern at the moment."

"No!"

I think I have now pissed him off as he turns quickly into the Oval Office from the paved walkway. A Secret Service agent is there to hold the door for both of us.

The Oval Office

With the door closed the President glances over his shoulder with a look that suggests I'm shouldn't be there. He moves to his desk chair, and sits, scanning several documents. Without looking up at me, he says, "I have no intention of briefing you, Jack."

"Would you be okay if I asked why?"

He rests both arms on the desk, head still down, and sighs heavily.

A heartbeat.

"Because you're not unbelievably stupid,"

And now a look right at me, "and I might just well be."

I'm beginning to feel his pain. Who the hell would want this job. I move to the desk, opposite my boss, and try a little light weight psychotherapy. Something I just might be good at given the fact that the President and I share the same kind of sarcastic streak. I often say to my friends and family, and anyone who'll listen, that such a quality shows superior intelligence and good mental health.

"People who trust you elected you, sir. They expect you to be honest. Take the heat. Make the hard decisions. Look what happened to that bozo from Arkansas when he lied."

I'm on a roll.

"That's not you, sir."

"I have no problem with reciting the pledge of allegiance, Jack. I'm still a patriot."

"Yes, sir."

"But I go with my gut."

"I tried that, Mister President. Look where it got me."

"I wish I could change that, Jack."

"Redemption. That's my new mantra."

"You'll have it. I'll see to it."

Okay. Good enough. I guess I shouldn't ask him if that's on his word as a politician, or as my Dad's best friend. It's a close call. I think I'll refrain from any further stupidity.

"So, Mister President, do I get briefed. Or do I march a team of over-rated White House lawyers in here?"

The boss now stands and moves behind his executive chair, looking right at me.

"That's the kind of thought that usually brings on bouts of stupidity, Jack."

Great minds do think alike. Although I'm not so sure how he's able to read my thoughts.

"I'm not ready for that call yet, Jack. I do hear your frustration, and I am truly sorry."

I'm struck by his simple honesty with me. Too bad no one is here to witness this revelation. I can't imagine telling Eiko about this conversation. She'd probably have my office ripped apart looking for drugs.

"I'll leave you alone, sir. You may be better off dealing with these issues without me."

I turn and head for the door.

"Jack!"

I stop and turn to face the boss, deciding to keep my mouth shut. But thinking, is he going to fire me, accept my *off the cuff* resignation, or recommend me for the Medal of Freedom?

"Tomorrow evening. Tuesday. 1800 hours, local. That's six pm."

And he turns to check the ships bell clocks while I wonder why he felt he had to tell me, an almost twenty year veteran of the United States Navy, that eighteen hundred hours was six pm.

Maybe he *did* read my personnel file.

"2400 hours, Zulu," he says.

Standing somewhat dumb-founded, not knowing what to say in response, I give him a little frown that hopefully will trigger an explanation of what he just said. Sometimes, standing before the leader of the free world, you get weak in the knees, afraid to ask a question that could be interpreted incorrectly, making you dumb as dirt.

Something like, "2400 hours Zulu – right – is that here or there?"

Fortunately, I catch myself just as he finishes.

"Everything, Jack.

Operation Silhouette.

Please, trust me."

Chapter 49

OEOB Office Corridors
Enroute to Jack Connolly's Office
1851 Zulu, 1251 Hrs. Local

Once again I feel like I'm bulling my way through this place. Head down. In some kind of rage. At this point I'm reasonably certain that I am being played. Although I can't say why. My best hope is that the President and whoever is in on this "incident" stuff with him think I'm way too bright to be part of their little scheme.

Or it could be the other way around where they think I'm a complete idiot. And, therefore, see no point in keeping me in the loop as it would likely be well above my head.

Then, maybe I don't want to know. That's the safer choice. The less I know the better chance I have avoiding pointed questions about serious intelligence matters that don't include sex, drinking, sex, more drinking and sex.

Actually, I do have a much higher opinion of myself, and would like to be in on the plan. At least it appears I'll be there sometime tomorrow evening. Eighteen hundred hours Zulu. Which, at the moment, is still six pm. As long as I'm still in this time zone. If I happen to leave this time zone, then things will get a little fuzzy for me. Like if Lauren says. "Let's go see my folks. They live in Ohio." That's another time zone. I think. I'm afraid to ask her because the mere mention of Ohio will lead to a directive that we visit Ma and Pa Miller out there. Somewhere. I heard it's somewhere on the other side of the Ohio River. No offense to Ohio, but I've got the perfect excuse not to go.

I haven't had my anti-union busting shot yet.

"Hey, good lookin'. Thinking about me?"

I hear that a lot around here. However, in this case, I recognize the voice. It's nice to have a hot babe cozy up to you. Especially where the entire male staff of single losers can observe. Lauren can have such a positive effect on me. Or anyone, for that matter. But I still feel a little down at the moment.

"I'm finished down in the dungeon. How'd it go with the boss?"

I'm still focused straight ahead, looking for the door to my private sanctum.

"I think I just quit."

"It's called self-preservation, Jack."

I have to think about that for a moment. Maybe that's why I just blurt out stupid stuff when I'm frustrated. I need to get that habit under control. One never knows who's listening. Although it was just the President and yours truly. No one else. I'm feeling a little better now. But I have to ask.

"Do they still record in the Oval Office, you think?"

Jack Connolly's Office

I go for the window and its view, sideways, towards the South Lawn of the White House. Not that I'm looking for answers out there, but the shear serenity of the vast landscape is somewhat calming. I'm getting more of a good feeling that the President is about to level with me. If he hasn't already, but on some lower level. I respect his honesty and integrity. Bringing me up to speed tomorrow will give me the strength to provide him with the best possible intelligence on this renegade sub matter. Giving it more thought, I believe we had a fruitful conversation. He recognized my deep concern for the issues at hand. And has shown a willingness to bring me closer to the situation.

You see? That's what a view out to the South Lawn will do. It builds confidence and trust. I'm pumped. I turn and face Lauren.

"Let's put together a time-line of the events we know. We'll try to draw some comparisons between that sub and the missing Veep. I think there's a connection."

Lauren steps closer to me and asks. "Did he take a cell call in there?"

"Yes. His wacky liberal daughter. We were outside, on the -"

"- It was the Veep, Jack."

Chapter 50

United States Capitol Building
The Rotunda
1919 Zulu, 1319 Hrs. Local

SENATOR JOE SYKES fast walks across the Rotunda floor, coming from the House of Representatives side, heading for the Senate side.

While he looks, with one of those political smiles, of course, at the visitors milling around the huge area, he secretly hopes no one stops him for an autograph or to ask some childish question as most constituents are prone to do.

Reporters are another matter altogether.

He avoids them like the plague, unless there's a specific message he wants to put out there. Usually if stopped by some annoying, whiney reporter, he smiles, but keeps walking hoping to make it past that point where only Senators and staff are permitted. The line of demarcation, known more conveniently as the DMZ.

He's not at all like some of his colleagues in the Senate. Like, for instance, Chuck Schumer who spends his day looking for TV cameras. Then runs to get in the picture, knocking anyone in his path to the floor.

The only positive thought on Sykes' mind, as he glides through the center of the Rotunda, is whether or not he'll lie "in state" someday in this location, a privilege accorded to former Presidents and other dignitaries.

Hard to say where Joe Sykes thinks he fits into that protocol. In the meantime, he's already directed his executor to make sure that happens.

Alongside is a rather severe looking woman. Someone pushing forty.

XENIA ZEITUNG is one nasty bitch. She proudly wears an earring - two dangling brass balls – on her right ear. She doesn't smile at anyone. Not even the Capitol Police officer that gives her a friendly wave from his post near the entrance to the Senate side. The only thing that comes to her is "peasant."

She carefully checks over her shoulder, then to either side of her boss, the powerful Senator Sykes, then says, "Simon Unger wants to point his ugly dick at the White House? Now I'm for that."

Sykes shakes his head, his eyes darting left and right, says, "Xenia. Please. A little civility."

Civility? That's the last thing on her mind. What she's thinking is how to keep this guy under control. Make sure his head is in the right direction. The United States Senate functions on a very clear system of seniority. Not Democrat verses Republican. And Sykes is up there. Regardless of the party in power at 1600 Pennsylvania Avenue, or the Senate leadership, for that matter, it's those senior members that ultimately call the shots. And her boss has that power.

She bites hard, saying, "I have a problem with politicians whose I Q is smaller than my bra size."

Sykes can only just bite his tongue and pretend not to hear her. She does have her strong points. Skills that go unmatched by most Senate aides. Skills that include an unflinching support of her boss. God help anyone who gets in her way, or his. Or anyone looking to make trouble. Rumor has it that most of his colleagues in the Senate avoid Xenia at all costs, usually sending a junior staffer to deal with her hard-ass questions and unflattering pronouncements. There have been many who have had the experience of leaving her presence in tears.

Nothing could be more annoying to her then what has just happened. Several feet in front of her and the Senator, Larry Mitchener has slid into their path from behind a marble statue.

"Excuse me Senator."

Larry flashes his credentials. Xenia glares with disdain at the wallet, and thinks to herself, "what the fuck does this guy want?"

"Agent Lawrence Mitchener, sir. United States Secret Service."

This stops Sykes. Xenia continues for a few steps, then stops, as well.

A friendly Senator Sykes, having a great deal of respect for the Secret Service and all of law enforcement, for that matter, smiles and says, "good afternoon, Agent. How can I help you?"

Xenia looks pissed, not unnoticed by Larry.

Larry eyes Sykes carefully, "I wanna hear what happened this morning at Burning Tree. Your version, sir."

Sykes chuckles a bit. Then adds, "I played golf, Agent. Poorly, I might add." He chuckles again, glancing at Xenia. She smiles thinly, not knowing fully where this is going.

Larry takes a moment to scan the nearby area, several yards in all directions. Then, eye ball to eye ball with Sykes, "why did the DCI - Director Unger - call you at Burning Tree?"

Senator Sykes feels his heart skip a beat. He momentarily has lost the smile so familiar to everyone as he runs through a list of serious issues in his mind that could have resulted in the Secret Service knowing he and Unger spoke. This encounter with Agent Mitchener has suddenly taken a dangerous turn.

Larry doesn't wait for a response.

"That was followed by a call you made to Thomas Delgado, of the Washington Post. Then one more call from your cell phone."

Larry pauses giving Sykes a moment to take it all in.

"At approximately 0902 hour's local time. A little less than one hour after the Vice President vanished from the golf course."

A very pregnant pause.

"A three minute call made to the Vice President of the United States...sir."

Chapter 51

The OEOB
Office of the National Security Advisor
1942 Zulu,   1342 Hrs. Local

EIKO NARITA seems totally unaffected by the simple fact that I have once again barged into her office, unannounced. Despite the fact I've now missed lunch, and, as a result, feel weakened, my adrenalin is rushing at warp speed. I could pass out at any moment. But the latest information currently being processed in my little brain has me, shall we say, really pissed.

Without looking up from her computer, she seems to have some idea why I'm in here, steamed. Although I haven't said a word. Just a slow eye burn on her.

"It's the DCI's plan, Jack." She pauses. "That's why he came over this morning to see the President."

"Unger?" I begin to stutter. "Simon Unger? That DCI?"

"He sent the guy on a secret mission."

Okay. I need to pace. And count to ten before I respond. Actually, I need to compute this information together with everything else I've learned this morning before I make a brilliant assessment of this new piece if intelligence. Then again, maybe she's playing with me.

"What? You're not serious, Eiko."

"The DCI is serious. It's happened, Jack. The guy's on his way to the fuckin' Seychelles."

"Eiko, what the hell is going on around here? You think we're back in the Nixon administration?"

She gives me one of those looks as if I really knew what went on during the Nixon administration, when I was about three years old.

Actually, my Dad had a lot to say about that time. Especially the decision not to allow Navy aviators flying missions over North Vietnam and use the newest electronically equipped A6E's. The thinking back here in Washington was "why put our guys in the best aircraft while attacking the north. If they get shot down, the Russians will likely get a hold of our latest technology, compliments of the North Vietnamese."

So much for politicians running a war.

Eiko stands, shuffles some of the paperwork on her desk, then says, again without looking up, "he's negotiating a jump-off base. We put 3000 Marines in the place – intercept the terrorists cells – you know, the training camps, and such – places like those no-name shit holes in East Africa."

I get eye ball to eye ball with her, "then what, Eiko? Have the Veep jump out of a tree and say boo? This is nuts!"

Eiko appears to ignore me. She gathers some of those papers she'd been shuffling and jams them into her large leather carry-all bag. She moves around her desk, and heads for the door.

She stops.

Her head down, thinking for a moment as I decide for once to keep my mouth shut, waiting for some pointed direction from my boss.

She steps closer to me, saying, "Jack. You're not supposed to know. Stay out of it! It's a small team here."

I'm momentarily stunned. Speechless, for once. But then...

"And I'm not asking, Mister Connolly."

Chapter 52

Lafayette Square Park
Across from The White House
2109 Zulu, 1509 Hrs. Local

The best place to set up a secret meeting at the White House is outside the White House and off the grounds. I get the feeling that everything is recorded in that place. Which begs the question, *who really is big brother?* I don't think I want to know the answer to that question. Not until I at least get some solid answers to the current crisis at hand. Since I've ruled out the President and the top National Security Advisor, I'm left with only my two friends, who are also involved with this mess.

Larry Mitchener, and Lauren Miller are both waiting for me as I stroll towards them standing near the Jackson monument in the middle of the park. One of the more compelling reasons this is a safe place to meet and talk is the fact that Lafayette Park draws an assortment of excessively vocal groups who have a thing or two to say to the President who lives and works just across the street. Of course, the guy in the Oval Office can't hear them. Nor can he see them since the Oval Office is on the other side of the West Wing. The only White House personnel that can see and hear these wing nuts is the White House grounds crew. And if these groups speak anything but Spanish, they're out of luck. So the whole fiasco is a waste of time. But they keep showing up day after day anyway. It's good to be on unemployment.

As I approach them, I ask Larry, "how do you know about the calls, Larry?"

"You don't wanna know, Jack."

I look around at the various groups chanting in an assortment of languages, none of them Spanish, of course, and their leaders blaring statements through portable microphones making it hard to hear my pals. But I press forward.

"Right, Larry. I don't wanna know."

Larry steps closer to me. Looks in several directions. Then says…

"Echelon." He pauses. Then, "forget I said that."

This guy's making me nervous. I glance over at Lauren with a wink and a smile. My soul mate. I trust her judgment. And desire to get to the bottom of the issues at hand.

She steps to me, and says, "I'm looking at e-mails – White House personnel, others that could be of interest to us, Jack."

I'm beginning to feel a bit queasy.

"Okay. The less I know, the safer I feel. Let's keep it that way guys."

"The FBI calls it third level Echelon, Jack." Larry just has to add.

"I don't wanna know. Really, I don't"

I beginning to freak out. This kind of stuff makes me uneasy. It shouldn't. I mean I've had the responsibility for a nuclear sub with, given the go-ahead, could blow a country back to the stone age. But this spy verses spy stuff is a bit unnerving.

Larry continues while taking in the protesters that surround us out here, "shoot man, it's always pissed me off, you know? The big brother watching thing."

I'm with him. Maybe we ought to just drop this thing. Let bigger minds in bigger positions work out the issues. Maybe that's not going to work. Lauren has already hacked into the White House e-mail data base. And someone will ultimately find out, connecting me to that little miss-step.

"Lauren. Emails? What on earth are you doing?"

Larry jumps in. "Eiko Narita. She's a player, Jack. In this thing deep."

"She's got a string, Jack." That's Lauren. "Direct to the DCI. Unger."

Larry adds, "now here's the really bad news."

"Don't tell me, Larry."

Laruen takes a nano-second to check the area, then, "Vice President Seth Greene's secret mission is not an official secret mission, Jack. There really is a secret."

My mind races at warp speed. I think of all the bad things that can and probably will happen and come to a conclusion as to why prosecutors prosecute.

"You mean as in a conspiracy?" I didn't think I was that smart. But I continue anyway. "Which includes the Secret Service, the National Security Advisor to the President, a United States Senator, and the CIA?"

Larry looks me straight in the eye and says, "and three of the players don't know there's a fourth player."

I shift my gaze to the front portico of the White House and start to bring the puzzle pieces closer together. Pulling them out of thin air and re-arranging their place in this mess. I can only think to say after a moment of thought...

"I'm bettin' on a fifth player, guys."

As I continue to stare at 1600 Pennsylvania Avenue, my android phone beeps with a text message. I lift it from my pocket. Tap the screen twice. And view the instant message. Then a look at both Larry and Lauren.

"The President?"

Chapter 53

The West Wing
Enroute to the Oval Office
2152 Zulu, 1552 Hrs. Local

Being summoned to the Oval Office via a text message by the big guy himself is pretty much an anomaly. Look what the Secret Service had to do just to satisfy Obama who refused to give up his Blackberry. I heard an entire new server and encrypted network had to be in place prior to the inauguration back in January of 2009. And that was done to satisfy Obama's love of video hoop games. Rumor has it he didn't even let Michelle in on the network for fear of her finding out he spends a lot of time out in the Rose Garden with jumpin' Joe Biden drinking beer and dreaming up stories for Joe to tell the press corps. As Obama was over-heard saying to Joe, "...my woman would gimme one hellava shellackin', Joe..." Joe cleverly responded by saying "...yeah, I hear ya man; it's some fuckin' deal." Joe has a one track mind.

Anyway, the President has over-ruled the SS - not those guys, but the good ones – and insisted he needs to use text messaging when summoning his minions. As I approach the outer office where the three admins are strategically placed, I make eye contact with the wicked-witch of the west. I mentally confirm that she is definitely a hold-over from the Eisenhower administration. And I also mentally compliment Bill Clinton for supposedly rebuffing her advances. At least I'll give him the benefit of doubt.

One of the cute ones waves me into the Oval. I give her a wink and a smile, and say "...thanks, honey." The old witch sneezes. Or did she say "horseshit."

Chapter 54

The Oval Office
2154 Zulu, 1554 Hrs. Local

PRESIDENT GIORDAN looks, not surprisingly, pissed. He paces slowly behind his desk. I'm sure he knows I'm here, despite not having reacted to the door being closed behind me by that cute admin. So I break the ice, having thought of something entirely appropriate to say on the heels of our last conversation several hours ago where I think I may have quit. But I'm not all that sure.

"Good afternoon, Mister President. And might I add it's a pleasure to serve you, sir."

"Sit down, Jack."

I take a seat in a chair that faces the desk. Not one of the two that flank the desk on both sides. I've learned those chairs are for the power players around this place. Like my boss, Eiko Narita, who, by the way, is not here.

Interesting.

Without looking at me, nor stating the objective of this little impromptu pow-wow, which is usually the protocol in the Oval Office, he starts to unload on me while still pacing.

"The war on terror has to be prosecuted in secret, Jack. Bush 43 and Clinton couldn't make that call. And in the absence of leadership, Obama failed to even acknowledge there's a war on terror. It's gone from a few radical groups to – hell, I don't even know anymore."

He stops, and pivots right at me.

"What I do know is the Iraq and Afghan wars created more enemies than pockets of freedom in the middle east. And all of these threats are coming at us like pecking ducks."

Still a moving target, the President shakes his head in either disgust or just simply acknowledging his limited options.

As he once said to me not long ago, his first few weeks in office almost four years ago would turn out to be a window into the trying times of his Presidency. Having sat through a number of highly classified intelligence briefings, he came away with the feeling that all options in this job were "lose, lose." Therefore, what is the best option that will do the least amount of damage? Like I said not long ago, who would want this job?

Clearly, with limited options on his mind and only me to vent to, which is another mystery unto itself, he continues his rant.

"We can't rely on our allies over there. Even our own intelligence apparatus is lost. Congressional over-sight has created a culture of wimps."

Looking right at me, "I'm not boring you, am I Jack?"

"No, sir. This is all…just fascinating."

"I'm sure you think so."

I think he's being sarcastic. Hard to tell.

Taking a long look out over the south lawn, a view I find particularly soothing and refreshing, he has more to say.

"Despite their stupidity, the French, with the help of the British, came across an interesting development. Those arrogant frog bastards tripped over their own intelligence and dropped a ripe peach in my lap."

I love the way this guy thinks. He really does have it all together.

"We have located what could be the center of the universe for terrorists."

The President moves to an easel that holds a map of an area I think covers pretty much the Indian Ocean. Keep in mind, my journeys in this part of the world have been largely conducted underwater, using only underwater navigation charts. Surface maps pose a problem for me.

The Navy brass would never say to me, "now listen, Connolly, just don't hit Madagascar while your scooting around the Indian Ocean chasing Russian subs." They would say something like, "when cruising silently past Madagascar, which, by the way is an Island in the Indian Ocean populated with animated cartoon characters, try to stay alongside the Mascarene Plateau…quietly. And no farting!" I made up that last part.

The President points to an area just east of the African coast. And to an island just to the north of Madagascar.

"It's an island in the Seychelles, Jack. A place called Silhouette." The President studies the island intently for a long moment. Then, "I sent Seth Greene to buy it."

I'm momentarily struck by the possible horrific pieces that could fall into place with this revelation. I follow the President with my eyes as I'm basically very skeptical.

"So you see, Jack. I had no choice but to send the highest ranking U. S. official to the Seychelles."

He pauses for a heartbeat.

"And in absolute secrecy."

What comes to mind instantly is that not just two hours ago Eiko Narita told me that the DCI, Simon Unger, had sent the Veep to the Seychelles. Who's running this candy store? So, I conclude that this piece of info from the Boss is miss - information. I don't believe it. I'm still of the school that the Veep is still "officially" missing. And the President and others are covering up a megawatt problem.

So rather than engage my mouth with my brain and keep quiet, I have to say to the President, "so you sent the Veep because you had a prior commitment – like a re-election campaign."

The President snaps in my direction, hardens like steel, obviously accepting the reality of the situation when he says.

"Fuck the campaign. I'm talking about a training camp with suicidal maniacs making dirty bombs."

He takes a deep breath, "and maybe, just maybe that dead American prick Anwar-al-Awlaki, the terrorist from, of all places, New Mexico, the good old USA, has put someone in the front of the classroom instructing these thugs."

Steamed, he jabs a button on his telephone console, and waits.

I say, "this is not how a superpower should behave, sir."

I guess that sounded like I'm a wacky liberal, which gets his attention.

"I inherited the body count mentality when I moved into this office, Jack."

"So change it."

"And wait for another nine eleven to unfold? The next time could undo us altogether. Thank goodness for Bush 43 who held off anything serious for close to eight years, putting in place the pieces to stop another attack. But the next guy let it unravel. A guy who happened to get lucky with finding and killing UBL. Those in the know, people hiding in the unknown dark corners of the White House, tell me that guy called Bush 43, not only to inform him of the kill, but secretly thank him for setting it up.

But now I'm in the hot seat."

I hear the door open and close over my shoulder. The quiet footsteps raise my concern as it could only be my boss, Eiko Narita. She moves to a spot alongside the President's desk, and, looking quite annoyed, scowls in my direction.

Just my luck. What I don't need right now is for her to engage the President in a conversation about this mess, telling him I ought to leave and let them work out the issues. So I choose wisely, and ignore her.

"You're telling me, sir, that your actions are proportional?"

"Yes, Jack. That's what I'm saying."

"So, let me get this straight. Did Clinton act proportionally when bin Laden bombed our embassies in Africa?"

Eiko spins, pointing at me, looking meaner than a rattle snake, "he didn't ram a Russian submarine in the ass, Jack."

I shift uneasily in my chair, silently counting to ten, once again. I need to hold my cool. If I were alone with Eiko, I'd have a completely different reaction. One that might include poking her in the eye with a sharp pencil. I focus back on the President.

"Actually, sir. Now that I think about some of the notes I've read concerning that incident..." Notice how I've slipped in that catch all, "incident." "Clinton let someone else make that call...sir." I pause for effect, giving them a moment to go back in time and think about what happened, and the result of a chief executive making a call that was more political in scope, looking like a wimp, and avoiding an all-out vocal battle with the American Jewish congress who didn't want Clinton to upset the Arab world for fear of reprisals. While they're giving this some thought, I jump back in...

"And Usama bin Laden got away back then. And so will the next guy if we don't get tough. What I mean is, screw the left."

The President moves around the desk, actually in a direction away from Eiko, and sits on the corner, arms crossed, looking down at me.

"What do you mean, Jack?"

"Did you let Simon Unger manipulate this plan, sir?"

"You're wrong about that, Jack. He doesn't know. It's the Veep, Eiko, myself. That's it."

To my left is Eiko, knowing full well what she has told me. And to my right is the President, also knowing what he thinks I know, but not knowing what I think I know. Which is going to cause me to explode at any second. However, for everyone's sake, we're saved by the bell.

The President's telephone intercom console hums, followed by the soft voice of a woman...

"Mister President! The Senate majority leader and the House speaker are in the map room, sir."

She pauses for a moment thinking the President may respond. But he just glares at the console. She continues...

"Were you expecting them, sir?"

The President and Eiko stare at each other for a long moment.

The President directs his attention at the console, "thank you, Grace." And he walks off to a door on the far side of the office.

And I feel that the temperature in this office has dropped to the level of arctic ice. And I don't mean the beer.

Eiko just glares at me. Then, says...

"You finally crossed the line."

"Unger's plan. You said –"

"– miss-information. It was deliberate on my part. I had no choice."

I calmly ask, "is the Veep secure?"

"Yes. Absolutely. It's over."

"Right. But my gut tells me it's far from over, Eiko. And I'm at the point of calling it quits. Your bullshit has reached new heights. If you haven't noticed- "

"– and just maybe it's your career that's over, Connolly."

She takes a hard step towards the door to the Oval Office. Stops and turns at me with another aggressive step at me.

"And you know what I mean."

Now seething with hatred, she says...

"It's time you need to tell the President what really happened."

Through clenched teeth...

"Why that Russian submarine was rammed."

Chapter 55

On Board the Bear Oscar Kim Jong
To the East, Mecca, Saudi Arabia;
To the West, Port Sudan, the Sudan
Monday, 2323 Zulu;
Tuesday, 0223 Hrs. Local (Red Sea)
In Washington, DC, Monday, 1723 Hrs.

Seated in the communications room is Park Kim, known to his friends as Pa-Ki (*Packy*) a North Korean. A young fella, maybe 20 years of age. And, by the looks of his body language, is clueless when it comes to understanding the equipment before him. His eyes scan the array of switches and dials. Needles inside meters that ark left and right, sometimes bouncing into the red zone. A movement that startles the inexperienced sailor.

Coming from several speakers, voices in languages not at all familiar to Pa-Ki. On close examination of the various dials and switches, the sailor attempts, in vain, to determine their significance.

Unfortunately, his knowledge of the Russian language is nil.

Racing through his mind at the moment is what to do should some vital piece of information come screaming through the equipment. How would he know if it's important? Better yet, who would he tell?

The Russian guy that put him in here, Chekhov, is one scary thug. He is too afraid to go looking for that guy. When Chekhov placed him in here he had shouted orders at Pa-Ki while holding a knife point hard against the young sailors' balls. Worse yet, the North Korean has no idea what Chekhov told him.

As sweat develops on his forehead, he's thinking that maybe the best solution at the moment is to simply fall on his sword when, just like that, the door blows open.

The North Korean kid spins in his chair expecting the worst.

Looking down, Vasili stares hard at Pa-Ki while spinning a key chain on his forefinger.

A long moment passes.

Then the young sailor jumps to his feet, and holds a salute while mumbling something entirely incoherent.

Vasili puts his hand up, ordering the kid to stop whatever he is trying to say.

Then says to him, *"ouberiysyi von!"*

Once again, Pa-Ki's Russian is non-existent. He looks totally confused.

Vasili thinks for a moment. Then points to the door and says, "get out!"

The North Korean bolts faster than a Hispanic kid leaving a bodega in the south Bronx...while stuffing a pistol in his pocket.

Vasili locks the door, then turns to take in the communications equipment, equipment he knows to be capable of encrypting everything going out and coming in.

He sits, and having complete familiarity with the equipment, grips a large dial to the right side of the center console, and dials in a specific frequency, noting the digital read-out that appears on the small LED screen just above the dial. It's a frequency that he had committed to memory, given to him directly by Putin.

Vasili adjusts a headset over his ears, and takes a moment to listen, making sure the channel is open. And, by carefully noting the presence of specific tones that run through the channel, he can determine if the secure channel has been breached by ease-droppers.

He flips several switches on the central console that give him the ability to check any "traffic" that may be on and/or near the bandwidth, or nosey ears, software that scans communication lanes. Different tones and beeps moving in and out would be a red flag.

After several minutes, Vasili is confident that his channel is secure and is now ready to proceed with an update to the mission.

He slides the Morse code key closer. Takes a moment to think through the message he needs to send while checking his watch.

Another few seconds as he waits for the sweep hand to land on the twelve, indicating the time to be exactly 2330 Zulu.

It's there, and he begins to tap away.

Chapter 56

The OEOB
3rd Floor Hallway
National Security Council Offices
0013 Zulu, (Tuesday), 1813 Hrs. Local, (Monday)

EIKO NARITA enters the hallway from her office suite. Alongside, is a young male staffer. She stops and turns to face the young gentleman. Her composure, hand gestures, are harsh and aggressive. She's reprimanding the dude, or giving very deliberate instructions for which she may feel he is not up to the task.

He takes it like a man.

Larry Mitchener and I are down the hallway, and around a corner, sort of. We can see the entire scene from our vantage point. As this little bit unfolds we figure she's dressing this guy down for some reason. Although, Eiko once lit into to me one day for taking too long to pee. While I explained to her that my routine, unlike hers, is to not drop my draws, sit on the throne, pee, stand and pull up my draws, which clearly requires more time, but to simply unzip, pee, then zip up, she looked me up and down. Then said I need to work on my aim.

There's simply no way of escaping her wrath.

We hear her mumble something about the Oval Office. Then the poor guy, chagrined, meekly says, "yes, ma'am."

I need to have a talk with him.

Eiko charges off, and disappears around a corner.

When she's out of sight, the guy flips her the bird, then hustles off.

Okay. Cancel that talk. He's gonna be fine.

At this point I lean into Larry, and whisper to him, "bad idea, man."

Larry, still focused on the area outside Eikos office suite, says, "follow me!"

And as he starts for the door Eiko has emerged from just moments ago, I reluctantly follow, pretending that I'm not really following Larry, just casually walking behind him. Larry, on the other hand, looks like what he's trying to do. Which is to sneak into Eiko's office suite, unnoticed.

"Larry, is this legal?"

"No."

We're now inside the office suite, moving into her private office space, and I'm even more convinced that this is not a good idea. Larry is a Secret Service agent, and has a badge. I've got nothing. Except a Buzz Light-year ball point pen my nephew gave me last Christmas. And as I've mentioned earlier, my request for a badge, as a Deputy NSA, has not even been addressed.

Larry says, "find something she always carries with her."

"She's not here, Larry."

Larry points behind her desk and says, "check her purse."

I'm amazed that she has left her purse which tells me she's not gone very far, and will likely be back momentarily, catching us red-handed. For which I will be summarily fired, then fired upon by a firing squad. But I comply with Larry's order and grab the purse.

I find a day book, which is odd. Who still uses these things. Then car keys, a brush, make-up bag, then, her cell phone?

"Larry, she always carries this. Why not now?"

Larry glances over at the cell phone, and says, "okay – good."

Larry grabs it. Then says to me, "watch the door."

"What?"

I give him a strange look, then say "you've gotta be kidding."

In the Hallway

KRISTEN SANDERS, Jack's admin strains to listen at the door having followed both Jack and Larry from Jack's office, suspicious of their conversation earlier. She turns for the ladies room, yanking out her cell phone.

In Eikos Office

Larry has got Eikos cell phone in several pieces on her desk. He plants a small device into the battery compartment. I lean in for a closer look.

"I'll be able to hear her fart, Jack."

"Nice, man." I'm trying to be sarcastic here. But Larry doesn't get it. He's way too serious about this stuff.

Larry reassembles Eikos cell phone, and drops it back into her purse.

"I'm done. Let's go."

"Yeah. Good idea, Larry. I need a drink. Maybe three…no, make that seven…"

Chapter 57

It's dawn in this tropical paradise where the sun rises from the east very early, being on the eastern edge of the time zone. There's no breeze. Just the soft sounds of calm waves as they lap onto the sandy beach that stretches for several hundred yards, flanked by towering palms. A setting so serene it could be easily mistaken for heaven on earth.

Birds chirp in the distance calling out a musical variety of matting calls that wake the Island to yet another day of peace and tranquility on earth. A day fit for the beachcomber. Someone with not a worry in the world. In a place one would never leave if suddenly stranded. Cast away from civilization, there would never be the longing for discovery by a search party.

With each lap of the waves on shore, a zillion sandpipers race to avoid being swept into the sea. Then, like hardened dare-devils, they follow the water as it washes back into the Indian Ocean, and wait for that next wave to once again scurry away from the quickly moving water.

One could spend hours watching this monotonous exercise wondering what these little birds know that we don't.

Or one could simply assume these little creatures need some serious therapy.

As the sandpipers move about haphazardly, the sand suddenly splatters in all directions, causing the birds to scatter in a near panic.

From a spot several yards off Nick's bungalow, the Jackel lowers a high-tech, small shoulder weapon and holds a hard frown, looking towards the scattering sandpipers, and mumbles...

"*Sheet!*"

Nick drifts casually to the Jackel's side, starring down-range at a spot where the sophisticated hand-made ordinance has left a large crater in the sand. He's thinking exactly what the Jackel is thinking. With so many targets close together, how could he possibly miss?

Nick removes an after breakfast cigar from his mouth and casually says, without making eye contact, "just don't miss tonight...*Monsieur Jackel*."

Nick turns to face the Jackel, giving him a firm, hard, no nonsense look.

"I never miss."

Chapter 58

The hip crowd is noisy.

Mostly young, yuppie types on the prowl for new friends.

And some casual sex with whomever.

Capitol Hill staffers showing off their make-believe power as close confidents to the rich and really powerful. Young men and women who have bartered their way into the halls of power up on the Hill or into the White House.

Most with the help a family member who has made a substantial contribution to those in power. While it's still Labor Day, these young folks must work today, and normally 24/7.

I never thought Dad or even Grandpa could do the same for me despite the fact both are Admirals, albeit, retired. So much for service to your country. In this town it's all about the greenbacks.

Especially those with lots of zeros.

Although, I did land a rather cushy job at the White House. With access, sometimes, to the Oval Office.

Except in my case the Navy brass view it as corporal punishment.

What do they know that I don't?

Interesting.

Anyway, I love this place. I often come here to eat, grabbing my favorite table underneath a large photo of one the Navy's most famous warships, the USS Iowa. Grandpa commanded that ship at one time.

Growing up on an Iowa farm back in the dark ages, i.e. the 1920's, and prior, it was only fitting he'd end up on that ship. And what no one else knows, except me, of course, is that he carved his initials into the wooden ships wheel. When it was discovered by the commander of the Pacific fleet at the time, Admiral Nimitz, he immediately blamed his executive staff saying that they love him so much they just had to leave a permanent remembrance on board the Iowa.

Grandpa's quite the character.

Dad says I'm just like him.

You think?

My attention gets quickly directed at the front door, mainly because every other guy in this place has done the same thing. Googgily eyes, drooling from their mouths, hearts beating at warp speed.

Suck it up, fellas. She's mine.

Lauren knows how to make an entrance. Can't tell whether it's the blonde hair, blue eyes, pouty lips, knock-out figure or that Naval officers uniform that just happens to be expertly tailored, highlighting every single curve of her body. In any case, much to the disappointment of every other swinging erect gold member in this place, she makes a bee-line for that incredible good looking hunk standing at the bar.

Me.

"Lookin' for a date, sailor?"

Several heads turn not knowing that I know this broad. I thought the guy next me was going to move in on her after that comment. However, my quick, yet charming whit kept him in place.

"Been there, done that, Blondie."

She scans the bar and restaurant area. I'm not sure if she's checking out the other babes in this place, worried that I'd dump her for someone else, or just the meat.

Usually I'd be afraid to ask. But in this case I can assure you she's not at all worried. Which is why I'm always worried when we visit a place like this meat rack.

I don't even want to hit the head, for fear of some rich, good-looking guy, dripping with charm, will hit on her. It's happened. More than I like to remember.

"Something to drink? Sorry. I've already started. It's been one of those days."

"Sure. What time is it?"

I quickly cover her concern, despite being in uniform.

"You're off duty, Lieutenant. Go for it."

She smiles, and says, "then make it a Cosmo."

Those mid-western Ohio chicks are really classy. Even the ones from Dayton, like Lauren. Never a sign of entitlement, nor that phony "upper east side" persona you find in New York. Just plain, down to earth women. Smart, focused, on top of their environment and the people they choose to call friends. Which begs the question, why me?

"So, Jack. You given this mess any more of your sharp brain power?"

"Actually, I've been making up teams. Mentally, of course. You know, who's who? And stuff like that."

"And?"

I think for a moment, then say to her, "except I can't place the DCI, Unger. He's definitely the wild card in this situation. Calling you directly, asking for a report on that sub. Something's real fishy with him."

Lauren takes a moment to process something. Then ads, "I thought he *was* the bad guy."

"That's the problem. In this town, it's hard to tell. Everyone keeps changing sides."

Lauren's Cosmo arrives. She examines the pale red liquid as if it were the result of some chemistry experiment.

But it's a thoughtful examination.

I wonder what's she's looking for. Maybe she's wants a cherry in it. That's when she says something, almost to herself.

I ask, "say something?"

"I was just thinking of Unger. And what surfaced while I scanned his e-mails."

I wisely decide not to ask her about Unger's e-mails, and how she was able to scan his. I mean, he is the DCI. I turn and check out the lively, youthful crowd when she continues with her quiet thought.

"There's a string that mentions a team. Like you said. A team. He refers to it as Tombstone. And it links to the Veep."

She pauses a moment.

Then, "it's a dead end. There was nothing more."

Since my little brain works on a 7 second delay system when alcohol is coursing through my veins, it takes that much time for me to process her comments and make a connection that suddenly scares the hell out of me. I turn at warp speed, facing her, but softly, trying to control my building blood pressure, and say...

"Tombstone? Lauren, did you say Tombstone?"

Lauren appears a bit startled at my sudden change in demeanor. But recovers quickly to firmly say, "Tombstone...yeah, Tombstone. Why?"

My mind races. Should I spill my guts on this one. Not just the part about what Tombstone is all about. But how I know what I'm not supposed to know. At least, despite my bullet-proof security clearance, I think I'm not authorized at the level of the President nor the NSA, the charming Miss Narita, to have intimate knowledge of Tombstone. But I'm sure Lauren can keep a secret. I cozy up to her, whispering in her ear.

"Do you wanna know a secret?"

She gives me a quizzical look that I interpret as "yes." At least I hope it's "yes" because I have to tell her.

Just to hear what our next step should be regarding the missing Veep, whom I'm beginning to surmise is not just playing hooky. But is definitely missing despite what the President told me.

"It's a classified directive. Tombstone, I mean." I'm still whispering into that lovely ear, but being distracted by the fragrance of her hair. Get it together, Jack!

"It's only authorized for use against selected terrorists. I mean a very narrow authorization. President Bush signed off on its use, and the strategic plan his administration developed against Usama bin Laden. That set the mission in place to be run exclusively by the CIA. No over-sight, nor further authorization. Obama simply confirmed its activation at the pleading of DCI Panetta to green light Seal Team Six hours before they whacked bin Laden. And by the way, Mister Panetta then went straight to church, while the commander in chief hit the links for a quick eighteen. Go figure."

I pause to give this next piece of info its proper importance given the fact that most Americans have a different understanding about the war on terror.

"It's an assassination team..."

Lauren takes a moment to process this information. Then asks, "how do you know this, Jack?"

Now the hard part.

"Several months ago I was working on Eikos computer, in her office with her sitting at her desk. Research of sorts that she had asked me to find immediately rather than head back to my miniature office and locate. I guess she thought I'd be goofing-off if she couldn't keep an eye on my progress."

Lauren makes one of those soft, guttural sounds that more or less confirms Eikos suspicions about me. Like I said, I don't think Eiko likes me very much. Now I'm wondering about Lauren.

Women! You can't work with 'em. And you can't kill 'em.

I think.

Anyway, on with my confession.

"I stumbled onto this document that outlined, in explicit detail, the Tombstone directive. I didn't read the whole thing. But enough to peak my interest. And concern."

Lauren interrupts to ask.

"So, by gleaning this document, you have surmised there is an assassination team out there, under the exclusive authority of the DCI, roaming the world for suspected terrorists. Then, when they find one, he, or she, is summarily whacked, Gotti style. Then the process starts all over, right?"

I can only stare, deer in the head-lights stare, at this assessment by Lauren.

"Jack. You really needed to read to entire document to get the full, sensible gist of this program. What you described is a blatant violation of all kinds of both U.S. federal and international – Geneva convention style – laws."

Whispering very softly now, I confess, "I e-mailed the entire document to me. Then deleted the transaction on her computer."

Now I get the deer in the headlights stare from her. Then she says...

"You do know the transaction is still on the White House server, right?"

"Oh."

Lauren takes a deep breath, then, as if to herself, "maybe I can make it disappear."

"Okay. That would be good," I say suddenly feeling confident.

"Or maybe the FBI will come late one night and take you away."

I attempt to get serious with her, "I guess this is a problem. What do you suggest, besides me heading for a remote Island in the South Pacific?"

She ignores my levity saying, "I'll need to read that document. I may be able to tie the DCI, Mister Unger, to the missing Veep, and perhaps to that rouge submarine. My guess is there *is* a connection."

"You know, Lauren, if you read that document, you may end up in trouble for violating the Official Secrets Act. I won't let that happen."

As she wraps her hand around my waist, she whispers, "then we'll both head for that romantic, very erotic, Island in the South Pacific."

Well...okay, maybe I'll let her read it.

Chapter 59

Office of Senator Joe Sykes
Capitol Hill, Washington, DC
Tuesday, 0249 Zulu, Monday, 2049 Hrs. Local

Senator Sykes is relaxed at his impressive mahogany desk, a gift from one of the more notable labor unions, a gift channeled through his PAC. His office is equally impressive with photos covering the walls of every famous living and dead politician going back to the Eisenhower Administration. The more important ones, regardless of party affiliation, fixed on the wall...below eye level.

Although relaxed, he's focused on his speaker phone as he listens intently to the condescending voice that permeates the high tech device. Sykes adds a rather sly smirk to his features as he swivels slightly to his right, glancing momentarily to someone on the far side.

Then back to the speaker phone, "you're risking a lot, Simon. I mean personally. Wanting to expose Tombstone, the executive order you insisted was needed in order to further secretly prosecute the war on terror, will likely cost President Giordan the election."

A low volume grunt is heard from the other end of the conversation.

More like an "I don't give a shit" grunt.

A clearly "gotcha" look on his face, Sykes adds with confidence, "you'd be breaking the law. Federal law that I, incidentally, helped draft many years ago, Simon. If you don't recall some of the specifics, let me remind you that's twenty years in Federal prison for someone with your lofty position in government. It's all about what you know, and choose to use for your own personal benefit."

At the other end, Unger scowls at his speaker phone. Then draws deeply on a Monte Christo, exhaling through a cynical smile at the thought just expressed by his friend, Senator Sykes. Unger considers his position in this conversation and the events that are about to unfold. And his role in forcing those events to bring his self-serving career path closer to completion. He rocks gently in his chair, eyeing some imaginary picture on the ceiling of his office.

He then turns his attention back to the speaker phone, "for the time being, Senator, I'll do my part with the Veep and his little game of hide and seek. And you, of course, will do yours, as agreed. We are still in agreement, correct?"

Senator Joe Sykes has lost his smirk, and now frowns heavily at the speaker phone looking as if he wants to spit on it.

"Pay back is hell, Simon."

Unger leans into the device on his desk, saying in a casual, soft manner that belies his alter ego, "and don't take it personally, Senator."

Unger jabs a finger on the disconnect button. Leans back, satisfied that his control over some of the highest levels of government is still safely cemented under his thumb.

Senator Sykes can only just stare at the speaker phone. A thin sweat line forms at the receding hair line on his forehead.

He's speechless.

Perhaps a fit of temporary paralysis for the moment.

But carefully thinking about the mess he has been thrust into by aligning himself with the very secretive Director of Central Intelligence, Simon Unger.

All the while oblivious to his immediate surroundings as…

XENIA ZEITUNG slips in behind the Senator.

Hands now on his shoulders offering a soothing massage, she looks down at the quickly ageing Senator, taking a moment to think.

Her eyes grow devilish, full of hate and anger.

Then, eyeing the speaker phone with contempt, she says...

"Prick."

Chapter 60

Early morning in Red Square and the down-trodden, heads lowered so as not to make eye contact with anyone, scurry off to their respective work places at this early hour. Since it's only early September, the severe Russian winter has not yet reared its ugly head. But the chill in the morning air is a subtle reminder that the frigid cold is not that far off.

The well-lit exterior of the Kremlin is seen in the back ground as steam rises from vents in the familiar cobblestone square, a distraction from ones' route across the famed area in what was once the most feared country on earth. Party workers contemplate what todays lies will bring from their leadership.

Inside the ornate Kremlin all is quiet.

Except for hard footsteps that grow louder, coming from the far end of a long, dimly-lit corridor.

One would instantly think the person to be a large man with significant body weight judging from the authoritative sound of the footfalls on the tiled floor.

Coming into view, however, is a slight, severe looking, middle-aged woman with facial features permanently tuned to evil. Despite the abundance of attractive women in Russia, this woman clearly belongs to another gene pool. Think Specter Agent Number 2 in the James Bond flick, "From Russia with Love."

She stops in front of an over-sized door, and raps, with authority, hard, several times.

From inside, a man's voice says, *"da."*

She enters the large, old world office, closing the door with a hard thud that appears to momentarily startle the occupant of the office. She moves swiftly to the desk, glaring with respect, but not that much, at Mister Putin.

"Excuse me, Mister President. We have just received this communique from the Chechnyan. Comrade Commander Vasili Bakura."

She hands Putin the document.

After a moment, she asks, "will there be an answer to his very interesting report?"

Putin glances up sharply, giving her one of his well-known blank, stone faced looks that speaks volumes.

She flinches.

Turns and leaves, mentally contemplating a craving to live a long life.

And one not necessarily in Siberia.

Chapter 61

If it were not for the screaming crowds at Nationals Park, home to the Washington Nationals, or the gazillion watt stadium lights that illuminate the entire neighborhood during night games, or the horrific traffic before and after baseball games, or the pervasive crime, this would be an absolutely wonderful place to live.

But for Kristen Sanders, none of that matters. It's a place to live in and crash in for the opportunity to call Washington, DC home, the center of power on the planet. And to meet the rich, famous and truly powerful men and women whose decisions shape our lives. But, for Kristen, it's about meeting the right lover, preferably a guy with all those qualities. And preferably one who's not married. Although exceptions have been made in many more cases than known by the rest of us. And to utilize the opportunities afforded a young, pretty girl no matter what it takes.

Including, perhaps crossing the line of good moral behavior...in every respect.

Kristen's apartment is small, but neat. One bedroom, tiny bathroom, a galley kitchen and an adequate living room.

It's a two story walk-up. With a lovely view of the Nationals Park parking lot.

In the darkened living room a shapely, young blonde girl holds her cell phone to an ear.

She's naked.

A soft, faint whisper, as her eyes dart towards the open door to the bedroom "oaky...I understand...no problem...see you in a minute." She disconnects the cell. Takes a thoughtful moment as she gazes off towards the bedroom area.

She stands and heads for the bedroom, stopping to switch on a lamp placed on an end table. The glow highlights the sexy features Kristen has worked hard to maintain despite the numerous invitations to some of the best restaurants in the District by the power brokers in this town whose key mission is to get in her panties. Certainly the mission not being unknown to her, she picks and chooses with deliberate care.

Kristen tip-toes into the bedroom and carefully slips into bed, between the fresh, linen scented sheets. She shifts closer, up against the body of another in the bed. And swings her arm over the other person, drawing closer to her bunk bunny as if a security blanket.

She whispers, "he's on his way up...sorry...he's down on the street...needs his car keys...sorry."

There's a rustling beneath the sheets. Then a larger person slips from the bed and disappears into the bathroom.

Kristen holds a stare on the bathroom door wondering if she needs to poke her head in and check on her friend. She gives this idea some more thought. Then decides to let the chips fall where they may, as they say. There are simply no secrets in this town.

In the living room, Jack Connolly has let himself in.

I'm here, and now I do a 360 in the small, dimly lit room, listening for any sounds. I see my car keys on the coffee table. And grab them. My superior intuition, and thorough knowledge of Kristen's life-style, I figure she's got company and I had better hit the road. Chances are it's someone who would not want me to know he's poking Kristen.

I turn for the door, but not before I catch a glimpse of the shade-less window, thinking maybe I need to buy her a set of drapes. I walk over to see what her view from this spot looks like. Taking in the empty parking lot at the Nat's stadium I remember that the Nat's just finished a three game sweep of the Mets up at Citi Field in Flushing Meadow today.

Freakin' Mets! What's happened to my team?

Then, from behind me, a soft, sexy voice that I know, "hi, sailor."

I quickly spin around and find myself now about 10 feet from her.

HEDDY DOWNS, I mean.

Despite being in her late thirties, Heddy looks incredibly gorgeous...and remarkably sexy. But showing some signs of heading over the hill. She stares at me with a Marilyn Monroe come hither look, and wrapped in an expensive fur coat.

"Heddy. Nice fur. Still kissin' ass, I take it."

"Beaver, Jack. It's a beaver coat."

She now moves in a very seductive way towards me. I can't back-up otherwise I'd fall right out the window. So I stand pat and hope for the best.

"Wanna wrap yourself in my beaver, Jack?"

I go flush. Things like this always happen at the wrong time. And place. I fight hard to come up with something to say when from the bedroom door...

"Hey."

It's Kristen, and she's wearing a flimsy short robe.

Hum...what's she been up to?

I know what you're thinking. But leave it to Kristen to save my butt right now.

"Hey, Kristen. Well, got the keys, okay?"

I give Heddy a friendly look, "so...Heddy. It's been..."

"Climatic, Jack?"

Heddy turns and saunters off towards the bedroom. And closes the door.

I let out a sigh, and say to Kristen, "how did you ever meet that woman?"

"She met me...I mean she, like, bought me a tall latte at Starbucks one day. It's been cool ever since."

Sometimes I think Kristen needs a smack.

"She's doing some married politician, you know. It's like a secret or something. But I don't get it. So…it's cool."

You see what I mean?

But I need to ask, "Democrat or Republican?"

I see she's thinking real hard about this. I hope it's not someone up on the Hill, which, in all likelihood it is. And if it's someone connected to the Intelligence community then we all need to move to a remote Island in the Pacific. Heddy is big time trouble. Like I once said, I'm good at reading people. The fact that she wanted me to jump her beaver is evidence enough. Although, in this town, that kind of behavior is common protocol.

"Jack! I hear something."

It's the text notification on my iPhone. Could be Lauren with an update. Or maybe she's naked and stuck on what to do next. Actually, she's back at my office working at some more hacking into an assortment of top secret data bases.

What a trooper.

I use the sound to bolt from Kristen's apartment with nothing more than a "I'll see ya in the morning."

In the bedroom, HEDDY has popped open her laptop and now pounds away at the e-mail screen. The message is brief and to the point…

"Dick. Our friend has been compromised. Lick."

She grabs a look over her shoulder, towards the closed door. Then back to the laptop. A heartbeat. Then…

She clicks, "send."

Chapter 62

Office of the Director of Central Intelligence
Tuesday, 0359 Zulu, Monday, 2159 Hrs. Local

SIMON UNGER, facing his computer screen, snaps
back in his chair, alarmed by the message that has just come
across and into his secure e-mail application. He glances
through the windows behind his screen to the darkened
grounds that surround the CIA campus in Mclean, Virginia
just several miles from the District.

His quick mind races through the various contingency
plans he had developed in anticipation of the events of the
past twelve hours, or so. The issue now before him involving
the compromise of someone that is part of his team has come
as somewhat of a surprise given the superior level of
intelligence and the important position this individual holds.

Whatever the mistake, this person must be held
accountable. There are no excuses in Simon Unger's world of
intelligence, spies, espionage, and secrets.

From his suit jacket pocket, he pulls out a Blackberry.

Not your typical Blackberry. But one that is unique.
Very high tech. Similar, but more highly sophisticated than
the one the Secret Service gave to Obama in 2009, discarding
the one he used in happier times to talk to his pals, Reverend
Jeremiah Wright and Bill Ayres. Unger takes a moment. Then
punches several soft key pads. Whatever the message, it's
brief and to the point.

He takes a moment to wipe the Blackberry screen
carefully of dust, lint, and smudge prints, examining the
device with affection before returning it to his suit jacket
pocket.

Chapter 63

**George Washington University Hospital
Washington, DC
Tuesday, 0404 Zulu, Monday, 2204 Hrs. Local**

All is quiet at the nurses' station on the fifth floor of this highly regarded hospital just several blocks from the White House.

It's where the Secret Service had taken President Ronald Reagan the day he was shot outside the Hilton Hotel in Northwest Washington. The early evening rush of visitors, dinner and meds for the patients has finally calmed down.

Except for the woman in room 508 who continues to moan. The only nurse on duty at the nurses' station, a post-middle age woman with a permanent scowl, hears the moans, but chooses to ignore the patient as she knows nothing further can be done.

Another nurse, younger and with a jaunt to her step and holding a clip board, steps out of room 502 and heads for the counter side of the nurses' station.

"Jane. 502 would like a large cranberry juice. He's such a sweet man."

Jane, the older nurse, doesn't bother to look up when she says, "he needs to sleep, not piss all night from too much juice."

The young nurse sighs, then frowns, "what's that beeping noise?"

This time Jane looks up. Then side to side.

Then, "you're hearin' things, honey. Go check that black guy in 536. He's been buzzin' for ten minutes."

The young nurse moves away quickly down the hall and around a corner.

A moment passes before Jane pops her head up, now looking up down the hallway, left to right. She hears the beeping sound, but can't place it. After a moment her glare settles on a door just several yards away marked "staff."

She shakes her head, mumbling, "answer your phone, jackass."

In the Staff Room

The soft beeping sound is surrounded by complete darkness making it impossible to know precisely where the beeping is coming from. Then, just like that, a man suddenly bolts up from a deep sleep, clicking on a fluorescent light that stuns his eyes. A moment passes before he gets his bearings and is able to focus his eyes in the light. He shakes off the mental cob webs as he takes still another moment to figure out where he is. It quickly comes to him as he rolls his feet onto the floor. The thin layer of his socks does not hide the chill of the tile floor. He mumbles, "freakin' hospital."

He stands, wearing blue scrubs that reveal a deceptively fit man of about thirty something, maybe pushing forty. He grabs the beeping device from a bench that is placed in front of a row of lockers that are surrounded by shelves of medicines, first aid crap, and other typical hospital junk.

We'll ID this dude as THE DOCTOR.

He focuses on the text message. Frowns. Then reads it again just to be sure. Now he stares off into nowhere for an extended heartbeat.

Now he's up, goes for the door, bolting it quietly. He moves to a locker, and works the combination. It's opened, and he pulls out a simple gray metal box. He lays it on the bench. Then from around his neck and tucked in his scrubs, he yanks out a key on a chain. The key is used to unlock and open the metal box. He looks inside for a second.

Then pulls out a SIG Sauer 357 magnum.

Its glinty black faux steel glistens.

He grabs a high tech suppressor from inside the box and fixes it to the barrel of the SIG.

He gives the lethal weapon a steady and careful examination.

Then, disengaging the 17 space magazine, takes a box of ordinance from the metal box and fills the magazine to its max with hollow-tipped rounds.

Cocking the weapon, smiling at the glorious sound, he stuffs the SIG into his waist band and hits the door with a plan in mind.

A problem to be dealt with somewhere in town.

Chapter 64

The White House
Rear Colonnade Breezeway, Outside the Oval Office
Tuesday, 0427 Zulu, Monday, 2227 Hrs. Local

I walk alongside the President. The conversation is tense, and one of us may come unhinged at any moment. Most likely me if I don't at least get some value from our little private talk. There's no one around except one of those elusive Secret Service dudes who pretend to only protect the big guy, but, in reality, digest every spoken syllable. When these guys retire, some write books. But, under pseudo names. Otherwise, rumor has it, they disappear. I think the White House staff is told that piece of information so we wouldn't have casual conversations with them when they're on duty.

Maybe one of them really knows the whereabouts of the not so elusive Veep. Surely, the Secret Service must know more than they're even telling Larry Mitchener.

The President says, as if an after- thought, "I don't want to lose you, Jack."

I'm hoping he's forgotten that I quit a little after noon time today.

"The voters may take care of that, sir."

"Jack, if I've made that mistake, then I'll live with it. We've talked about mistakes before. About redemption."

"Is that based on the current course of stupidity, sir?"

He turns sharply at me, "it's based on my trust in you, Jack."

He could've called me a smartass, as many have in the past, oh, say thirty years or so. But I sense more integrity here than anything else. Sometimes I think he tries to fill in for my Dad when Dad is not around. Like now. Somehow they both know I need to be re-directed in the right direction, despite being a grown-up.

"Should I feel that you're still trying to earn me my redemption, sir?"

"No. You're doing that all on your own,"

We walk a little bit more. Although the gap between us and the Secret Service guy hasn't changed. He's good.

The President holds a stare out onto the South lawn looking, perhaps, for that same inspiration I sometimes look for. He appears deep in thought so I hold off bringing up the subject of "me" until he says something. Hopefully, he's not on a new line of thought.

"After the election, Drew Cardinelli, the White House Chief of Staff, will step down. It's not going to be easy for me, Jack. He's truly a superman in that job."

Knowing the bullets Drew has taken, figuratively, for the Boss these past three years, he really is superman. However, I sense a play here.

"On his own. Or am I still missing it?"

"Cancer. It's terminal, Jack."

He stops and gets eyeball to eyeball with me. And softly says...

"At that time, I will announce that you're taking over as White House Chief of Staff."

He looks over my shoulder at the Agent, then back to me...

"It's just between us...for now, Jack."

He scoots past me to a door to the Oval Office now held open by the Secret Service Agent, who seemed to know when to open it.

Chapter 65

The White House
2nd Floor Private Residence
Tuesday, 0542 Zulu, Monday, 2342 Hrs. Local

A depressed President Giordan fingers a Frederick Remington sculpture – a warrior on horseback, an arrow in his chest. He bought the sculpture when he and his wife moved into the White House almost four years ago. It was to honor his friend and hero, in addition to FDR, the greatest President in the past 100 years, Ronald Reagan. It is meant to shore-up his mind, reminding him of the battles that need to be fought on a daily basis. And that some may not turn out so well. Battles, the ones both foreign and domestic - i.e. Congress - that define the office and its leader. And to demonstrate solid moral behavior, a quality cast away during the Clinton administration, and decisive leadership, absent during the entire Obama administration, to the 310 million Americans who yearn for both.

The living room in this part of the private residence is altogether quite fancy. Expensive trappings like antique furniture, and china and silver knick-knacks. The sofas and over-stuffed chairs are upholstered in expensive Asian silks. Paintings on the wall could cause one to mistake the residence for a high quality museum.

At the moment, none of this matters to the President. His demeanor illustrates a need for a stiff drink, or perhaps some Prozac.

Still focused on the Remington, he says, "my expectations by this point were somewhat higher."

His national security advisor, Miss Eiko Narita, sits back on the very comfy sofa, saying in her usual tone of "I'm smarter than you" confidence, "if we can locate the submarine, we take it out. The world will never know it was even an issue."

The President turns quickly towards Eiko, drilling her with a rhetorical question, "then what the hell has the Vice President accomplished?" He slams his fist into the wall behind the Remington, "I blame this whole mess on Unger. He's out to fuck me."

The silence in the room is deafening. Yet heavy breathing can be heard as there is someone else present for this impromptu, late night chat. Unseen, from the far side...

"Then fuck *him*, Mister President!" Approaching the steamed President from across the room, Senator Joe Sykes, scotch on the rocks in hand, gives the leader of the free world a slight grin...

"We'll pin this mess on his ass."

Eiko leans in, "oh, come on Joe. Unger is one cleaver son of a bitch. How do we get the better of him?"

Senator Sykes is still grinning. He downs the remainder of his drink. Sets the glass down on a coffee table in front of Eiko. Now, standing ram-rod straight, faces the President. "Mister President. You remember executive order 1871, sir?"

The President takes a brief moment to think about that. Then nods at Sykes, but holds a look on Eiko, as Sykes continues...

"The Tombstone directive?"

Chapter 66

The OEOB
Jack Connolly's Office
Tuesday, 0607 Zulu, Tuesday, 0007 Hrs. Local

Despite the late night hour, all is quiet as I wander down the hall here in the OEOB towards my luxurious suite of offices frustrated at not being able to form an intelligent, coherent thought. As a matter of fact, I'm not so sure I can form any thoughts at all. The likely cause is due to the fact that my brain cells are bouncing around the inside of my head like Mexican jumping beans on Quaaludes. And here I thought I'd be able to learn the ins and outs of working in the White House maybe after two, three weeks, tops, on the job. It's been over a year, and I think I've evolved into a complete moron.

But maybe I'm not an idiot as my boss, Eiko Narita, once told Kristen. I just can't seem figure this whole process out. I need to call my Dad. He'll have a point of view that should help iron out the sticky quirks in dealing with the President.

I hope.

I mean, he does know the Boss. They're still pals.

I hope.

I slip into my office, and behind Lauren, who's at my computer likely violating another batch of obscure Federal laws known only by the nerds over at the DOJ. Emphasis here, *my* computer. Which reminds me. I need to report my computer missing...I'll tell 'em it disappeared from my office, let's say...four months ago? That ought to drive the nerds bat shit.

The big question is, did the President of the United States just bribe me?

Lauren peeks up at me, "hey, sweetie. How was your little chat with the Commander in Chief?"

I'm still not totally here, my mind being in some other universe. But I manage to respond, "I guess it's a learning curve thing for me..."

She hammers away at the keyboard.

"What've you learned, honey?"

I start to wander around my office seeing everything but noticing nothing.

"Of course, on the other hand, White House staff work does involve dealing with people who are not very bright. You know. Political patronage?"

"Jack. I hope you're not talking about me."

"Uh? Oh...right, okay. It's the Obama doctrine that still runs amuck around this place. You know, run it like partisan politicians, and not like leaders."

She spins around and faces me, "you know, Jack, hearing others requires listening."

She always has some intellectual spin on everything. Smart women do that to us guys.

"What you don't hear, Lauren, is this whole mess crumbling around me. I may be the only one in the White House that's interested in the truth. The people deserve that."

"And the press will not report it the way they should, Jack. Maybe that's your deep, hurting feeling right now."

I don't know what I'm feeling other than perhaps going for that one way ticket to a remote Island in the South Pacific.

"I'm sure of one thing. People around here don't wanna know my opinion."

"Jack. Some people do think you're damaged goods. That you should've retired after that incident with the Russian submarine."

"I can't help that."

"No...but it bugs you. Look, Jack. Everyone makes mistakes. It's how people deal with those mistakes that sets them apart. Some just go to pieces and never recover. Others move on and come back twice as strong."

She eyes him with a little bit of caution. Then...

"It took me - and the Israeli's, for that matter – two weeks to unravel the mystery about that submarine after it left the Sea of Japan." She grips his hand. "You studied the data, the photos, the communication information, and figured out the whole Russian scenario in less than fifteen minutes, Jack."

My only thought right now is I hope the President didn't hear me quitting. Maybe there is more to this mess. And I'll find it. I wish I could be more like my Dad. He always says the reward is in the fight.

Lauren moves back to the keyboard, hammering away.

"I'm in, Commander. Where to?"

I move for a look over her shoulder...

"Start with the Veep's Blackberry. Download everything. Let's see what this hot shit ex-Marine is up to."

Chapter 67

Republic of Seychelles, the Western Indian Ocean
Office of the President in Victoria on Mahe Island
Tuesday, 0635 Zulu, Tuesday, 1035 Hrs. Local
In Washington, DC, 0035 Hrs.

JACQUES AMIEL, at sixty two years of age, relishes the twilight of his long career in public service now as President of the Seychelles, an Island country that secured its independence from Great Britain in 1976. Although the first inhabitants from overseas were the French, they subsequently lost control when Napoleon was defeated at Waterloo.

Jacques Amiel stands at a window that overlooks the vast, aqua marine Indian Ocean that surrounds all of the country's 115 granite and coral islands just south of the equator, and east of the African Coast. The view is magnificent, even to Jacques who has viewed the lush environment every day for all of his sixty two years. And it's why he gets at least one round of golf in every day. A passion that everyone knows takes absolute precedence when scheduling a meeting with the legislative branch, or tea with a high level foreign dignitary.

However, his mild demeanor and gentle, calm voice masks an inbred craving that can be best described as greed.

"Yemen pays us handsomely, sir. Thanks, of course, to our most trusted benefactors, the French, who brokered the arrangement."

A slight snicker is heard from another part of the President's massive office. It does not go unnoticed by Jacques. But, then again, he's a crafty negotiator, quite capable and willing to sell his mother for a better financial deal. Known to look the other way when questionable people, those with unsavory ties to God knows who, enter his country for perhaps some planned mischief.

A deposit made in a numbered account in the Seychelles National Bank buys the depositor an automatic "get out of jail" card.

He turns and moves to the over-sized executive chair at his desk and plops his six foot four figure down with a thud. Smiling, he holds a stare at the far side of the office, making a definitive statement that is more than just words...

"Money is everything for our small, impoverished country, sir."

Then, suddenly, his reflexes kick-in. He sits up, ram-rod straight, his right arm shooting up above his head, and then...

Smack!

He's caught a golf ball.

A golf ball?

Jacques studies the ball with some intensity, then says, "Titleist four..."

A nearby voice says...

"I found it yesterday, Mister President...in the woods."

And U.S. Vice President Seth Greene slides into a leather arm chair that faces Jacques Amiel. He crosses his legs, staring at the Seychelles President with delight, and a firm sense of confidence.

"How 'bout we double the ten million a month for six months."

Jacques Amiel leans back, listening intently.

"And I'll build you a Jack Nicholas golf course. Just for you."

The Veep pauses, then says...

"I know Nicholas, personally."

Jacques Amiel feels as if he just died and gone to heaven. The good Lord has finally answered his prayers. In his mind, it opens other doors for his poor country. For instance, if they build him a golf course maybe they'll build a huge military base for the Air Force or Army on land that Jacques may just happen to have available for sale to these rich Americans who will certainly pay his *fair* price.

Veep Greene takes a cigar from his jacket pocket, "may I, sir?"

Jacques approves, still smiling at just winning the lottery as Greene lights up.

"That money from Yemen? It came from banks in Iran. Not Yemen. Those are the bastards behind this whole mess. And those towel head pot heads running around the beach up on your Island, Silhouette? They're being paid by Iran. You gotta know they're up to their nipples in shit, Mister President. And the French? They screwed you. More likely they didn't know what they were dealing with when they came to you with that bogus lease arrangement."

Jacques shrugs.

"Well, anyway. We'll clean up that shit. Just give us to go signal."

Jacques Amiel tosses the golf ball from hand to hand, giving the Veep's information some thought. Not happy with the circumstances, he may seek revenge, using his mercenary contacts from Somalia. But on the other hand, the Americans are offering a great deal more money. And a new golf course. It's not a tough decision.

"You may have the Island, Silhouette, Mister Vice President. It's all yours."

Chapter 68

On Board the Bear Oscar Kim Jong
Tuesday, 0659 Zulu,
Tuesday, 0959 Hrs. Local (Red Sea)

In the communications shack, VASILI has shut down the transmitter and receiving devices. He removes the headset he was wearing while communicating with Moscow. He takes a few moments to transcribe notes into a journal. When finished, he leans back, studying the notes to be sure he got the instructions the way Putin had intended. Often, there are times when Putin has been less than clear in his instructions to Vasili during highly sensitive missions. It takes Vasili more time to sift through the political hazards that Putin generally throws in front of different phases of a mission.

Putin of late has become more aware of the world view of him as a leader. And now fears certain other leaders around the world who may view him as an irrational leader.

He is not unaware of the consequences of performing in such a way as to piss-off respected leaders around the world. He has only to look at the likes of Saddam and Gadhafi, both of whom acted irrationally, and are now dead. And not the result of old age. Then there's Mubarak and Assad, whose future wish is to be able to fog a mirror. Both leaders remain in limbo, with the possibility that their lives will be cut short any day now.

From behind Vasili, "so, what's up, Comrade?"

LUBIN drifts over to Vasili. He smokes like a bloody chimney, the stench alone irritating Vasili's stomach and eyes.

Vasili eyes Lubin with concern. He knows Lubin to be an ally, but is unsure about his relationship with the two Chechnyans on board. If they talk behind Vasili's back, then that could mean trouble.

On the other hand he looks to Lubin to help keep Chekhov and Zoyan in check. Relying on his street smarts, Vasili concludes Lubin to be his right hand man for the task ahead.

"Putin has verified our orders. We are to take out the target as planned at the prescribed time."

Vasili checks his Rolex.

"Approximately fourteen hours from now." His glance shifts up to Lubin who draws on his smoke, saying...

"Da. We're ready." Lubin holds a stare on Vasili. Then...

"Then what, Vasili?"

"We surface. But not before we eliminate our two friends."

Lubin likes that idea.

"Then we sink this piece of shit boat. Putin is sending the Barracuda for us."

Lubin reacts with a sense of revenge in his tone.

"That bastard, Marat? He owes me."

Vasili, very much aware of the bad blood that exists between those submariners who got high profile commands, and those, like Lubin, who got discharge papers.

"Let's hope Marat Ivanov thinks so, my friend. And the American CIA has transferred our money."

Chapter 69

Alexandria, Virginia
Home of Simon Unger
Tuesday, 0710 Zulu, 0110 Hrs. Local

SIMON UNGER'S face is concealed by a shadow cast from the drapes that hang from the double hung window of his sparsely decorated bedroom despite the bright moon light that casts a brighter than normal twilight over old town Alexandria. The soft, classical number that plays from his cd player on the dresser calms his rough edges. The music fills the room, the only noise at the moment. It's this quiet solitude that Unger relishes. A time for reflection on the day to come, and his plans for the agenda set in motion.

While he still has a loose end or two that will be dealt with shortly, his level of satisfaction is only compromised by the possibility that something can still go wrong. He stands, now with his eyes closed, in a short silk robe, mulling over another devious thought that involves the lovely Miss Eiko Narita. He's never been all that fond of her. And, frankly, thought her political aspirations were a bit far-fetched. He's concluded that she cannot, nor should be, part of his team going forward.

A woman adds too many emotional issues to any plan. They're just not mentally fit for high stakes politics. Their views are generally irrational, and usually affected by "menstrual" timing issues.

Which probably explains Unger's commitment to the single life.

His thoughts now wonder to President Giordan's administration. A smirk develops as he takes in the outside. Then, as if carrying on a conversation...

"Idiots! My little ruse has worked. Those fools are focused on that Island, Silhouette." Thinking some more, he says, "Greene would have made his deal by now."

Unger stifles a soft chuckle.

"And that submarine, with our two shills, those dreadful Chechnyans? Long gone, my friend. Not far from the target."

Now he chuckles even louder.

"And no one knows a thing."

Unger leaves the window area and paces his darkened room, while lighting up a Monte Christo. He takes several satisfying puffs before saying...

"President Giordan will suffer a significant set-back. And it'll cost him the election once word gets out."

Now turning and facing the bed, ram-rod straight...

"And I'll be the next Director of Intelligence. A perfect stepping stone to the next election in four years."

A broad smile crosses his vile features.

But only for a moment.

Another puff as he contemplates another not so pleasant thought.

"Still, I'm worried about Senator Sykes. Something's wrong there. Something our lust-filled angel will learn very soon."

A telling pause.

"She's quite good, you know."

He stares hard at the bed for an eternity. Then...

"Why so quiet, my special munchkin?"

From under the bed linens in the darkened room, the naked body of a fit, young man swings out, stands for a brief moment.

Then heads in the direction of the bathroom.

On the way, TODD GITELSON, his voice raised, and unpleasant, says...

"You promised me an evening with Heddy."

Now, really pissed...

"I'm taking a shower...alone!"

The bathroom door gets slammed shut.

And a cell phone buzzes from the dresser.

Chapter 70

HEDDY DOWNS stands at a window in a darkened bedroom. She gazes absently, almost paralyzed, at the outside. Her body, with well-defined curves in all the right places, is wrapped tightly in a plush towel. The moon light accentuates her mature, yet sensual features. Her mind computes the latest information and how best to use it. Although, she mustn't get too excited. She needs to remain "clueless," for lack of a better strategy, at the moment. Act as if it's a dream come true. As if life is just too wonderful to believe.

As she morphs into her alter ego state of mind, a naked, yet taller body cuddles up to her from behind and slips long arms around Heddy, gently cupping her breasts. Thin fingers loosen the towel that drops to the floor, the sound barely noticeable.

Heddy develops a "happy to see you" smile as she turns to face the erotic and sweaty features that cover Xenia Zeitung's face.

Xenia's hands work Heddy from her breasts down to her genitals, carefully massaging every inch of territory along the way.

Their tongues now meet, and Xenia groans, grabbing Heddys butt cheeks and pulling both their steamy bodies together.

Breathless, Heddy manages to say, "it's all true?"

Xenia's lips find Heddys' neck, planting soft, wet kisses in several different places before answering.

"Hum...the President told Senator Sykes..." more kisses..."he's gonna be the new Director..."

Heddy moves her hand between Xenia's legs. And slowly massages with her middle finger. "Director?"

Xenia presses her lips to Heddys' lips. Then pulls away, but only an inch, or less, "National Intelligence…" a long wet kiss. "right after the election. Sykes can't stop spraying his shorts."

They both chuckle at that thought.

Heddy whispers, "wow!"

Xenia takes Heddy by the shoulders. Pulls back to arm's length and just stares lovingly at Heddys voluptuous body for an extra-long heartbeat. Then, softly saying…

"Heddy, I just *know* Senator Sykes will adore every luscious inch of you."

Chapter 71

The OEOB
Jack Connolly's Office
Tuesday, 0805 Zulu, 0205 Hrs. Local

I think I'm stretched out on a sofa that barely fits inside my office. I can't say for sure, but I think I'm sleeping. You may recall I've had very little sleep these past twenty four hours. Largely the fault of one hot Navy chick, as well as complications surrounding a pesky little incident, namely the bizarre disappearance of the Vice President of the United States. The latter having several people here in Washington, DC a bit skeptical. Mostly yours truly. As they say, there's something fishy in Denmark. Which is where I don't think the Veep is currently hiding out.

Eikos comment to me yesterday morning when I arrived at Camp David, as well as Gideon Margolies' comments later that morning, has me thinking that the Seychelles are somehow involved.

Then there's that Russian submarine.

I know the dots are connected. But right now, it's a blur.

I really need some deep, brain-cleansing sleep to get this whole mess sorted out. I sense that light, cushy aura of a deep sleep starting to come over me.

Now there's a hand. Soft and aromatic. A woman's hand. Gentle. I love these dreams. She works her gentle fingers slowly up my right arm, then over my shoulder. Then fingers now caress my cheeks, then work their way up and into my hair. I have good hair. One of my more seductive qualities.

I feel her breath on my face. Minty. Then a soft kiss on my cheek, which, instinctively, mind you, causes me to flip my left eye lid into the open position.

In my one eye open, one eye closed dream, I see her. Clearly. As if it were not a dream. And she sees me. She smiles, then plants her lips on mine. And slides on top of me. And starts to grind.

Which causes me to open eye lid number two.

And I'm now wide awake with this gorgeous blonde on top of me. Despite it being dark in my office, I, of course, know this hot skirt.

So I say, "that was fast."

"I'm not finished, sweetie."

"Right. Hold that thought." I push her back a little, taking a moment to readjust my vision, just in case it's not Lauren, but one of those sex-starved interns who work in the White House. They all want a piece of me. Yeah, I know. It's tough.

"What'd you find out?"

She lets out a sigh followed by, "it's in the Red Sea."

"Where?"

"Heading for Duba. That's on the Saudi Arabian coast."

I take a long moment, looking past her and running through several targets in my mind. Anyone of which would be a serious national security issue for us, not to mention potential devastation to some part of the Middle East.

"Oil fields, you think?"

She swings her legs to the floor, now sitting on my legs. She tries to unfasten my belt buckle with one hand while moving a finger around my lips.

In a sly attempt to distract me, she says, "no, don't think so. At least there's no confirmation. Unger, however, has been sending encrypted e-mails to someone in the Seychelles. Perhaps an operative, or one of his spies keeping an eye on that Island the Israeli ambassador talked about."

So Unger is deeply involved in this. And President Giordan knows this because why would he say that he's worried about Unger?

You see how clever I am. Whatever is going down, the President fears Unger could be that proverbial fly in the ointment.

"And something else, Jack. Unger refers to a "target.""

With that, play time with Jack and the family jewels is put on hold as Lauren jumps off me and grabs some papers from my desk. She scans through several pages before silently reading one for a moment.

Then, "here's a piece of news I find particularly troubling, Jack. Interpol, in France, reported a known brutal assassin simply walked away from a prison in Algeria three days ago." She pauses for effect, while looking right at me, "he was serving four life sentences."

"I don't suppose he was released on good behavior."

She gives me that look, then adds, "no, more like payments to high government officials in Algeria according to Interpol. Funds channeled through banks in the Cayman Islands."

The Caymans'. A favorite of crooks, spies, the very wealthy, and high government officials, some of whom reside right here in DC. All of whom share the same goal. Screw us poor folks.

Interesting.

Lauren adds, "Interpol thinks they know where he is."

"How many guesses do I get?"

She tactfully ignores my insightful question, saying, "not only does Unger know this, he's got a partner…besides his operative, or whatever, in the Seychelles."

Folding her arms, she holds a long stare at me, then says, "wanna venture a guess, Mister smart ass?"

I think for a moment.

Deceitful.

Deceptive.

Manipulative.

Someone just like Simon Unger.

But, hopefully better looking.

Who could it be?

And then it hits me. I bolt straight up from the sofa, swinging my legs onto the floor.

"Holy shit!"

Chapter 72

The Underground Garage
The Watergate Apartment Complex
Tuesday, 0856 Zulu, 0256 Hrs. Local

A black Lincoln Town car pulls into the half empty quiet garage. It moves around the aisles, perhaps looking for a place to park. In the process it passes several empty spaces, at least a dozen, before it settles on a spot amongst some shiny new high-end rides like Beamers and Mercedes.

Its lights and engine die. And it's an eternity before a rear door opens, and a man slides out. Although the area is dimly lit, and the man makes an effort to conceal himself in the shadows created by three foot square concrete posts, it's obvious he's in a black trench coat, the collar pulled up, and wearing an out of character sporty looking fedora. On his mind at the moment are the not so cleverly hidden security cameras, the location of each known to him. Which goes to explain why the Lincoln Town car, while gleaming from a recent detail job, carries dirt smudged tags, both front and rear making it difficult to tell not only the letters and numbers, but from what jurisdiction amongst all the states and territories.

The man walks slowly towards a dark corner of the garage, the sound of his shoes clicking on the concrete floor accentuating his confident, yet casual stroll. He stops, and turns for a look back at the Town car. A moment passes before the Town car moves slowly from its spot to the opposite side of the garage and out of sight.

The man continues several more steps towards the darkened corner. He stops. A lighter flicks, a flame dances as it finds the end of a Monte Christo cigar.

Its glow highlights the rough features of Simon Unger.

He draws slowly on the Monte Christo, its end an easily seen bright orange glow. Taking the smoke from his mouth, he says...

"This had better be worth my time."

There's an odd moment of silence, followed by footsteps on the concrete floor. These are softer, yet quicker steps as they approach Unger's concealed place in the garage. From the shadows, a slight, female shape appears, her silhouetted figure blending with Unger's.

"You're fucked, Simon."

Unger draws once again on his Monte Christo, taking time to respond as the woman drifts closer to him, stopping just short of several yards away as a plume of smoke swirls up from Unger's distasteful scowl.

Drilling a hard look at her...

"Then we both are, Miss Narita."

Now unsteady, Eiko Narita lets the inference sink in, her composure changing perceptibly.

Chapter 73

The OEOB
Jack Connolly's Office
Tuesday, 0920 Zulu, 0320 Hrs. Local

Even though it's dark in here, the moans coming from Lauren are a little much considering the possibility that someone could be at the door listening. Around this place, ease-dropping is commonplace. Unless, of course, you're outside the Oval Office. In the event you're caught the Secret Service punishment involves strapping you to a chair in front of a television set. Your eyes lids are surgically fastened to the open position, i.e. like in the Clockwork Orange flick. And you are forced to watch one hundred hours of Rosanne reruns starring the delightful, Rosanne Barr.

Next stop, the funny farm.

Just as I'm wondering if someone is really out there, the door flies open. My eyes dart to the door jamb where a large man is silhouetted, standing motionless. I hope it's someone I know. My wish is confirmed when he says...

"Shoot, man. Get a freakin' room!"

Larry Mitchener fumbles for a light switch on the wall. As the lights click on overhead, Lauren and I are already up, standing. Lauren unevenly buttoning her once sharply pressed Navy blouse.

Me, zipping up.

I take several steps towards Larry. Mostly to cover his view of Lauren. But, Larry being Larry only gives this incident a brief musing. Then heads for my desk.

"I got something."

"Good news, I hope, Larry."

"There is no good news, so why don't we start with the bad news."

This is why I like Larry. He always gets right to the point. No B.S. Larry pulls out a device from a soft-sided bag that looks like a small tape recorder and places it on my desk.

"Nothing adds up. Starting with my boss, Director Mcguigan. Listen carefully."

Larry hits the play button and a mechanical voice announces, "new message at 7:08 AM." Then the voice of Mcguigan comes through...

MCGUIGAN
"Agent Mitchener?
This is director Mcguigan.
I need you at Homeland Security. My office. ASAP."

I got nothing. But I know Larry is a professional and has an explanation to this rather bland message. I give him a shrug. He gives me a sigh.

"Think about the time line, Jack."

And boom. I grab some papers off my desk, scanning them two at a time. It's a heartbeat before I make the connection.

"Right. Here it is. Secret Service Agent Phil Witte reported Veep Greene missing at 8:10 AM."

"You got it, man. One hour and two minutes *after* Mcguigan left me that message."

I'm beginning to see the handwriting on the wall, literally. It reads *conspiracy*. Inside the *hallowed halls of government* kind.

"There's more."

As Larry sets up another tape, and Lauren now fully dressed, my mind is racing, once again trying to set up teams. If Unger and Eiko are one team, who's part of the other team? My guess is the Veep, of course, and the President, which would have to include the Secret Service. Now the big kahuna question. How does that Russian Oscar class sub fit in?

I know it's part of this mess mainly because I think the Israelis, who brought another piece of the puzzle to us yesterday, are on top of their game and know more than their letting on. So, what else is new?

The Veep's disappearance is clearly a secret mission of sorts perhaps designed to boost the President's poll numbers during the re-election campaign. That is, if he succeeds at whatever it is he's supposed to be doing. Talk about a bold, audacious strategy. I guess it gives new meaning to the phrase, *the audacity of hope, change, and,* of course, that all-time favorite, *transparency.*

"Okay. Here we go. Listen up. What we got is Simon Unger and Eiko Narita about ten, fifteen minutes ago." Larry hits the play button...

EIKO
"The team – covers the target when?"

UNGER
"A little anxious, my dear?"

EIKO
"This shit's by the clock,
Simon – so we'd have time
to re-think."

UNGER
"Fourteen hundred Zulu –
under six hours."

Larry hits the stop button. Then moves his look from me to Lauren. And then back to me. I see Lauren going through a bunch of mental hoops. So, I give her one of those looks, like, "so?" I'd say something a little more provocative in order to get her to spill her thoughts. But Larry is here and I think the guy writes down everything everybody says. Lauren finally jumps in...

"Six hours doesn't work."

Larry and I give her a "huh?" look.

"The Russian sub…six hours leaves it too far away – seven hundred fifty kilometers," she adds.

"Right. Range to Israel has to be less than six hundred kilometers."

Although I impress Larry with my knowledge of firing ranges, which, by the way, is top secret, he gestures to us, "wait."

Lauren finishes her thought, "maybe some other target."

"There's more." He punches play…

EIKO
"I don't know – I just don't know…"

UNGER
"Too late, Miss Narita, you're already in.
And it's a good plan…hell, it's a great
plan…for both of us."

EIKO
"I hope you're right, Simon…

UNGER
Hard ball politics…with a
special twist…"

EIKO
"Yeah, right, Simon…it's known
as murder…that's twenty five to
life. Has that for a twist?"

UNGER
"Except you're the one who needs
to be Vice President…Miss Narita."

Larry hits the stop button.

It's an unreal moment as we all just stare at the recording device that sits now quietly on my desk.

After a long heartbeat, I look at both with some trepidation, and say…

"Tombstone's been activated."

Chapter 74

The Watergate Apartments
Home of Eiko Narita, NSA to the President
Tuesday, 0937 Zulu, 0337 Hrs. Local

EIKO NARITA removes the key from her apartment door. Closing the door, she latches the double action security lock, and moves slowly through the dark interior of her apartment living room. The only light a soft glow from the outside that gets filtered through shear drapes that hang from a large picture window at the far end. Without turning on any lights she moves to the picture window for a view down onto the Potomac River that moves slowly, typical for this body of water in the late summer.

To her left she watches a jet aircraft depart from Ronald Reagan National Airport as it tracks over the river, heading in a north westerly direction. Most likely a Fed EX aircraft on its way to the Memphis distribution center. Operations by commercial passenger aircraft are severely restricted at this hour of the night, or rather the very early morning.

Eiko is struck with a decision of severe magnitude. A decision that takes her to that line between patriotism and personal career. Her few years here in Washington, DC have changed her. Once a thoughtful, intelligent thinker who was capable of making clear choices, she has now been re-shaped into a political animal, often times taking positions that align herself with the politicians on Capitol Hill rather than the other 300 million Americans not living and working in the District.

Then as if suddenly getting religion, yanks out her iPhone, punches in a key code followed by a classified number. She has the phone to her ear, listening for a moment.

Then, "connect me with the President."

The order given with authority to some minion on the other end judging by the tone of her voice.

Then a sense of frustration as the other side of this call is delivering a brief message.

An obvious sigh, then, calmly, she says, "then wake him...please...it's critical."

She turns and drifts away from the picture window, moving slowly, but with signs of tension in her body language, towards the middle of the darkened living room.

From the galley kitchen, the simultaneous sound of a SPIT and a FLASH.

The hollow tipped round has found the center of Eikos forehead.

As she stumbles backward, dropping the iPhone, another spit and flash, and the second round has found her center chest.

This round pushes her into the picture window with a thud. She slides down the drapes to the floor, landing in a sitting position, blood gushing from both wounds.

The bleeding suddenly slows.

Her heart has stopped.

From the shadows of the galley kitchen, the DOCTOR emerges.

While he removes the suppressor from the weapon, he casually walks over to Eikos body, placing two fingers on the carotid artery at her neck.

Satisfied, he moves to the door, and is gone.

Chapter 75

The White House
The President's Private Residence
Tuesday, 0946 Zulu, 0346 Hrs. Local

I stand about ten feet from the President as I watch him work the keys of his special, highly secure Blackberry. Lauren stands next to me. And we're both anxious. Now that we've identified the threat to the Vice President, and finally, the President providing full disclosure on what the hell has been going on, we're hoping that the Commander in Chief can make contact with Greene and get his sorry ass back to Washington, ASAP.

He turns towards us having finished his message.

"I copied Secret Service Agent Wierda...just in case."

"One agent may not be enough, Mister President. Considering Simon Unger's contacts, assuming his plan is to assassinate the Veep, there may be a team of operatives out there."

"Jack, I can tell you for certain that Seth Greene is quiet capable of protecting himself."

It's not like me to put the President on the spot. But, in this case he needs every point of view. Then some.

"Against a Tombstone assassin, sir?"

A uniformed Secret Service Agent has knocked, opening the door. He gets the President's attention instantly.

"Special Agent Michener, sir?"

The President nods, but Larry was not waiting for the high sign. He barges past the uniform, and into the room. Just several steps from President Giordan, he says,

"I've sent a team of agents to Miss Narita's apartment in the Watergate, sir. I presume you want to see her. She's not answering her cell phone."

A dispirited President thinks for a moment, his eyes drifting towards the floor. Then he says, "she was on the line just a few minutes ago. Wanted to speak with me…urgently. When I picked up, the line had gone dead."

The President moves over to the window for a look outside at the South Lawn, and perhaps to escape the reality of the moment. For a man always in charge and usually barking orders, points of view, or just talking about anything as politicians do, he's uncharacteristically quiet.

Once again I feel the need to bring all elements of the situation into view. And my role as a deputy NSA to him for Naval matters, he needs to know everything we know at the moment. And what we think.

"My bet, sir, is the sub has a firm target."

President Giordan gives this some thought. Then without turning, he says,

"Lieutenant Miller, what else do you think?"

Lauren grabs a look at me, looking like she's landed on the hot seat. I give her a wink, which I know she'll understand that he wants her unvarnished opinion.

She says, "she'll sit in the Red Sea…near Duba…she'll run silent, and deep. And almost impossible to find."

The President turns and takes a steps towards Lauren, "and the target?"

A moment while a cautious glance moves between her and me. I step up to the plate, "Tel Aviv, sir."

And Giordan just simply freezes. Facial grammar paralyzed. Maybe his breathing has stopped. Had to tell.

Then, at the top of his lungs, he comes back to life…

"Shit! Everyone to the situation room…now!"

He grabs a handset, punches a key. Waits a moment. Then…

"Is Admiral Hasslinger, and his team still in the situation room?" He pauses and I note a determined expression. Then, "make sure he doesn't leave."

He slams down the handset, and bolts from the room.

Larry follows the President out, and as Lauren and I watch, she says...

"You going to tell him the bad news?"

Chapter 76

The Situation Room
Underground in the West Wing
Two levels below the Oval Office
Tuesday, 1012 Zulu, 0412 Hrs. Local

It's not every day that a mid-level White House staffer gets to parade into the Situation Room. And I'm not talking about that phony hype of a news program on one of those cable channels that have not so cleverly lifted the name. I'm referring to the real deal. The place buzzes with activity that comes mostly from the half dozen or so giant LED screens that surround the remarkably small space. And not activity coming from the military and civilian personnel that have been here all day, all night, and into the wee hours of this morning. At least, from what I can tell, they're focused on the missing Veep.

This should vindicate Larry Mitchener's fear that he was the only guy looking for the Veep. Who, by the way, is really not missing but on a secret mission for his boss, the Prez. Which I still hope is not a re-election stunt.

I don't know all the players here, but do recognize some of the military brass that advises the President on a variety of National Security issues as they relate to the military.

Who I don't see is Eiko Narita. Where the hell is she?

Anyway, the President is conversing with several civilian and military big shots when I notice Admiral Hasslinger step up to me.

"The boss has filled me in, Commander. So why are you here?"

With that, he turns to the President who has walked to us.

Admiral Hasslinger redirects his attention to the Commander in Chief.

"Mister President. Thirty minutes, by our mission clock, sir. We're ready to activate at ten forty five Zulu as called for in the mission. But, on your order, of course, sir."

"What's the latest, Admiral?"

Hasslinger points to one of the larger LED screens while he nods to one of his minions.

"Our best Intel puts at least two Russians on board the North Korean submarine."

I focus on the LED screen. It shows, what appears to be, mug shots. Two hard, meaner than rattle snake faces look back at us.

The Admiral adds. "Likely Chechnyan dissidents. We've sent the photos to the FSB in Moscow. General Kaspersky. Waiting for a reply."

Interesting.

There was a time when we would not even officially acknowledge the existence of the FSB, the Russian successor to the famed KGB. Now, we're like bridge partners. Hopefully one of us is not trying to out trump the other.

The war on terror really has become a front where we can be on the same side as the Russians. But, hopefully we're smarter.

I guess we're not the only ones that know these jihadists Muslims are bastards.

And by the way, Thomas Jefferson, third President of the United States, but not on Obama's list of the top four all-time best Presidents, which, by the way, includes Obama himself, thought so back in 1803 when he declared war on those guys by issuing an executive order, accusing them of raiding our merchant vessels along the Barbary Coast of North Africa. Unlike Washington and Adams before him, Jefferson refused to pay the ransom those towel-head terrorists demanded.

Instead he chose to simply kill them off.

With a brand new military force.

Events that resulted in the creation of the Marine Corps.

That has given us mission crazy, Veep Seth Greene.

Who happens to be knee deep in this shit.

Interesting.

And, oh by the way, I don't think Jefferson's executive order has ever been rescinded.

The current President, Donald Giordan, takes a pensive moment to quietly analyze the latest facts.

Then, "Admiral, I authorize you to activate the USS Ronald W. Reagan's battle orders. And by the mission clock."

Hasslinger doesn't even bother to acknowledge the President's instructions. He goes right for the nearest secure handset.

I, on the other hand, take a long look at the two mug shots up on the screen. I simply cannot believe they're submariners. There's more to this equation than meets the eye right now. As I'm studying the photos, Hasslinger has finished his call and slips in next to me.

"Whatdaya think Commander? I'll put my money on those two running that sub a ground."

I'm only half listening. I decide the President needs my valuable input here.

"Mister President. Israel will retaliate. They'll pick someone at random. Like Iran."

Admiral Hasslinger can't let my view go untouched. "It's a sophisticated boat. A few Chechnyans...poorly trained North Koreans, if trained at all...fire a missile and hit a target?" Hasslinger gives me a scowl. One that signals that I may never see the inside of a submarine again.

"Let's hear Commander Connolly out, Admiral."

Maybe he does like me. And didn't hear me quit earlier. So I give it my best shot.

"Your assumptions are too logical, Admiral."

The Admiral quickly takes a call on his secure Blackberry before I get to have him reconsider my highly regarded level of Naval intelligence and perhaps suggest I be given a new submarine command.

But the boss is still tuned in. So, I focus on him.

"It's what's not logical that makes no sense, sir." I pause and take a look at Lauren. She can read my mind most of the time. And this time she gets it right. She jumps in, "a brief communication intercept several hours ago, sir, puts a new spin on it."

Hasslinger is back in saying, "Centcom will activate Operation Silhouette at ten forty five Zulu, sir." He turns at me, "forget the Bear Oscar sub, Commander. We've got an Island nuke factory to put on the bottom of the Indian Ocean."

Lauren bravely gets between the President and Admiral Hasslinger. But I quickly give her the look that says let me.

"Sir, that intercept? It was a coded message for the crew of the Bear Oscar sub." Another pause for a deep breath. "In Persian...and it originated in Tehran."

Chapter 77

VASILI observes the other three - Chekhov, Zoyan and Lubin – with a taste of contempt. On his mind at the moment is a wish that this mission be over and done with as quickly as possible. He's had about enough of the others, especially Chekhov. As he watches the others mock the clueless North Korean crew, he spins that special key even faster. First in one direction around his index finger. Then unwinding it in the opposite direction. A constant reminder of his duty. Wind it up, tight as a drum. Then unwind it.

The North Korean first officer barks a command at the dumb-founded crew. This cracks up Chekhov who pulls a small caliber weapon from his cargo pocket, placing the barrel at the temple of the first officer.

"I don't think they understood you." Chekhov cocks the weapon. "Try again."

The first officer stands frozen. A steady stream of sweat rolls off his forehead, down his cheeks. Staining his stiff, white roman collar.

"That's enough, Chekhov." Vasili jerks his head at Chekhov, indicating for him to move away.

Chekhov holds a threatening look on Vasili. He lowers the weapon, stowing it in his cargo pocket. Turning, and pissed, he grabs a smoke from Lubin's mouth and jams it between his lips.

A moment of silence before a short, weak looking man in a military uniform appears in the control as if out of nowhere.

The Russians, except Vasili, are surprised. They look to Vasili - who secretly brought the visitor on board during their stop in the Seychelles - for an explanation as to who this sudden interloper is. Their looks are accompanied by expressions of astonishment as the visitor could easily pass as the twin brother of the Iranian President, Mahmoud Ahmadinejad. Perhaps not a twin brother but one of the many known doubles Ahmadinejad employs when traveling away from the Presidential palace in Tehran, around Iran, and around the world.

His uniform displays the rank of General, including a chest full of medals. But more importantly, a gun belt that holds two Russian made Markov pistols. His facial countenance is not friendly. It's simply down right evil looking.

He scans the room, holding looks on Chekhov, Zoyan and Lubin. Then, a look at Vasili, "approximate time to launch, Commander?"

Vasili gives him a hard look, confident that the Iranian General, sent personally by Ahmadinejad, knows that this is Vasili's mission and to ask the mission leader a question with such a tone is out of line. Vasili's look sends that message to the General.

But first, the formalities.

"Gentlemen, our *guest* is General Najaf Tariq. Formerly part of the Shiite high command in Baghdad who worked on behalf of Iranian President Ahmadinejad. I should add, worked in a covert manner, correct General?"

The General's look is not pleasant. And Vasili chooses not to push the envelope any further than he has. He checks his Rolex.

"Thirteen hours, twenty two minutes, General."

Tariq takes several steps around the control room observing the North Koreans in the process. He stops at the weapons control panel and gives it a very long stare. Without taking his eyes off the now extinguished red and green lights at the weapons control panel, he asks, "we have no problems I trust, Commander?"

Vasili, arms folded across his chest, and hiding the special key, takes a long heartbeat to answer Tariq's question.

As Tariq turns at Vasili, looking for his answer, Vasili says, adding a stab of sarcasm, "with this crew, or the mission, General?"

General Tariq takes a few hard steps towards Vasili, getting in his face with vengeance in his eyes, "the Supreme Ayatollah, a great and religious leader of men, and our President, have agreed to pay you for your…services, as they may be, once completed. Then you may return to your beloved homeland."

Tariq turns to leave the control room, taking only two or three steps away from Vasili. He turns with a slim smirk on his evil features.

And says, "but first you must depart this boat…alive."

He moves quickly out of the control room.

Once out of sight, Lubin flips him the bird.

Chapter 78

Somewhere on the Indian Ocean
East Southeast of Kenya
Off the Eastern Coast of Africa
Tuesday, 1041 Zulu, 1441 Hrs. Local

A sight to be seen at this hour of the day on the calm Indian Ocean. Mid-day calm in all its splendor on this aquamarine colored water. No oil tankers in sight at the moment, nor the occasional luxury sailing yachts that once dotted the shipping channels not long ago. But now a scarce sight.

The problem, Somalia. And its unfriendly capital, Mogadishu just 700 miles to the North Northwest from this quiet spot. A haven for pirates and their well-financed efforts at raiding vessels of all stripes and sizes.

The serene calm of the ocean surface is suddenly broken by the hum of engines that grow steadily, squeezing in on this stunning view. The hum of engines is now replaced by an almost deafening whine that quickly approaches the ear-splitting level.

Then the appearance of an enormous V-shaped bow of a Naval vessel pushes all the quiet serenity aside as it cuts through the Indian Ocean, throwing sea water left and right at least forty feet away from the huge ship.

And if this were a Steven Spielberg flick we'd be watching perhaps the greatest Naval shot in the history of cinema as a gigantic aircraft carrier steams past.

The USS Ronald W. Reagan, CVN 76, is surrounded by various other, albeit smaller, Naval vessels that make up its battle group. The Reagan's position is more or less in the middle of the fleet. The Reagan is one of the newer Nimitz class nuclear powered aircraft carriers, and a viable threat to any and all rouge nations that dare intimidate the U.S.

From the flight deck, sailors move in and out of the super structure through one of several hatchways that lead to the interior corridors. A quick climb up the staircase where sailors make way for the human traffic finds the way through two more hatchways that end up in a large, open space walled in glass on three sides with all sorts of high tech equipment up the ying yang.

The Bridge is staffed with a Helmsman stationed at the huge brass ships wheel. Sailors and Officers cover the Ocean in all directions with sophisticated binoculars. Radio communication is heard coming through several speakers highlighting preparations on the flight deck.

Fleet Commander, Admiral Keyes, the USS Reagan his cushy flag ship, sits comfortably in the leather captains' chair near the port side of the Bridge. He sips his third cup of joe, a mocha decaf, since lunch, expecting further instructions from either the Commander in Chief or his designee at the Pentagon regarding Operation Silhouette.

Only Keyes and his XO, Captain Sablan, are aware of the special mission. And why the Reagan battle group is positioned in its current location. Admiral Keyes mulls over the various scenarios in his head. The one open issue that is somewhat perplexing is why the Vice President was sent on this mission in the absence of adequate protection. The Admiral concludes it was Greene who would have insisted upon the "covert" nature of the mission, although knowing that Admiral Keyes' fleet was relatively close-by in the event of a problem. On board one of the escort destroyers is a unit of Seal Team Six that could be deployed at a moments' notice should the Veep's mission spin out of control. Although Keyes had recommended a team of sharp shooters and back-up assault Marines be placed covertly in the Seychelles.

The President, and Greene, fearing notice by the press, nixed the plan. So this whole thing may come down to a rescue mission to be carried out by Naval personnel standing by, waiting for the order from Admiral Keyes.

Keyes concludes, as if to himself but in a barely audible voice, "politicians...stupid bastards."

"Sir?" That was Captain Sablan.

Keyes, realizing he was heard, waves Sablan off, "nothing, Captain."

As the Admiral recovers from his brief mind journey, a Communications Officer arrives on the Bridge, walking briskly to Admiral Keyes and handing him a folded note.

"Admiral – sir, - urgent message from Centcom."

Unfolding the note, he gives it a look. Then, from a breast pocket, removes a small laminated card. He reviews the note, making reference several times to the small card. Then, on his feet, his attention is directed at the XO...

"Captain, my quarters, please."

They both leave the Bridge, quickly as the other officers and seamen frown with concern.

Moments Later - The Admirals Quarters

Admiral Keyes works the combination of a safe that was hidden behind a simple looking cabinet door beneath his wet bar. From the safe, Keyes pulls a legal size white envelope, its border bright red. Across the front and back, the words "Top Secret."

On one side, a date in large type that Captain Sablan just happens to notice.

"Dated ten days ago. Hope we're not too late, sir."

Admiral Keyes gives him a harsh look as he uses a sterling silver letter opener to slice the Tyvek edge of the envelop. He removes a single page document.

After a moment reading the directive twice, he slaps the document onto his desk, and like a machine, gives the order to his XO...

"Turn the fleet, heading to coordinates fifty four degrees east, four degrees south, Captain." He takes a beat. "A place called Silhouette Island. In the Seychelles. Looks like that's our hot spot. Let Colonel Harris know his Marine platoon will go in with the beach head landing strategy, not by chopper."

He pauses for a heartbeat. And a deep breath. Then...

"It's what the Veep ordered."

Admiral Keyes takes a long look to the outside through one of his two windows seriously wondering if this mission will fulfill Veep Greene's expectations in every respect. Right now, he's a bit skeptical knowing what he knows.

Then sharply back to Captain Sablan...

"Let's make Vice President Greene proud."

Chapter 79

In the Situation Room
Tuesday, 1129 Zulu, 0529 Hrs. Local

A quick look around this tight space and one would conclude that everyone in this high tech room presents caffeine over-load symptoms. The long night, and prior day coupled with the early morning hour makes for a dicey situation when high level intelligence data needs some careful thought.

For me, I've simply given up trying to figure out when it was I last slept. Not including those one or two cat naps along the way. Especially the one which ended with Lauren on top.

Okay, Jack...focus, focus, focus.

My eyes are glued to several monitors giving us real time video and communications with the Seychelles, and Admiral Keyes' battle group, presently steaming at flank speed towards the Seychelles. What's missing is a feed from the Vice President who is supposedly packing in some z's at one of the more fancy resort hotels in Victoria, the Seychelles capital. My guess is, since his meeting with President Jacques Amiel went well according to Giordan's last briefing with me and Hasslinger, he's got a round of golf planned for the day. Forget the fact that a big chunk of the 5th Fleet is heading his way in the event a rescue mission is required.

Greene being the object of a possible rescue mission.

For Veep Greene, it's just another walk in the park. Except today it's more likely to be a golf course. Although the Secret Service report outlining the events of yesterday at Burning Tree Country Club indicated that the Veep left his sticks behind when, somehow deciding that finishing the round with a Democrat who was beating him after only three holes would be political stupidity, he bolted.

Somehow I don't think Greene would have gone halfway around the planet to a lush Island resort kept secret by the British for a zillion years without a spare set of clubs. I bet he made Agent Don Wierda carry them.

While I'm still studying the monitors, the President saddles up next to me and softly says, "you know the risks, Jack."

Lauren Miller, on her new secure iPhone, is not that far away, so my take is he didn't want her to hear that last comment. Which, by the way, was not a question.

But Admiral Hasslinger fixes that by calling over to the President, "Admiral Keyes will have to okay putting Commander Connolly on board the Reagan, sir."

Whether Lauren heard that or not is apparently not relevant as she hands the President a note. He takes a moment to read it carefully.

Then, he says to Hasslinger, "I have another idea, Admiral." He waves Lauren's note at Hasslinger. "This one is better…and it's my decision."

He glances back at Lauren's note and mumbles to himself while checking his Luminox Swiss Army watch, a gift from the Swiss Prime Minister after spending a long weekend at the President's Park City, Utah condo at Deer Valley. In case you didn't know, it's where the rich folks ski. You know that one percent Obama wanted to stick up.

He says, "twelve hours from now."

He signals for me to follow him over to a more private corner of the room, obviously for a little face time. I hope he doesn't wanna know why I quit. Because I was only kidding. I need the job.

He checks over my shoulder to the group in the room, then says, still holding Lauren's note, "you'll have my full authority to act as you see fit, Jack."

Since I guess this has something to do with putting me on the USS Reagan, which might not be a good idea, I try to deflect the conversation to what's been bugging me for, oh, about a year now.

"There's something you need to know, sir."

"I already know, Jack."

He does? Holy shit, now what?

"Your mistake was taking the blame for something you didn't directly do at the time of the incident."

"It wasn't like that, sir."

"Temporarily transferring command to the nuclear commander, what was his name? Wilson? Your equal on that boat...that was okay, in my view."

"Please, sir. I need for you to listen."

The President nods, okay go for it.

I check the close in area, a bit nervous as I wring my hands, and put the facts together in my head.

"Wilson got my spot – right out of the Naval Academy. I was the one who was supposed to get a nuclear command. My Dad wanted that more than anything. He calls those guys the Navy elite."

I pause, taking a deep breath.

"I had Wilson take the conn. But not before I gave him some compromised data on that Russian submarine under the command of Marat Ivanov. Who had shacked up with one of my dates when we both attended a UN conference in Tokyo. He a Russian military attaché, I was the American attaché. It was supposed to be a friendly exchange of safety ideas for sailing the high seas."

The President folds his arms, and scans the others in the room. Then back to me.

I take a swig from my bottle of Fiji water, which I almost hoped contained a dose of cyanide.

"I left the bridge. It was a deliberate miscalculation that would have taken my boat too close to the Russian submarine, you know, to scare them off a bit. Maybe force them to engage in an evasive maneuver."

Another deep breath, "Wilson miscalculated my miscalculation and collided with the Barracuda...it wasn't an accident, sir."

The President looks troubled, perhaps even angry.

"I see, Jack. So, not only was the Russian submarine in danger, but you, your crew, and a billion dollar submarine."

"Yes, sir. And I'm sorry. I've disgraced my Dad. You know him, he'll..."

"Yes I do, Jack. I also know he's very proud of everything you've accomplished in your career." The President gets eye ball to eye ball with me.

"But you'll need to tell him...I already knew what happened."

Giordan drops his head. Then back to me, he says...

"You're not the only officer that has carried out a stupid stunt. During the Vietnam war, I deliberately sank a Russian merchant ship docked in Haiphong harbor...then worked at covering it up...with your Dad's help. We were both pissed at Nixon for not allowing us to have the more advanced A6E to fly into the North."

He looks off to the far side of the room.

"That's between us, Jack."

I nod, waiting for another shoe to drop.

"As your Commander in Chief, I'll find it difficult to have you return to the submarine fleet. Commanders have had their careers ended for lesser incidents."

I nod, followed by a meek "yes, sir."

"Like that poor fella who commanded the USS San Francisco. Two hundred feet below the surface and hits a rock out-cropping south of the Sea of Japan. The impact killed a sailor in the engine room.

The Navy found it was an accident, plain and simple because that out-cropping was on no known chart."

The President shakes his head, "finished out his career at a desk in the Pentagon."

This little chat is going down the tubes fast. But the President has more to say.

"Jack, right now I need to know who you are. Can your country count on you?"

"I'm prepared to follow your orders, whatever they may be."

I said that in all honesty and with my best foot forward.

"Good. Just what I needed to hear." A pause. "Jack. I'm ordering you to fast-jet to the Middle East."

"You'll be put on board the USS Virginia, one of our newest fast attack submarines, and go after the Bear Oscar Kim Jong. I want you to sink the bastards."

Chapter 80

Central Intelligence Agency
DCI's Office Suite
Tuesday, 1255 Zulu 0655 Hrs. Local

SIMON UNGER has a very worried look on his face. He should be worried. His undercover contacts tell him the other side is moving in closer. Getting closer to the real truth. His conversation with Eiko Narita was a tell-all sign. Able to read between the lines and capture the subtext, he has concluded that additional counter measures need to be further activated. Looking out onto the huge expanse of lawn from his 7th floor window, the dew succumbing to the rising sun, he sketches out his next chess move. A move to add shock and awe to the equation that has formed the bizarre set of events the last twenty four hours.

He grabs his high tech Blackberry from his desk, and knocks out a text message. It's slow going because of the coded nature of the message, not to mention the need to be as perplexing as possible should the message be captured by Connolly's whiz kid of a girlfriend. Satisfied with the content, he hits send.

Georgetown University, NW Washington, DC

The Starbucks coffee café is coming to life with bleary-eyed students who wander in from all directions on the campus of this elite Jesuit University in the heart of Washington's premier residential neighborhood. Not only known for its superior educational reputation, its championship basketball teams, its high profile graduates, but also known for the location shooting of the 1970's flick, "The Exorcist."

Most of the small outside tables are occupied with students talking about the new semester, professors who are really cool, and those that are jerks. A few guys talk about the new crop of hot chicks that make up the freshman class and who will be at which weekend frat parties. Guys being guys are rating the ones they've seen or even have met.

A cute blonde junior, knock out figure and sexy legs being shown off sticking out of a skimpy skirt, is transfixed on someone on the far side sitting at a table alone.

He's a little older, mature looking for his actual age of twenty-four, and looks like a preppy Robert Redford. He's in Chaps, head to toe, good looking with great hair. The subject matter of the text book he reads while nursing a Grande latte is titled "Diplomacy for the Twenty First Century."

And we'll ID this guy as THE GRAD STUDENT.

Then, just like that, the Blackberry on his table, one identical to Simon Unger's, pulses. He grabs it quickly. Noting the text message, his eyes widen just a bit. And he reads the text again. Then, with two fingers he deletes the text message.

He stands, gathers his books into a soft-sided bag, and moves away at a fast pace.

Simon Unger's Office at the CIA

A frustrated Unger pounds away on his Blackberry, unable to raise NICK.

He checks the time after several minutes then re-checks the small high tech device.

"Son of a bitch!"

Chapter 81

Andrews Air Force Base
Washington, DC
Tuesday, 1327 Zulu, 0727 Hrs. Local

The F-15E Eagle taxis fast out onto runway 01 Right. The pilot, Lieutenant Colonel Dave Evans, a quiet, but big guy from Kansas, either forgets or just ignores the protocol of asking for take-off clearance. I can hear the communication inside the crash helmet they've strapped to my head, which, by the way, seems a bit tight. I have no comment at the moment regarding the term "crash." But that's what the young airman said when he jammed the little helmet onto my humongous head.

Colonel Evans has turned onto the runway, and with a loud continuous blasting sound, has thrown the throttle all the way forward to the fire wall. As we race down the runway I feel my eye balls move the back of my head. I open my mouth to say something but now my lips are stuck in a place that makes me look like I'm trying to swallow a hockey puck. Then I hear the Colonel say "rotating" and the nose of this multi-million dollar fighter jet instantly points at Mars.

I try looking off to my left but all I see is a miniature city that looks to have been constructed with my nephews' Lego set. Then everything goes white. And I realize we're zipping through the cloud cover the weather guys talked about when Colonel Evans was getting his briefing. I no sooner filter that thought when everything turns blue. And getting darker blue. Heading for black. As in outer space black. I hope the Colonel got it right. It's Saudi Arabia, not Mars.

So I say into my headset microphone, trying to sound calm, not giving any indication that my breakfast is about to end up in my lap, "this bird really moves along."

"Yes, sir. We'll hit Mach 2.5 once we get to our assigned altitude."

"Right…got it…what's that, two, three hundred miles per hour?"

No response.

I guess he has to think about that. I'm more use to the speed of a submarine which, by the way, is classified so I can't mention it. Anyway, all I see looking forward is really dark blue sky. And from what I can tell we're still pointing at Mars.

It appears we're leveling off. And looking off to our right, I see another F-15E Eagle no more than 30 yards away. The two pilots look over. So I wave. They just look. So, I ask the Colonel, "who are those guys, Colonel?"

"Our back-up escort, Commander."

"Right. So if we have a problem, you drop me into that other plane?"

No response.

I get the feeling this is going to be a long flight. Now I'm wondering if, in the rush to get me to Andrews, and onto this rocket ship, did I remember to hit the Head? I don't think so. I better ask Colonel Evans what the plan is for a pit stop.

"Colonel. How many stops do we make before we get to Saudi Arabia?"

"None, sir. We've got four air to air re-fuelling hook-ups scheduled along the way."

Oh.

"What if I have to pee?"

No response.

Was that a Grande or Vente Latte I had earlier?

Chapter 82

KIMBA is not the sharpest knife in the draw. There's no need for him to be. It's not a requirement for the low paying job of doorman at this luxurious resort hotel. But the sounds of invisible night creatures that suddenly appear as soon as the sun set off in the West startles the lone doorman. He's already a bit nervous having been given specific instructions involving a certain VIP guest who is about to depart the hotel's ornate main entrance. And, wanting to not screw up the assignment, begins to over-think his simple duties.

As various confusing thoughts ping around his brain, the revolving door moves and Secret Service Agent Don Wierda appears. He takes a long moment to carefully scan the immediate area. His view is limited due to the lush vegetation that is part of the entrance portico. He then turns to Kimba, giving him a slight nod.

Kimba catches the signal and takes off at a sprint towards the far end of the entrance driveway, stopping at a parked black limo. He waves it forward, pointing to a spot where Wierda is standing. The limo driver shrugs, and then waves his arm at Kimba who just happens to be standing in the way of the limos' path to the front door. Kimba studies the drivers' arm signal for way too long. Then gets it. He moves to the side and the limo pulls up to a spot 5 meters from the revolving door entrance.

In the hotel parking garage about 40 meters from the front door, the JACKEL hides behind a concrete pillar. He lifts the uniquely designed weapon to his shoulder and takes aim through the telescopic sight at the hotel entrance.

He zeros in on the back of a man casually walking passed the revolving door. The man stops, and turns, now revealing NICK's head in the cross-hairs of the telescopic sight.

At the revolving door, Agent Wierda takes a long look at Nick, his expression and body language going from casual to high alert, as he shifts his weight to the balls of his feet, bending his knees just slightly. At the same time his head turns at the revolving door for a quick look, then back to Nick. And in this quick motion, Wierda has moved his right hand to the inside of his jacket, gripping the hand-hold of his Glock 357.

At that same moment, Vice President Seth Greene is spit from the revolving door.

Wierda shouts while drawing his weapon "get back inside…now!" Wierda now points the weapon at Nick, as a surprised Greene just stares instead of going back into the hotel.

Nick's arms go into the air while saying. "Hey – hey, man. I'm just here for dinner. Please put the gun down."

Spit! Spit!

In rapid succession.

Blood splatters, silently, onto the revolving door.

Seth Greene crumbles. A thump, the sound of his dead weight hitting the pavement.

Wierda spins, taking his eyes off Nick and looking down at Veep Seth Greene. He takes a step and kneels, feeling for a pulse at Greene's neck. There is none. All at the same time Nick has pulled a 9mm Beretta from seemingly nowhere, and now has it leveled at Wierda.

Nick takes aim, ready to fire as he develops a bizarre grin, when…

Spit! Spit!

Again, in rapid succession.

Nick is knocked off his feet and blasted backwards into a line a shrubs, spread eagled, and quite dead.

Wierda dives to a safe position in front of the black limo that had just pulled into position moments before the chaos. It's a long, sweaty moment before he inches up for a look in the direction he thinks the shots came from, an area near or in the garage. Then he scans the entire area. Not a soul in sight. Kimba has vanished, as well. The limo driver is jammed under the steering wheel, now crying for help, as he's stuck.

The only other sounds are those of the night creatures.

Agent Don Wierda sits hard on the pavement, leaning back on the front of the limo and dropping his weapon to his side, he takes several deep breaths. From another pocket inside his jacket, he pulls out a secure satellite phone and punches in a seven digit code, waits for a two level tone, then punches in thirteen more digits.

He holds the phone to his ear, and begins to weep, silently.

Chapter 83

SENATOR JOE SYKES and Secret Service Agent
LARRY MITCHENER come barreling out of the Senate Office
building, walking briskly towards the exclusive parking area
reserved for United States Senators, only a quick walk from
the offices. While the area is out in the open and preferred by
some Senators who would rather not park in the garage, it is
only patrolled by the Capitol Police on an irregular basis.
Senators who don't mind surprise intrusions by the press, and
those that can't wait for an opportunity to get in front of a
camera, like Chuck Schumer of New York, usually park in this
area. Although a few members of the press corps spot Sykes
and Larry, their quick pace sends a signal. Not today, guys.
Although, a fella from the New York Times catches them in
his peripheral vision, and makes a bee-line for both men who
are now 50 yards ahead.

At Sykes' car, they split. Sykes to the driver side, Larry
to the right. Before getting into the car, Sykes leans across the
top of the car, saying to Larry...

"Do I trust Simon Unger has played his last card?"

Larry fires back, "shoot, Senator. You don't know what
I got."

Sykes can't help but smile at the Secret Service Agent
while shaking his head...

"Agent Mitchener. Whatever you do, don't ever
underestimate his reach. He's the personification of George
Orwell's 1984."

They both jump in the car.

About 100 yards away, the GRAD STUDENT walks casually away from the area, holding what looks like a cell phone, and heading for Union Station. Perhaps just another student going for extra credit by doing some Capitol Hill research. On the way, he covertly pulls an antenna from the cell phone-looking device. He mentally counts to five, then pushes a small button. Then goes for a look back over his right shoulder, without stopping.

Sykes has started his car, about to put it into reverse when...

KAAAAAAA BOOM....

Flames, debris and body parts litter a wide area around the exclusive parking space. The explosion has also activated every car alarm within 100 yards of the spot where Senator Sykes had parked his car.

The New York Times reporter who had been running after Sykes hangs upside down from a tree limb ten feet off the ground. His press pass, hanging from his neck, sways in the light breeze.

Two U.S. Army officers running up to the scene instantly develop the same thought, giving each other a look. This carnage looks all too familiar.

A scene they both witnessed too many times in Iraq.

Chapter 84

The Oval Office
Tuesday, 1703 Zulu, 1103 Hrs. Local

DONALD GIORDAN has his back to the office as he gazes, somewhat comatose, to the outside and the South lawn. His shoulders slumped in a posture of defeat. His mind in another universe. Perhaps a parallel universe where no evil exists. Where the bad guys are cast away much like the three villains in Superman were cast away to forever slide throughout space stuck in a flat, confined space for all eternity. But the thoughts quickly vanish as he comes to realize that as the leader of the country, one who is not a political ideologue dependent on unions, the liberal media, big government hand-outs for the benefit of a welfare state, nor one whose mantra is spend, spend, spend, Giordan's role is to be a leader of *all* the people. And it requires much of the man or woman who occupies the Oval Office.

Giordan wrote an op-ed piece long before his first campaign for the Presidency. In it were a variety of sound, noble ideas for a President. One idea still stands out in his mind that should put the political priorities to rest. On inauguration day, the newly sworn-in President will be required to resign from his political party, and thus swear complete and total allegiance to the American people exclusive of any other individual, party, state, organization, or public and non-public entity. And serve just one eight year term.

More or less, personally codifying the values of the Constitution.

Such leadership would perhaps negate any and all political stunts he or she may contemplate. It fell on deaf ears, which now places Giordan in a rather dicey situation.

During his little mind journey, the DCI, Simon Unger was escorted into the Oval, and now stands quietly at the opposite end of the President's desk.

The President holds a look out to the South Lawn.

"Simon, you never liked Vice President Seth Greene."

"I don't understand, sir."

"No, Simon, I'm sure you don't."

"Clearly, Mister President, you're not suggesting anything improper..."

Giordan turns hard on the balls of his feet, and eye ball to eye ball with Unger, teeth clenched, "what I am doing, Director Unger, is initiating a criminal investigation. On two fronts. One, dealing with the murder of my National Security Advisor, Miss Eiko Narita. And secondly, with regard to the assassination of the Vice President of the United States."

Unger stays motionless. Not even blinking. Thinking that his tracks are perfectly covered. It would be a stretch to connect him to both incidents. The planning and execution all handled quite cleverly and via secure communications. So much for boastful rhetoric from a politician. Someone who, come January 20th, will be out of a job.

Now, and with restrained rage, President Giordan has cut the distance in half between he and Unger, and adds, "clean out your desk, you son of a bitch."

Standing ram-rod straight, he continues, "and don't forget to take your boy-toy, the young Mister Gitelson."

Chapter 85

Over Eastern Europe
On Board a U.S. Air Force F-15E Eagle
Tuesday, 1946 Zulu

We just finished our third re-fueling maneuver provided by a huge USAF tanker out of Ramstein Air Force Base in Germany. Colonel Evans thinks we can make it to Saudi Arabia without another fill-up. He's doing the calculation now.

I'm a little worried since he just said he can't find his calculator and was going to do the math in his head.

And fly this bird at the same time.

I'd offer to help find the calculator but I'm strapped into this seat so well the only thing I can move is my right pinky.

The trip so far has been very informative. The Colonel pointed interesting sights like Iceland, the Arctic Circle, Mars, the Scandinavian Peninsula, and just a moment ago, a place he thinks is either Romania or Russia.

He then added, "if it's Russia I'm not sure we're authorized to shoot back."

"What?"

Silence.

Then a soft chuckle.

I'm glad this guy has a sense of humor because I was just about to ask how to administer CPR on myself.

I can't wait to get this fly boy on a submarine someday. He'll wish he should have never left Kansas.

Anyway, there's a chopper waiting for me when we land to get me out to the Red Sea and on-board the USS Virginia. I can't wait. Except for just one small problem.

His name is Captain Mike O'Flannigan.

Chapter 86

Somewhere Beneath the Red Sea
Egypt to the West, Saudi Arabia to the East
Tuesday, 2037 Zulu, 2337 Hrs. Local

The USS VIRGINIA glides through the murky blue/green water, its stealth presence a real head scratcher to those we classify as the "enemy" and who spend every waking hour trying to find one of Americas' newest and most lethal weapons.

Its enormous hull - 377 feet, longer than a football field, 34 feet on the beam, and 1.65 billion US dollars, that is taxpayer dollars from those happy taxpayers who support the worlds' best military machine – would be too big for the screen if this were, in fact, a Spielberg flick and not a cleverly written novel.

A fast attack submarine capable of neutralizing even the boldest enemies of the US should the President give that order.

The towering Sail sits 100 feet forward of mid-ships. On both the port and starboard sides of the Sail, 20 foot long winged planes cut the distance in half from the top of the Sail, known as the Bridge, to the deck below.

On board the Virginia, CAPTAIN MIKE O'FLANNIGAN, a well-worn Boston Red Sox's ball cap firmly seated on a round Irish head of red hair, studies a coded message handed to him by his Communications Officer.

He crumbles it up in his hand while gritting his teeth. A moment passes before he says to no one in particular... "Son of a bitch...I hope it's not who I think it is."

Chapter 87

On Board US Navy Chopper "Air Tebow"
Heading Southwest from Tabuk, Saudi Arabia
Tuesday, 2213 Zulu, Wednesday, 0113 Hrs. Local

AIR TEBOW is the moniker adopted by the pilot, Navy Commander J. O. "Skip" McKnight, Jr., a native of Boulder, Colorado. It comes from his expertise at delivering personnel from his chopper onto an assortment of naval vessels in all kinds of weather. Whether they are rescue missions or transfers, he is the best when it comes to this kind of mission. The same way pro football super-star quarterback, Tim Tebow, can deliver a football into the hands of his wide receivers while being rushed by the biggest guys in the NFL, and do it with unmatched expertise. And it's the praying, what we all know as "Tee-bowing," that has kept him from serious injury.

McKnight can do the same on the high seas. And without losing a single man or woman in the process.

At least, not yet.

As we fly past Duba, Saudi Arabia, heading out over the Red Sea, my mind stays tuned to Commander McKnight's piercing words to me before take-off from Tabuk.

"Not yet," is what he said.

By the time I get on board the Virginia, I'll be a basket case unable to carry out my mission. I wonder if Captain O'Flannigan has a bottle of Scotch on board.

Probably not.

There's something about that in the policy manual.

Speaking of the aforementioned Captain Mike O'Flannigan, we do have a history together. Unfortunately, it's not Navy related.

Which may make matters worse.

Actually, Mike and I have been friends for quite some time now.

And it's dissolved to simply acquaintances.

I think.

We've served together on various submarines in lesser positions the past fifteen years.

Mike is Boston Irish inside and out.

He grew up in the famed North End in a neighborhood where outsiders were usually greeted with, first, getting their asses kicked, then, second, asked why they were there in the first place.

Kind of backwards. You gotta be from there to understand, I suppose.

Despite his roots, Mike landed a ticket to the Naval Academy, and it has taken him almost to the top of the Navy food chain.

And he's a die-hard Red Sox fan.

So much so, he's the only Officer in the Navy that gets away with wearing a beat-up, 30 year old Red Sox ball cap on his boat. Despite dress code rules to the contrary, the Navy brass has simply given up talking to him about it.

The fact that I spent part of my youth in New York I can honestly say that I'm not a Yankees fan.

If so, we would've been at each-others' throats long ago.

No, our problem is - you've probably already guessed -
A woman.

I didn't know she was his fiancée.

Really.

I didn't.

Anyway, it's a long story that Captain O'Flannigan has kept simmering on a back burner. One day, we'll talk it out. I hope not in Boston where I know he has lots of tough buddies.

I'm about to board his boat with the full authority of the President of the United States.

Whether he understands and follows his orders is an open question.

If I end-up in a torpedo tube, and it gets aimed at the Egyptian coast, that'll be a good indication of how our little get together went this evening.

Chapter 88

Beneath the Red Sea
Close to Duba, on the Saudi Arabian Coast
Tuesday, 2331 Zulu, Wednesday, 0231 Hrs. Local

The BEAR OSCAR KIM JONG, an Oscar Class Russian submarine, shows its age as it whips through the murky blue/green water at 26 knots, 6 knots less than its designed submerged speed. The peeling paint and barnacles obviously contributing to its less than adequate performance in deep water. The engine room is a whole other issue for Lubin. They will make the time frame assigned to the mission, but with only minutes to spare.

In the control room, the handsome General Tariq stands alongside the clueless North Korean Captain. While he stands at ridged attention, Tariq shouts commands at the crew who have no idea what he is saying. These guys are simply scared shitless.

He turns to the Captain, and in English, a language both seem to understand, he demands, "open missile doors five and six...now!"

The North Korean Captain repeats the order in a language his crew can understand. Several crew members look at each other as if who is supposed to do what.

Zoyan is at the Ships Control Station, also known as the SCS.

Tariq is quickly losing his patience. He shouts, "now!"

Chekhov is on the opposite side of the control room, and out of Tariq's line of sight. He foams at the mouth, ready to spring into action like a caged tiger. Letting Tariq call the shots at this point in the game is just counter-intuitive to the former Russian Navy warrior.

As Chekhov mulls over his move, Vasili and Lubin slip into the control room without any fanfare. Almost unseen, as it may. Vasili scans the area looking for any sign serious trouble. His scan ends at Tariq who has now noticed Vasili standing several yards from him.

Tariq has a bizarre, out of character smile for the Russian Commander. This causes Vasili to frown with suspicion, but careful to be politically correct with this former Iraqi military leader turned Iranian wing nut.

He asks, "General, is everything to your satisfaction?"

Tariq responds, "as those American bastards say in that land of Satan, Commander – show time, no?"

Vasili holds a long, expressionless stare on Tariq. In his mind he's wondering just how crazy this guy is. Tariq's eyes tell Vasili this guy has gone completely off the reservation. Time to get back control.

Vasili moves slowly towards the Weapons Control Panel, but not taking his eyes off Tariq, while spinning his key chain at a mad pace around a finger.

Tariq has now lifted his head for a look above and aft. No one is sure what he sees, but some of the North Koreans do follow his gaze...

In the Water - Outside the Bear Oscar Kim Jong

...and noting just aft of the huge Sail, two large round manhole-type covers groan as they swing open, pointing towards the surface, 75 feet above the ship. Further aft, and behind the rudder is the giant six-blade screw. It spins menacingly clockwise creating a broad range of turbulent baffles that could easily be picked up by sonar as far away as the Mediterranean Sea.

Perhaps a strategy employed by Vasili, but unknown to Tariq.

Further aft of the Bear Oscar, about 8000 meters aft to be more precise, it's deathly quiet. Except for Pings that now travel from the Bear Oscar, across an 8000 meter stretch of the sub-surface Red Sea. And grow louder, radiating from the water's deep shadows.

Then, as if through a veil in the blue/green murky water the black nose of another submarine bears down in the direction of the Bear Oscar, hot on its trace. It slides quietly through the water because it's the quietest submarine on the planet.

The USS VIRGINIA, SSN 774 is about to demonstrate why it's considered a mortal fast attack submarine with the motto, "thus always to tyrants."

On Board the USS Virginia

A motto embedded deep into the mind set of each of the 134 officers and sailors on board. And a motto I find particularly appropriate at the moment having some idea of who may be on board the Bear Oscar, or at least who they represent.

On close examination I see everyone is wound tight, at their battle stations. This ship is being run the way a nuclear sub needs to be run. By the book.

Except for that crappy looking Red Sox ball cap Captain O'Flannigan is wearing. I think it even smells. But I'm not going to say anything. I've already heard enough from the guy, telling me about the danger of having to surface to pick me up. He's still trying to estimate how many enemy satellites took our picture while he waited for me to scramble into the aft deck hatch. Actually, I fell into the ship through the hatch door, thanks to a really big guy named Senior Chief DeLorenzo. I guess he didn't want me to take my time climbing down the incredibly dangerous stairs.

So, he pulled me down.

Ass first.

When he asked if I was okay, or maybe if I needed to see the ships medic, he didn't wait for my answer.

I'm sure this was O'Flannigan's way of welcoming an old friend on board. What a swell guy. The crew is glued to the various video displays that surround the control room. I note Captain O'Flannigan has moved over towards the sonar shack with that well-known street-wise tough guy look, and calls out, "where is he, Borrelli?"

From the sonar shack, I notice a fresh-face sonar guy with a large head-set over his ears. This must be Borrelli. And, like most everyone else, except the Captain, he's wearing a Virginia ball cap.

He lifts one side of the head-set, and shouts back, "8000 meters, sir – he's popped two aft missile doors…and both could use a lube job, sir."

These sonar guys are the best. They can ID any sound, anywhere. I need to make certain I don't cut the cheese since I'm sure O'Flannigan, with Borrelli's help, will have everyone pointing at me.

Back in the control room, O'Flannigan looks over at someone else I know. Commander George Huntington takes charge of a panel know as Fire Control. The Captain gives the order, "Mister Huntington, flood tubes one and two. Lock in a firing solution."

Huntington responds, "aye, skipper.

Huntington moves his ear microphone closer to his mouth and says, "launch commander, flood forward tubes one and two. Safety's off."

Now the atmosphere is highly charged. And I'm beginning to feel that rush I've experienced in the past on board a submarine. And I know now how badly I miss it. And I also know what a dope I am to have blown it all away.

Captain O'Flannigan takes several steps towards me, a wry smirk on his face. I guess he knows how I feel and is probably going to rub it in. Or he's going to take a shot at me for poking his ex-fiancée.

Maybe not.

He hooked up with an ex-girlfriend from the old neighborhood. He moved back to North Boston from his bachelors' pad in Groton, Connecticut.

They married. And he has three young boys now.

All red heads. And, from the pictures in Mike's quarters, all tough looking characters, and all wearing Red Sox ball caps.

I need to make a note to never visit North Boston.

Mike stops, and just looks at me for a long heartbeat.

Then, "Commander Connolly. Tell the boss the USS Virginia is armed and fuckin' dangerous."

It's the smirk that's scary. But I know he's best guy for this mission. I grab the red handset over my head that's already connected to the situation room, and the President of the United States...

"Mister President, ready here, sir."

In the Situation Room

Deep beneath the West Wing the Situation Room buzzes with activity as most of the occupants are still on way too much caffeine. Some do nothing more taxing than work a cup of morning Joe. The President, holding a red hand-set, examines multiple LED monitors simultaneously, on edge, as he tries to make up for lost ground. And a few bad decisions.

Voices still radiate updates from various speakers around the room, although now turned down to a lower pitch at the request of the President. He needs space in order to better comprehend the horrific losses thus far today.

Four people he knew and respected are dead. He's particularly mortified over the death of Secret Service Agent Lawrence Mitchener. Larry had been chief of the Presidential protection detail when Giordan took office. The President admired his professionalism and never once felt in danger with Larry at his side.

But the time for deeper reflection will come. Right now he needs to lead his nation out of the current crises. He's ordered the destruction of a major terrorist camp in a foreign country, and has ordered the sinking of a foreign Naval vessel likely crewed with officials from North Korea, Iran, and Russia. On that thought, he senses a need to speak with Putin.

Holding the red hand-set, he focuses his attention on Admiral Hasslinger who is carrying on two conversations at once.

"Admiral. What's the bogeys' range to Tel Aviv?"

Hasslinger responds, "Bear Oscar is approximately six hundred kilometers from Tel Aviv, sir."

"You said he must be under five hundred fifty K to fire and reach the target, Admiral?"

"Yes, sir. If, in fact, Tel Aviv is the target."

As the President gives this more thought, a young Army officer approaches with a document in hand.

"Read it to me, Lieutenant."

"Yes, sir. From Central Command in St. Petersburg, they confirm Kill Kim is airborne out of Kadena Air Force Base in Okinawa, now 1800 kilometers from the North Korean target."

The President nods, dismissing the young officer while he turns to face a recent addition to the Situation Room.

Ambassador GIDEON MARGOLIES, the Israeli representative to the United States, can only just stare at Giordan, his expression packed with fear. This is one guy on the verge of a panic attack.

"Mister Ambassador. You'd better call your Prime Minister, sir...just in case."

Margolies snaps out of his brief journey through hell and responds, "you *will* give the order, Mister President?"

Giordan lets out a noticeable sigh, then, "please, sir, make your call."

Invisible daggers fly from each, clearly a sign that these two are certainly not the best of drinking buddies.

"Like I said...sir...just in case."

The President turns, red hand-set at his ear, "what's our next move, Jack?"

On Board the USS Virginia

I replace the secure hand-set back onto the rack above my head. Then I cringe as I look over at a visibly unfriendly O'Flannigan, arms folded, and who is perhaps scheming for a way to get me into that forward tube. I'd love to bring up a happy discussion about the wonderful Red Sox, but they just dropped two out three against the Yankees this past weekend. At Fenway, in Boston, no less.

I get a firm grip.

"Put the safety's on, Captain. Bounce two off his hull."

"Then what? Tell 'em, you're it? This is not street tag, Commander. I don't play games like you did chasing Russian subs all over the ocean."

"Right. I understand. But, please, hear me out. We need a chance to get 'em on the surface. They'll know we're here and on to their plan."

O'Flannigan fumes. But keeps it in knowing that he's been over-ridden by the Commander in Chief. At least, I hope that's what he's concluded and not a way to stuff me into number one tube. He unfolds his arms, shifting his stance over to Huntington at Fire Control.

"Mister Huntington. Safety's on. Let's go a knockin'."

Huntington doesn't like that order. Not one bit as he fires a look at me that says he's already volunteered to help the Captain stuff me into number one tube. But a quick glance at Huntington from the Captain brings Huntington back to planet earth.

"Yes...sir."

On Board the Bear Oscar Kim Jong

GENERAL TARIQ is in the midst of an adrenaline rush as his eyes move from terminal to terminal from his central vantage point in the Control Room. The crew, on the other hand, is showing signs of a collective nervous breakdown in the making.

VASILI watches the show from his station at the Weapons Control Panel. He casually winds that special key around his finger so as not to attract too much attention as he keeps a careful watch on Tariq. The over-arching thought that has Vasili a bit on edge is Tariq's right hand that keeps moving to the weapon holstered to his gun belt. This lunatic is quite capable of firing the weapon, something not particularly recommended on board a submarine at any depth.

CHEKHOV stands behind a sweaty North Korean in the sonar quarters just off the control room deck. With Chekhov fumbling for another smoke, Lubin sticks his head into the confined smoke-filled area saying, "you're going to kill that boy with all your smoking, Chekhov."

Chekhov exhales, then smiles at Lubin saying, "no my friend, with this."

And making sure the young North Korean can see, Chekhov pulls a closed switch blade from a pocket, snapping it open with great fanfare. A second North Korean sitting in the next chair blows his lunch when, suddenly, the young fella in front of Chekhov jumps in his seat as if pinched in the ass.

Chekhov moves like an animal, grabbing the head-set off the young sailor, strangling the cord around the startled man's neck in the process. He listens intently, eyes glued to the computer monitor an arm's length away.

Then, shouting into the Control Room, Chekhov barks, "Americans! Virginia class attack submarine! Eight thousand meters aft! Closing fast!"

Vasili stands up straight, moving just a few steps away from the Weapons Control Panel towards Tariq, and says.

"Well, General, maybe the Americans do have the best of you after all."

From the sonar quarters, Chekhov shouts, "two in the water!"

Tariq shifts his attention momentarily to Chekhov. Then, instantly back to Vasili, ordering, with a twinge of retribution.

"Take your post, Commander!"

Tariq stares at the monitors in front of him. To his left, the North Korean Captain stands motionless still wishing he was any other place but on this ship. Without looking at the Captain, Tariq says, "Counter measures, Captain!"

Nothing.

Tariq spins hard at the Captain.

"Counter measures, you idiot!"

Again. No response.

Tariq draws the weapon from his holster. The muzzle gets placed against the Captains' temple just as Chekhov shouts again into the Control Room, this time a little bit more relaxed, "wait...wait..."

The Generals' eyes shift up to a spot where the periscope moves through the Sail and up passed the Bridge and towards the surface.

And from a spot looking off the Bridge and towards the stern of the ship, two Mark 50 Lightweight torpedoes, 112 inches in length and traveling at 40 knots, hit the starboard rear quarter of the Bear Oscar Kim Jong.

And shatter into a zillion pieces.

And as the crew listens to an assortment of torpedo parts rattle across the deck with all eyes focused above, a new visitor enters the Control Room...

"Traitor!"

Bang!

The North Korean Captain drops hard to the deck. A bullet hole through his forehead. And now all eyes are on the newest player standing near a hatchway...

COLONEL SALAAMAN HABIBOLLAH SAYYARI, a senior officer in the Iranian Armed Forces. As a matter of fact, he's the eldest son of the Iranian Navy Commander, a close ally, and possibly another twin, of Mahmoud Ahmadinejad.

General Tariq, fully understanding the political pecking order, despite his rank, nods in respect to the young Colonel from Tehran. Then glances quickly down at the very dead North Korean Captain. Noting the stunned silence amongst the other North Korean sailors who can only stare at their dead Captain's body, Tariq says while pointing to two sailors, "remove this traitor, enemy of the great Supreme Ayatollah!"

Several sailors jump at the order, but the General selects two. The others drift back to their posts, pretending to know what to do next, but avoiding eye contact with the insane General.

In the meantime, Chekhov has moved into the Control Room, now facing Tariq, says, "the Americans want us to surface. I suggest we flood two aft tubes, General."

General Tariq blows him off with a wave, "not yet, Mister Chekhov."

At the Weapons Control Panel Vasili tries like the devil to mask his anger. Tariq directs his order to Vasili...

"Slow us down, Commander. Close the distance with the American criminals."

Vasili, jolted by the ill-advised order, spins his key and chain as he nods at Lubin, seated at the SCS, to follow the order.

On Board the USS Virginia

That fresh-faced sailor in the sonar shack - Borrelli – jumps to his feet, poking his head into the Control Room, "yes sir, that's what I think it was – a gun shot. And that ship is not heading for the surface."

I'm standing next to Captain O'Flannigan at the OOD – a location in the Control Room known to us as the "Officer of the Deck" post. Somehow I think Borrelli's latest development from the sonar shack is not good news for me. Like I've said, I'm good at reading people and O'Flannigan's angry body language has my prints all over it.

"Well, Commander Connolly, any more brilliant ideas?"

He doesn't bother to wait for a response, which I don't have at the moment. He speaks into an over-head microphone that connects him directly to Borrelli.

"Range, Borrelli?"

From the over-head speaker, Borrelli says, "six thousand meters, sir. Missile doors still open."

Trigger happy Huntington chimes in, "we've got a firing solution plugged in, sir."

Before O'Flannigan can reach up and depress the mike button to ask Borrelli another question, Borrelli is firing at us, "he's slowing down, sir. Real slow. Distance closing fast."

O'Flannigan looks over at his senior chief, DeLorenzo, "Chief, gimme ten knots."

"Aye, aye, sir."

"I guess things will never change with you, Mister Connolly."

Right now I know this is some serious shit going on. So, I'm not about to get into a childish pissing contest with this guy. Anyway, he still is the Captain. And I truly respect that despite the orders given to me by the President. I'm gonna lay low.

"Captain. Let's not get too close."

Chapter 89

From a small mountain top outside the city the view reveals a city cloaked in the dim lights of late night.

Or, in this case, the very early morning hour, well before sunrise on the eastern Mediterranean.

While there are no crowds in the streets at this hour, nor many cars traversing the city, there still is some activity.

Then, from the same mountain top location the whining, screaming sound of an air raid siren penetrates the entire area.

A sound not unfamiliar to the residents of this city.

The few cars on the streets come to screeching stops. Men, women, the young and the old, coming from a night out or perhaps on their way to an early shift at a factory or hospital, dart into the nearest buildings, some ripping gas masks out from tote bags carried over shoulders, just in case.

A rather common accoutrement to ones person in this highly charged city in a country surrounded by violent enemies.

The few pedestrians, mostly young people, exiting popular night spots run back inside, only to disappear into under-ground shelters.

Chapter 90

The White House
West Front Lawn,
The Press Pad
Tuesday, 2358 Zulu, 1758 Hrs. Local

TOM DELGADO of the Washington Post faces a remote TV camera, rehearsing his six o'clock news hour report as a scheduled guest on Fox News while he waits to file a live report.

Delgado is skeptical.

He knows something's up in the West Wing, that expensive, well-appointed structure just behind him. Having no briefing since the President did his one man stand yesterday regarding the Vice President raises all kinds of red flags.

He's stumped and regrets having agreed to speak with Bret Baier at Fox without something news worthy.

Other journalists, as well as activists from MSNBC who call themselves journalists, stand by, shiftless, taking in the small group of pedestrians out on the blocked-off section of Pennsylvania Avenue. Someone mentions to no one in particular that there's a report air raid sirens are going off in Tel Aviv.

This peaks Delgado's interest, but just for a nano second.

Still others talk to their respective producers via cell phone wondering if their lead-in should be what the President had for lunch on his first day of the re-election campaign.

The real news obviously has not yet been released to the news media. And for good reason. It's being held by a small group of folk's under-ground in the Situation Room no more than 45 yards from this spot.

The Situation Room & USS Virginia

The President, with the red hand-set in hand, and flanked by Lt. j.g. Lauren Miller who's working her iPhone, spins quickly around towards Admiral Hasslinger. Speaking into the red phone, but with eyes on Hasslinger...

"A gun shot?"

"Only the Captain would have a side arm, sir." As I say that, I zero in on O'Flannigan and wonder where he's hiding his side arm on his person.

Admiral Hasslinger gets closer to the President saying, "the Virginia has a firing solution programmed in, sir. Let's move."

I hear Hasslinger in the background and remember, while he's a senior officer with loads of medals, he's not a submariner. I need for the President to have the best possible picture of what could be going on.

"Someone else is on that boat, sir. Maybe trying to take control."

"Admiral, we could be dealing with a mutiny. That changes the equation."

"Mister President. Someone that smart wouldn't fire a weapon inside a nuclear submarine."

I jump in, "right, someone just plain stupid, maybe. But perhaps someone else is on that boat. Perhaps someone on our side of this problem. And not the person who fired that weapon."

Giordan looks over at Lauren Miller saying, "go back over everything you've tapped into, Lieutenant. Every transmission. I wanna know who else is on board the sub.

The President takes deep breath. "We missed someone."

On Board the Bear Oscar Kim Jong

General Tariq steps to the Ship Control Station, the SCS, and stands behind Lubin. And barks...

"All engines stop!"

He then shifts, holding a wry smile, towards Vasili at the Weapons Control Panel. Vasili, standing rock solid, still spinning his key and key chain, his only movement.

The looks between the two signal a collision of minds about to happen.

The Situation Room

Lieutenant Lauren Miller shifts towards the boss, a panic stricken President, and says, flatly, "he's opened two missile doors, sir."

From the far side, a young, but confident voice is heard, "Virginia less than one thousand meters, sir."

The President, in a moment of frustration, kicks a chair.

And then paces back and forth for a moment.

Then...

"We've gotta a rouge submarine with two nuclear missiles pointed at Tel Aviv!

He scans the faces in the Situation Room.

"And I've got to take a guess?"

On Board the USS Virginia

Captain O'Flannigan moves quickly from the OOD watch post, around the type 2 periscope. While still a confined space, the big Boston Irishman moves like an NFL running back with ease.

A man in control of his environment.

From there he glances at the Weapons Control Panel, on stand-by, and lit-up like a Christmas tree.

Then, a look over at me, standing at the starboard plotting table, drumming my nibble fingers, and in deep thought.

I perk up, returning his glance.

He smiles, saying, "I wanna stay on his cute ass."

He winks at me.

Then turns to Chief DeLorenzo, "chief, put us in reverse...one third."

"Aye, Captain." A pause. "Reverse engines. Set your speed at one third."

"Aye, sir."

I think for a moment, then add. "He won't fire, Captain. Not at this close range."

"And he knows we won't fire at him, Commander."

"Right. Maybe someone's told him that."

"Still. I wanna be at a safe distance, Mister Connolly."

Then, as if a sudden awakening, I have a thought. I reach for the red hand-set still connected to the Situation Room, and give O'Flannigan a knowing look.

"You think you know who's on board, Mister Connolly?"

The Situation Room

AMBASSADOR MARGOLIES has just wiped his face with a now very damp handkerchief. He moves carefully towards the Presidents' command position near the head of the long and highly polished mahogany table. The one with Dick Cheney's initials carved into one of the legs.

"Mister President. I would like to add a simple fact to your thoughts."

"Go ahead, Mister Ambassador."

"Sir, the population of Tel Aviv, the surrounding area and countryside, is approximately 3,325,700 Israeli citizens."

All eyes have shifted to Margolies as he pleads his case.

"The USS Virginia is, what one hundred twenty sailors, give or take, Mister President?"

Those close by go silent and stiff as stone as the President turns his flushed, infuriated face at the Israeli Ambassador. And to make sure there is no miss-understanding...

"Eleven officers, one hundred twenty three enlisted men to be exact. All of whom volunteered for submarine duty. And a senior advisor to the President of the United States. All Americans, Mister Ambassador."

The President stands, and, indicating the two Marine guards at the door...

"Escort the Israeli Ambassador out, please, gentlemen."

The two tough looking leather necks, dressed in battle fatigues and armed to the hilt, approach Margolies, grabbing him by the arms. They leave, quietly.

From the far side, that young officer is once again heard...

"Virginia is less than five hundred meters, and in reverse, sir. Making a gap, sir. They're looking for the order, sir."

"I'm not ready to give the order, god dammit."

Lauren steps over to the President, and pointing at the red hand-set...

"May I, sir?"

Giordan hands her the secure hand-set. And, sitting at the mahogany table and cupping the mouth piece, she says...

"Hey, sweetheart. Got an idea."

I melt with hearing the dulcet tones of her voice. But, I get it together and respond with a loving complement...

"Time to save my ass, Lieutenant?"

Lauren swings in front of a computer monitor, her fingers moving swiftly over the keyboard. She transfers the link with Jack to a head-set and boom microphone and whispers into the mike.

I hear a name I don't normally like to hear from her.

"If he's connected, he'll answer right away. He's like that with me, you know?"

"Must be love...love."

"How would you know?"

"I should've stayed for breakfast."

"Are you begging for a second chance?"

"I deserve a second chance, you think?"

"I don't like a man who eats and runs."

"You said shoots and runs the other day."

Lauren has now perked up, her eyes widen at the message coming across her computer screen.

"Jack, I've got something interesting coming across..."

She finishes the read, then, "you bastard! Why didn't you say so?"

I hate being left out of the loop. Actually, I hope she's not referring to me.

"Lauren, who?"

In the Water, Outside the USS Virginia

The huge sub slides in reverse, its hull covered in the screws' wake turbulent baffles. It moves further into the murky blue/green water where it disappears from view.

Only to be replaced several seconds later by the Bear Oscar sub as it drifts in a backward direction, probably with the strong current, its screw in the neutral position.

It appears almost dead in the water.

And the only sounds are pings that fill every inch of water space between the two submarines.

On Board the Bear Oscar Kim Jong

CHEKHOV moves to a position alongside VASILI who is stationed at the Weapons Control Panel. The tobacco stench is revolting to Vasili. But he sucks it in, not letting it interfere with his next steps. Chekhov chuckles.

"We get to do what Moscow never let us do, huh, Vasili?"

Vasili, suddenly stunned by that statement gives Chekhov a look that may show a slight pang of compassion.

"We may never see Moscow again, Chekhov."

From the OOD, General Tariq shouts, "on my order!"

Chekhov glances at Tariq, then smiles at Vasili.

"Like I give a shit."

"Fire first missile!" That was Tariq.

Chekhov reaches up to the Weapons Control Panel, above his head. His finger on a red button, now lit. A sardonic smile at Vasili. Then...

"Fire!"

Chekhov slams the button.

A moment.

Then a loud, muffled, thunderous sound permeates the control room. All the men standing on the deck shake – much like standing helpless on a diving board when someone jumps off into the water from the far end.

But way worse.

Earthquake worse.

And it scares the shit out of the young North Koreans in the control room.

Not understanding what they are saying, Vasili assumes, correctly so, they're praying out loud.

Tariq, smiling and gripping one of the many hand holds, shifts his look straight up through the hole leading to the hatchway to the Bridge.

From there, and looking aft, a missile leaves the deck from inside the ship, heading straight up to the surface of the Red Sea.

The 24 foot missile breaks the water.

A moment before the secondary engine ignites, sending the flaming projectile up. It now bends, its on-board guidance system adjusting the heading to 359 degrees.

A trajectory that will take it directly to Tel Aviv, Israel.

Tel Aviv, Israel

The empty streets, the darkened homes and office buildings, only serve as a ghostly backdrop to the whinnying sirens that continue to blare around the entire Metropolitan area.

Lights, both public and private, have been extinguished.

No point in making it easier for the bad guys to find them if, in fact, waves of aircraft are on the way to Tel Aviv.

The only signs of life are the junk yard dogs that roam the neighborhoods late into the night, scavenging through the trash for a quick bite to eat.

The Situation Room

The stunned room has gone silent. The President looks over at Hasslinger.

"Admiral, let me know if the Patriots intercept that missile."

"Yes, sir."

The President lifts a black, non-descript telephone.

"General Zimmerman. Operation Kill Kim is authorized." Holding a small laminated card, he continues. "Authorization code, Charlie zero niner two zero one niner four six."

Giordan listens as General Zimmerman, on the other end, reads back the code.

Then, "affirmative, General."

The President disconnects. He grabs the red hand-set.

"Jack, I've just authorized a B-2 squadron to bomb six targets in North Korea." A measured beat, as he pauses. "They're fifteen minutes from the first target."

Concerned the President is not familiar with all the facts, I have one thought that's been pinging around my brain for several minutes to pass on, thanks to the expert hacking performed by Lauren Miller. How she got this, no one knows. But it's truly valuable information from what we know about the Iranian threats the past few months.

"Sir, someone on that sub knows not to take aggressive action against us. As a matter of fact, they probably didn't expect us. Otherwise, they would've fired at us by now. Certainly after we bounced two dead bullets off his hull."

"What are you suggesting?"

"I'm suggesting it's an Iranian operation. Not North Korean. The Russians are there, first to run that boat, and second, as a red herring of sorts. We smell the wrong fish."

"I'm listening, Jack."

"Kind of a counterpoint to the bluster from Tehran related to the sanctions we've imposed."

"I gotta a whole lot of folks over here who'd say you're flat wrong, Jack."

"Yes, sir. I know."

My mind is burning brain cells at warp speed right now.

"And one more thing, sir. Part of the planning, in order to involve those Russian dissidents, had to have come from our side."

"I'm not ruling out the possibility of what you're saying is far-fetched. But what part, Jack?"

"Money."

The President's thought process now runs the gamut of possible agencies that could conceivably finance such an operation, under the radar. And like an awakening, his mind settles on the CIA, the only agency with tens of millions of dollars stashed away overseas.

And the infamous DCI, Simon Unger.

Make that former DCI, Simon Unger.

"Jack, I've connected the dots. When you're at a safe distance, you can take out the Bear Oscar."

I hang up the red hand-set and turn to find Captain O'Flannigan not far away. Certainly within ear shot.

"Gotta hand it to you, Mister Connolly. Maybe you've learned a thing or two working at Camp Peary."

Okay, that was...different.

Although, I still think he would like to kick my ass.

On Board the Bear Oscar Kim Jong

The Iranian Colonel, Sayyari, has joined a gleeful General Tariq who offers an arm in Chekhov's direction.

"Colonel. Your pleasure, my good friend."

Sayyari glares with level disdain at Chekhov. Then, firmly...

"Fire second missile!"

The Situation Room

From across the room, in a nervous, flat voice, the young officer says to no one in particular, "second missile away..."

It's unclear at this point whether or not President Giordan, his body ridged, his eyes appearing to be glazed over, heard that statement.

While everyone in the room holds a look on the President, the same young officer adds...

"Virginia now at a safe distance, sir."

He snaps back to real time. "Have the Patriots hit the first missile?"

"Negative...sir."

"Is the Israeli Prime Minister still on the secure line?"

A female voice this time, presumably Lauren, says...

"No, sir."

On Board the Bear Oscar

General Tariq and his new best friend, Colonel Sayyari, are now embracing. Hugs and kisses all around as they are joined by that thug, Chekhov.

At the Weapons Control Panel, his back to the joyful trio of embracing idiots, Vasili stops spinning his key and chain. Quickly, he inserts the key into the small recess above the launch buttons. This is the Command Control Detonate Sub-Panel, or what is commonly referred to as the CCD.

Now a quarter turn counter-clockwise. He hits the green button to its right, holding it for a moment as it turns from green to red. Then it's released, sending an electronic, coded signal to a small explosive charge built into the missile's central core.

At the moment of release, and from behind Vasili...

Chekhov shouts, "Vasili! *Octahobut! Octahobut!*"

Vasili spins in the direction of Chekhov's command to stop! But Vasili sees only Tariq's weapon pointed at him. Tariq's eyes then go quickly to the CCD. And, not surprisingly, this is one electronic device on board the submarine the General has read about in his spare time when not confirming delivery of his seventy-seven virgins in paradise.

"You bastard, you Russian scum. You will die!"

Lubin moves quickly in front of Tariq, his hands raised to stop Tariq from making a rash decision.

"Comrade, General. He has only locked the weapon. Preventing the American Patriot missiles in Israel from destroying it in flight."

Chekhov screams, "bullshit, you ass!"

No sooner has Chekhov delivered his rebuke of Lubin's claim, when Tariq fires.

Lubin is shot square in the heart. He drops, dead, onto the deck of the control room.

In Flight, Above the Red Sea

A massive explosion that lights up the night sky, can be seen from both the Egyptian and Saudi Arabian sides of the Red Sea.

Missile number one has been detonated.

And debris rains down onto the black, calm sea.

On Board the USS Virginia

Captain Mike O'Flannigan is at the conn where, from a speaker above his head, Borrelli comes through, "two more gun shots, sir."

O'Flannigan takes a moment to think, then to Huntington…

"Are we ready to fire one and two, Mister Huntington?"

"In all respects, skipper."

Again, from the speaker, it's Borrelli…

"Holy shit! What's this?"

My first and only reaction standing here next to the Captain is to whip my head over towards the sonar shack because I think I know what has just alarmed Borrelli.

On Board the Bear Oscar

VASILI, the target of Tariq's second shot, has landed on top of a young North Korean sailor, who was functioning as a weapons officer, and who was seated just to Vasili's right.

Blood oozes from Vasili's shoulder all over the young sailor who makes an effort to squirm away.

Vasili looks up, seeing Tariq step closer, his weapon pointed at Vasili's head. A long moment of painful distress as Vasili glances quickly at the CCD and notices the detonate button is still red. A quick glance back to Tariq, then again, back to the CCD just as the button cycles to green.

Chekhov is back in the sonar room.

He's placed the head phones back on, listening to the activity.

"General! Americans have reversed to a safe distance. Ready to fire!"

Tariq turns towards the sonar room, looking across the control room at Chekhov, shouts, "flood all rear tubes! Now! Fast!"

And at that same moment, with Tariq distracted, Vasili has elbowed his body upward, and reaching the CCD with his good arm, slams the green button, straining to hold it in until it turns red.

As the detonate button goes from green to red, Tariq turns back to Vasili.

Reading the situation, his eyes go wide, filled with evil vengeance...

Bang! Bang! Bang!

The Situation Room

The eerie silence for such an important place is suddenly broken by the sounds of a young officer's voice from the far side of the room.

"Both missiles detonated, sir."

The President leaps from his chair at the head of the mahogany table, grabbing the red hand-set on the way.

"What the hell's going on, Jack?"

"Someone on board the Bear Oscar keyed the detonator program, sir."

That same young officer, again, "Virginia sonar officer reports multiple shots fired on the Bear Oscar, sir."

I heard that report in the background and was about to tell the Boss. But Borrelli beat me to the punch. So, I fill in the blanks, my best thinking on this terribly bizarre situation.

"It's who we missed, sir. From Lieutenant Miller's hacking activity," oops, I should re-word that one, "I mean…her brilliant Intel investigation…we always thought there was someone else on that boat. Now I'm convinced it was a Russian agent of sorts. Perhaps put there by someone in the Kremlin."

I think some more, this time grabbing a glance at O'Flannigan.

"Let's step back, sir."

I listen to the Commander in Chief, then disconnect the hand-set. Stepping towards the Conn, I notice everyone in the control room is coiled like a spring, ready to rock. I take a deep here-we-go breath…

"The President has rescinded the shoot to kill order, Captain."

O'Flannigan stands up straight, drilling me with a, "I'm gonna kick your ass" look.

He says, "Connolly, you sonofabitch!"

I think that's better than a right hook from the big guy.

Just then, Borrelli is back on the speaker.

We're gonna need some valium for this poor guy.

"Russian Sierra Class submarine – six thousand meters – haulin' ass, sir."

In the Water, 150 feet Below the Surface

The unmistakable shape and size of a Sierra Class Russian Nuclear submarine zips through the murky blue/green water of the Red Sea at better than 30 knots.

It's 111 meters in length and 14 meters on the beam. It carries a complement of highly lethal and accurate Starfish and Stallion torpedoes.

A force to be reckoned with, it takes the lead in the Russian Navy's quest to hopefully dominate International waters in a Naval confrontation.

A quest that is more like a long shot given the fact that the Russian Defense budget clocks in at a mere 20 billion US dollars compared to the US's 700 billion dollars plus.

This ship is ID'd as the Barracuda – Sierra II 945.

A Russian Navy submarine that Commander Jack Connolly is all too familiar with these days.

The Situation Room

Spinning in his new executive chair, the President locks onto Admiral Hasslinger.

"Another Russian submarine? Where?"

"Directly behind the Virginia, sir. Closing fast, thirty knots."

Giordan turns to a young female staff officer, and says...

"Get me Mister Putin at the Kremlin – on the red line."

On Board the Bear Oscar

Tariq looks down on the very dead Vasili. After a long look, disgust filling his face, he spits.

"You ass. You had forgotten about the presence of Allah on this mission."

He kicks Vasili's lifeless body. Then he kicks it again.

"I will not accept failure!"

He marches to the OOD post, and shouts at the crew…

"Open missile door seven!"

From behind, Colonel Sayyari, rests his hand on Tariq's shoulder.

"Be at peace with Allah, my good friend. Just be peaceful."

General Tariq, turning for a careful study of Sayyari, takes a moment to let those words sink into his now trembling body.

He pees in his pants.

On Board the USS Virginia

In the sonar shack, O'Flannigan and I are hovering over Borrelli. I see the need to make a safe suggestion. That is, for all of us.

"Captain. Let's move out of the way. Let the Barracuda deal with him."

"It's my fight now, Commander. Anyway, I don't know that he's not after us."

"I don't think he wants us, sir. There's another reason he just happens to be in this spot at this time."

"Back off, Commander! It's my boat!"

"Yes, sir."

Now what. I go into "throw up some obstacles" mode. Anything to get O'Flannigan to give this some more thought. Particularly, given the last piece of Intel Lauren provided.

"Rules of engagement, sir, state…"

"Rules of engagement state in a threatened situation, Commander, it's my call. I know the rules. Especially the one that says *kill the bastard before he kills me!*"

"If it's who I think it is, I know this guy."

O'Flannigan seems to have ignored me for the moment.

"What do you think, Borrelli?"

"Another torpedo door is open. That makes two, sir."

"Jesus Christ."

Above Borrelli's head, O'Flannigan reaches for a mike activation button.

"Ready forward tubes one and two – flood aft tubes three and four – safety's off."

From the speaker, I hear Huntington, "aye, skipper."

I jump in, "Captain, I think I know what he's up to."

The Captain, again, ignores me as Borrelli's entire body has just flinched in his seat.

"Sir. Russian Sierra class, now dead astern – two thousand meters...and he's flooded two forward tubes, sir."

"Get clear, Captain. Let him shoot. He's not after us. He wants us to move."

O'Flannigan stiffens, turning at me...

"You gotta be kidding, Commander."

"I'm not a comedian...Captain."

The Situation Room

President Giordan stands next to a nerdy looking character, a translator to be exact as to his identity. His name is Boris Sullivan. A guy somewhere north of forty years old. And closely examining his dress code, someone who's stuck in the 1970's. Give him a pocket protector for his pens and pencils and he'd look like an IRS agent. It's the black horn rims that give him away.

He speaks clipped Russian into a secure telephone. Then waits.

The President holds a receiver to his ear.

"He says he knows all about it, sir."

"What the hell does that mean, Boris?"

Boris asks Putin for clarification. There's short conversation between the two, in Russian.

"He says not to worry about the Barracuda, sir."

"Don't worry about the Barracuda? His freakin' sub is on the Virginia's ass, for chrissakes. Has he lost his mind?"

Boris is once again in conversation with Putin.

Then, Boris has just a blank stare for the President. And replaces the phone onto the hand-set.

"Well, Boris?"

"He heard you in the background, sir. Said to calm down. He'll deal with it. And then...he disconnected."

The President, fuming, throws the receiver across the room, accidentally hitting Admiral Hasslinger in the leg.

He paces in a tight circle.

"So, that's it?"

Boris removes the black horn rims, wipes his forehead of a massive amount of sweat. Then, replacing his glasses, he looks at the President with a shade of mystery...

"During our brief conversation he made a quick reference to an individual - I didn't get the name - on board the Oscar Class."

Boris thinks a bit.

Then, "clarification about two passengers picked up in the Seychelles."

Giordan instantly grabs the red hand-set phone connected to Jack Connolly on board the USS Virginia.

On Board the USS Virginia

I replace the hand-set, but hold my hand on the receiver, standing there, attempting to sort out this mess. Despite the fact my brain is now in full bore overload, I sense it's finally kicking-in to computing mode. My inclination to somehow feel the Russian connection was more than just a few dissidents on board the Bear Oscar seem to have been, not just confirmed, but fleshed out based on the conversation with Putin.

I'll need more time to fully pull these puzzle pieces, dangling in thin air, down to a hard surface, and then draw my conclusions.

However, right now we've got trouble both ahead and astern.

I turn and O'Flannigan, once again, is right there. He's good at sneaking up behind nervous nellies, like me. I need to slip a pack of tick-tacks into the Captains' pocket.

"Can I shoot the bastard, Commander?"

Now I need to choose my words carefully.

"I think I know that guy, Captain."

Indicating aft, O'Flannigan says, "on the Barracuda?"

"I'm dating his girlfriend. And it's not platonic."

O'Flannigan's complexion seems to have turned pasty.

"Does he know you're on my boat?"

O'Flannigan immediately suspects I don't want to answer that question.

So I spin around and grab the red hand-set, feeling O'Flannigan's fury building behind me.

"Mister President. We knew he'd be there. I mean, we had an idea last weekend when Lieutenant Miller was told he was in the Middle East. I never made the connection."

Actually, I was pissed at Lauren for still having a relationship with what's his name. So, I failed to realize that by telling her where he was, which was way out of the way of his normal patrol - we do know where these Russian guys are most of the time - he was really giving us a heads-up. But I guess I shouldn't tell the Boss about another screw-up on my part.

"It's more of Putin's play here. The Barracuda has been assigned to clean-up the mess."

"So, Jack, why the hell is he *behind* the Virginia?" I hear the Boss ask.

"He knows something we don't, sir."

The overhead speaker crackles with Borrelli's voice...

"Russian Sierra class has two in the water. Bearing three five three degrees, sir."

I jam the hand-set down, disconnecting the Boss. Hope he's not angry about that but I'm pulling together more of the puzzle piece floating around my brain.

Huntington turns at the Conn, "that's right at us."

O'Flannigan shifts towards DeLorenzo, "emergency blow, Chief!"

"He's not shooting at us, Captain."

"You've been wrong so far, Commander." Meaning, "Chief!"

Opposite the Conn, Chief DeLorenzo reaches up for the two handed emergency blow grips.

"His target is the Bear Oscar. And, like I said, we're in his way."

"So he blows us outta the way, then another two at the Bear Oscar?"

"And there's another problem, Captain."

"What's that, Connolly? I know you're just full of surprises."

"We're too close to the Bear Oscar."

"We're too close. So, we need to back-up closer to the Barracuda just in case he misses us, he gets an easier second shot?"

O'Flannigan sighs, turning away from me as if I'm no longer there. He reaches for the mike button…

"Borrelli?"

From the speaker, "fifty one seconds to impact, sir."

O'Flannigan turns back to me, "stand down, Mister Connolly."

Before I have a chance to make one more plea, the speaker crackles with Borrelli's now high pitched voice, "something's not right, sir. I think they're wide…and they're not yet active."

DeLorenzo eyes me with a look of contempt. Then a look at the Conn...

"Ready with emergency blow, skipper."

I watch as DeLorenzo has now leveraged himself to pull the dual handles that will cause water in the ballast tanks to be literally blown out the side and forward resulting in the bow turning sharply up, towards the surface at about 30 degrees.

This is the part of training where they tell to grip anything with one hand, and grab your nuts with the other.

I notice the Captain has taken a second, not like before, but this time he's thinking real hard.

"Chief! Reverse! Flank speed!"

DeLorenzo freezes. Deer in the headlights frozen.

"Chief!"

He snaps out of it.

"Aye, Captain."

O'Flannigan looks my way as we all feel the boat jerk sharply backwards.

"Not just for your sake, Commander, let's hope he's got the distance right."

Feeling a bit vindicated, I give O'Flannigan a thin smile, and then add...

"I've heard this guy's a really good shot."

Mike O'Flannigan leans on the starboard plotting table, gazing at the ceiling of the control room...

"Let's see...what do we know about you and this Russian Commander behind us? First, you ram the bastard, come *this* close to sinking a commie boat without authorization, then you go home and fuck his girlfriend."

He makes eye contact with me, "no wonder you ended up in the White House with a cushy job."

He moves back to the Conn, "I hope he's not sick with retribution."

I think to myself, you're not the only one, Mike.

On Board the Bear Oscar

General Tariq shouts from the OOD watch, "fire missile three!"

At the Weapons Control Panel, Chekhov flips the fire control key back and forth, waiting for the engagement light to signal the system is ready to activate the firing mechanism. Chekhov, having trouble with the activation key, mumbles…

"Piece of shit submarine."

"Fire! I said fire!" That was Tariq, growing impatient, not just from Chekhov's inability to fire missile number three, but perhaps because of the presence of Colonel Sayyari and what he's thinking, who stands right behind him.

"It's not engaging, god dammit!"

Tariq waits no longer for any other explanation.

Bang!

Chekhov keels over, dead as Tariq moves quickly to the Weapons Control Panel. He presses the red button, proclaiming, "bye, bye you Zionist bastards!"

Nothing.

A moment as Tariq can only just stare at the Panel. At the same time capturing Sayyari in his peripheral vision, glaring. Then, the light goes green. And now Tariq looks over at Sayyari, all smiles. Instead of slamming the button, he takes a moment to give thanks to Allah in a short prayer.

On Board the USS Virginia

A speaker crackles with Borrelli's voice…

"Ten seconds to impact! Still not active"

And we're all bracing ourselves at the various, oddly spaced hand-holds that are available throughout the Control Room.

And I can't help but think the engineers at General Dynamics certainly have taken every conceivable hazard into consideration in the design process.

Like, when a Russian submarine is shooting at you, get a good grip!

I shift my look up, and try to imagine the path of the Barracuda's two bullets as they travel, hopefully, past us, and find a bull's eye on the Bear Oscar. Eyes now jammed shut; I paint a picture in my brain...

From a position aft of the Virginia, two torpedoes whine as they pass on either side of the Sail, under the horizontal planes in a shot that looks like threading a needle.

I hear Huntington say, "I think the guy missed."

I let out a deep breath and say, "he didn't miss."

O'Flannigan shouts at DeLorenzo at the ballast control, who is still holding the emergency blow handles, "Chief! Emergency blow all main valves. Put us on the top, pronto!"

"Aye, Captain." He pulls both handles. "Emergency blow!"

The blow is ear-splitting. The boat angles at 30 degrees up, and equipment not battened down flies across the control room. All hands have grabbed the hand-holds, holding on for dear life.

Chief DeLorenzo calls out the shrinking depth...

"fifty feet...

forty feet...

thirty feet...

twenty feet..."

His eyes fixed up as the Virginia breaks through the surface of the Red Sea like a giant whale in heat.

It splashes down suggestive of Fat Albert diving into the neighborhood swimming pool.

It displaces what looks like a zillion gallons of the Red Sea.

On Board the Bear Oscar

General Tariq has finished his short, but poignant prayer. He now reaches for the execute button on the Fire Control panel as he smiles over at the evil looking Colonel Sayyari.

And, for these two terrorists, it's their last vision of life on earth.

On the Surface of the Red Sea

And several thousand meters from the USS Virginia, the surface suddenly vibrates causing a rippling effect on the water that travels out of sight.

Then a white and murky green cap of water rises into the air followed by a massive explosion of water.

Then browns and grays, mixed with debris, boat parts, and other trash that litter the surface as the momentary, instantaneous under water rumbling begins to subside.

And there does not seem to be any survivors.

Chapter 91

On Board the USS Virginia
On the Bridge
Wednesday, 0021 Zulu, 0321 Hrs. Local

I make it up to the Bridge with Captain O'Flannigan and Commander Huntington and quickly breathe-in the calm, serene setting.

The moon light is bright enough to provide good visibility across the surface of the Red Sea. O'Flannigan and Huntington scan the surface with special binoculars, perhaps looking for my Russian pal, what's his name.

Huntington says...

"He's probably not gonna surface."

Captain O'Flannigan sticks his head down towards the Control Room.

"Chief. Gimme a position on the Sierra Class Russian submarine. Pronto."

I hope he's not planning on surfacing.

Since he carries a weapon, he may take a shot at me if we're close enough.

Then I remember the walls of the Bridge are bullet proof. So, I know to drop down with any sign of aggressive behavior from that Russian Commander.

As I'm running through several duck and cover options in my mind, 60 meters to port the Barracuda surfaces.

Oh, shit!

And DeLorenzo yells up at us.

"I think the guy is right next to us, Captain. Off our port beam. And coming up."

Now I begin to wonder if our underwater surveillance equipment is running too many nano seconds behind real time. Need to make a note about that issue. Then tell DeLorenzo to next time take a peek through the type 2 periscope before telling the Captain what he "thinks" is happening.

There are two Russian officers on the Bridge of the Barracuda.

They turn their night vision binoculars at the Virginia. Then they lower them. And we all just stare at each other.

I break the ice, and throw up a salute, commenting to O'Flannigan and Huntington.

"I don't think we want anyone to know how good a shot that bastard is."

O'Flannigan winks at me, and follows my lead, holding a salute.

Then the two Russians salute, sharply, but only for a moment.

Thanks to the bright moonlight, I can clearly see what's his name.

And I give him a smile and a little wave.

He flips me the bird.

Chapter 92

I enjoy these early fall rides through the Nations' Capital. While it's still considered summer, the light coolness in the morning foretells of cooler days to come, perhaps just weeks away. I take in the sights as if never having paid much attention in the past. Which is probably true. When you work here you tend to take your surroundings for granted and therefore miss the beauty of the Federal Buildings, specifically the architecture and landscaping.

Although, there is a tendency on ones' part not to give too much thought to what goes on inside these buildings. Flies on the walls of most of these places are no doubt undergoing some serious therapy.

Not just up on the Hill, but also inside the West Wing.

The President has promised, sometime today, to address his decision to send Seth Greene to the Seychelles. We'll see what happens. The bigger issue, of course, seems to be what happens to his re-election bid. The attempt to secretly take over a major terrorist camp in the interest of National Security seemed genuinely defensible. But purely as a political stunt raises some serious questions about leadership.

From my last briefing with the President it's been concluded that the Bear Oscar incident was an Iranian mission. Luckily, he called off the Kill Kim mission with only minutes to spare. Some of the data that has now been secured came from the Russians. And the mission had nothing to do with North Korea, other than using its Navy as a scapegoat.

Putin authorized the sale of the sub to North Korea. It was paid for by the Iranians. Suspecting something fishy, Putin put his own people on that boat to keep an eye on things. He also sent the Barracuda ahead of time to watch from a distance. Also suspecting an outcome that could disrupt the world order in the Middle East, Putin, through the FSB, knew of Simon Unger's plan to upset that order for his own personal gain.

So, he played along.

Putin certainly is a crafty fella. He hides his involvement from the Iranians because it's a country where he has a serious economic relationship. But I think he also has his sights on someday making Iran's Persian Gulf coast a Russian military beach-head and nudist resort, not to mention access to the enormous oil reserves.

Then he decides not to tell the President what Simon Unger is up to, but waiting until the end to ride in on his white horse and save the day. Had Unger not been able to pull the USS Dallas off the tail of the Bear Oscar, the whole mess would never have happened.

But the real upshot of the whole incident is that it *never happened!*

That what's the National Security Council has ordered.

It's kind of like a Mission Impossible scenario. The intelligence apparatus of the U.S. government along with the Russians will disavow any knowledge of the incident, despite what the Iranians or Israeli's may have to say. It'll be interesting to hear how Ahmadinejad explains the sudden disappearance of General Tariq and Colonel Sayyari, two senior Iranian military officials.

I was thinking of sending Ahmadinejad an e-mail saying that I heard those two fellas were gay lovers and have since defected to Key West, Florida. They've been spotted sunbathing naked with Kim Jong Dope, or whatever his name is!

As for the North Koreans, the NSC says "screw 'em." That was a quote.

"Jack!"

As we cross the Potomac River via the Arlington Memorial Bridge, I spot a commercial aircraft departing Reagan National Airport down river. My thoughts settle on the fact that I need to get out of this town. And fast.

"Jack! We're almost there."

Maybe California. The Napa Valley. Wine. Warm weather year round. Wine. Great food. Wine. Hot chicks. Wine.

"Jack! Are you with us?"

"Huh? Oh, sure. Yeah. Just…thinking."

I look over at Lauren seated next to me in the back seat of the White House limo that is taking us to the Arlington National Cemetery. And I suddenly realize I don't wanna go where we're going. This is not going to be a good day.

The limo stops and two Secret Service Agents sitting up front jump out, opening the rear doors. I walk around and take Lauren's arm, accompanying her to a gravesite.

There's a small crowd, not over-flowing the immediate area.

No press.

The White House decided to keep it as private as possible under the circumstances. I'm sure there are those paparazzi guys off in the bushes somewhere with telephoto lenses capturing every nuance.

Lauren and I are seated in the front row on one side of the flag-draped coffin, several seats from the President. I look right and note the honor guard that will undoubtedly fire off a twenty-one gun salute at the appropriate time. Looking around the group, there are only a few faces that I quickly recognize. But, not many.

Then my eyes lock onto a middle-aged woman directly across the top of the coffin on the other side. Her eyes are telling.

This is indeed, a tragedy.

Lou Ann Mitchener always knew that Larry's job was dangerous. But she also knew he could take care of himself, despite the peril at protecting the President of the United States.

The tragedy is further brought home as I glance to her left, then her right.

Larry's two kids, I think, are maybe seven and nine. Their expressions are more than a profound sense of loss.

And I immediately focus on where my life would have gone had I lost my Dad when I was seven or nine. I simply can't imagine.

The President stands, and moves to one end. There's no microphone, no podium, nor a teleprompter. Nor does he have notes in his hand. He looks at Larry's coffin, then over to Lou Ann and the kids. Then, back to the crowd.

"I know the friendship with those close to me is perhaps more important than even my job as President. And there are those who, because of the position I hold, were even closer. It's a tragedy that brings us to this place on this day. The third and final funeral I've attended in as many days."

He pauses.

"This nation has lost a dedicated servant. Secret Service Agent Lawrence Mitchener served his country protecting the values we sometimes take for granted. He gave his life for his country and I'm here today to make sure we never forget."

He moves over to Lou Ann, kneels on one knee, and takes a long moment to express his personal condolences.

In the distance, a twenty-one gun volley salute starts.

The bugler finishes, and the flag is now presented to Lou Ann. Ten minutes pass before Lauren and I walk towards a small crowd that has assembled near the President's limo. He seems to be holding an impromptu news conference much to the loathing of his press secretary who appears to be suffering a coronary near-by.

"I think I wanna hear what he has to say."

Lauren and I tune in to the President...

"I asked Vice President Seth Greene to take on this mission, and he willingly stepped up to the challenge. It was my decision to engage in what some may believe to have been election year grand-standing. I take full responsibility for that deception."

With that, he glances quickly over to me. Perhaps what I had said last week to him in the Oval Office hit home.

"Under my authority as President, I have ordered the arrest of the DCI, Simon Unger...the man I hold responsible for the death of Vice President Greene."

The President thanks the small group, and as they all drift away, with the help of the Secret Service, of course, drilling them all dirty looks, the Boss signals for me to join him.

As I walk up to him, he says, with a smile.

"I hope you have some smart ass remark about what I did wrong today, Jack."

"I wish it were that simple, sir."

"I was afraid of that."

"I was never cut out for politics."

"Which is why you'd make a great politician, Jack." He looks over at Lauren, with a friendly smile, then back to me, "I still want you to write my memoirs someday."

"You don't know what I'll say."

"Yes I do, Jack. And by the way, don't retire from the Navy so fast. This morning I issued an executive order re-commissioning you back up to the rank of Captain. That should help with your retirement benefits. Plus, you've earned it."

I hesitate, then say, "thank you, sir."

My hesitancy probably sent a message to the Boss. So he added...

"Under the circumstances, you know I can't give you back a submarine command. But I do have the ability to get you most any other assignment you want. Maybe something in the Intel arena...at the White House...the Secret Service plays a big role in this area. Under the radar, of course."

"At least until you're no longer the President."

Fortunately, the President understands my sense of humor. Otherwise he would have had me re-assigned to the weather station at the North Pole doing Intel analysis on Eskimos and Polar Bears.

We shake hands. He gives Lauren a pat on her elbow, and then jumps into the Beast, what the Service calls his ride.

I take Lauren by the hand, seeing Lou Ann Mitchener not far. We catch up with her and the family.

"Larry never stopped loving you and the kids. It's all he ever talked about."

Holding back tears, she says. "He always said you were the most honest friend he had, Jack."

"I'm leaving the White House, Lou Ann. So, no more free passes to the Easter Monday egg roll."

She laughs, and I'm glad to bring a smile to her pretty features.

"Actually, it's a conflict of morality, Lou Ann."

"Jack, tell me something. How does one promote good moral and ethical behavior in a town that so artfully skirts it? Leadership has just been simply lacking around here."

"Good moral behavior runs contrary to the way this town works."

I give her a peck on the cheek, and we part ways.

Lauren says, quietly, "that was nice, Jack"

I look over at the Iwo Jima Memorial in the distance and take a moment to think. "We want to trust what is not true about our elected officials, Lauren. Who really wins at the end of the day?"

After a long silence, as we walk the Cemetery grounds, Lauren perks up.

"So, when do I get to meet your family?"

Uh oh.

"Well, I guess we should start with my married sister. She lives in the Hamptons."

"The Hamptons! Wow, fancy. She must've married well, huh?"

Okay. Now I think it best to start being honest with Lauren. All the stories I've told about my family came out during some rather intense sex. And, as I've said before, I need to put most of those into the re-wind bin.

"What's he do?"

"He's a retired Wall Street lawyer."

"Cool. Must've made a fortune. How'd they meet?"

It's probably not appropriate to go into the various pros and cons about Ron. By the way, that's' his name. Ron something. At least, that's what he has told us.

My Dad thinks otherwise. His real name and social security number are buried somewhere in the NCIC data base, aka, the National Crime Information Center.

Very few people make a ton of money on Wall Street doing really good things.

So, the question is what did he do that attracted my sister's attention?

"So, Jack, how'd they meet?"

Note to Editor: Insert a long pause here...

"I think my sister picked him out of a police lineup."

To be continued...

Follow Jack Connolly in his new career at the White House as Assistant Director of the Secret Service in a political thriller, available now on Amazon:

Succession

Melissa Callen's life is turned inside out as the newly elected Vice President of the United States finds herself unknowingly the victim of a ruthless conspiracy.

The President is assassinated on November 22, 2013 in Dallas, Texas commemorating the 50th anniversary of the JFK shooting. Melissa's evil twin sister, Linda, is sworn into office as Melissa is in the throes of fighting off the effects of a psychotic drug with the help of Jack Connolly and Dr. Andres Devendorf, a handsome and resourceful psychiatrist.

While Jack and Andres work to get Melissa secretly back to Washington, DC, and along the way battling one life-threatening hurtle after another, they are stalked by two assassins – Henning and Pellicane - assigned to take her out. However, their mission to capture Melissa is routinely and humorously foiled by Julia, a mental patient with tons of baggage.

We learn the conspiracy goes all the way to the White House and the Senate, and includes a pair of Iranian terrorists.

In the end, it's Melissa's wealthy but ancient mother who needs to step in and make the key identification.

Novels, screenplays, audio books, and/or treatments for cable television by M. Charles McBee currently in outline form, draft, production or finished and ready for publication:

The Sodality
Sign of the Cross
Negative Action (a/k/a – Soft Money)
The Monticello Protocol
Absolution
The Winery
Monticello Lake

Check out cool tidbits of information about the author, how to e-mail him, novels in production, screenplays, and other truly stirring ramblings at:

www.mcharlesmcbee.com

Made in United States
Troutdale, OR
10/06/2023

13474503R20213